An Order from the Sky

AND OTHER STORIES

Celebrating
30 Years of Publishing
in India

Mission Statement

This is an initiative of the Tamil Nadu Textbook and Educational Services Corporation (TNTB & ESC) under the aegis of one of the announcements for the year 2021–22, by Honourable Minister for School Education Thiru. Anbil Mahesh Poyyamozhi to identify and translate into English Tamil literary works, that they might enhance the reach of Tamil antiquity, tradition and contemporaneity and enrich world literature and to also translate significant literary voices from other Dravidian languages into Tamil. Both ventures are to be undertaken as either independent or joint publications with collaborating publishers.

Members, Academic Advising Committee (Translation)

Dr. R. Balakrishnan, IAS, Researcher and Writer

Thiru. S. Ramakrishnan, Writer

Thiru. S. Madasamy, Educationist

Project Execution Team

Thiru. Dindigul I. Leoni, Chairperson, TNTB & ESC

Tmt. R. Gajalakshmi, IAS, Managing Director, TNTB & ESC

Dr. S. Kannappan, Member Secretary, TNTB & ESC

Thiru. R. Dhayalan, Financial Advisor, TNTB & ESC

Dr. T.S. Saravanan, Joint Director (Translations), TNTB & ESC

Thiru. P.A. Arumugam, Deputy Director (Publications), TNTB & ESC

Dr. P. Saravanan, Assistant Director (Publications), TNTB & ESC

Thiru. M. Appanasamy, Consultant, TNTB & ESC

Tmt. Mini Krishnan, Co-ordinating Editor, TNTB & ESC

An Order from the Sky

AND OTHER STORIES

IMAYAM

Translated from the Tamil by
VASANTHA SURYA

HARPERPERENNIAL
An Imprint of HarperCollins Publishers

First published in English in India by Harper Perennial 2023
An imprint of HarperCollins *Publishers*

HarperCollins *Publishers* India, Cyber City, Building 10-A, Gurugram, Haryana-122002, India

www.harpercollins.co.in

2 4 6 8 10 9 7 5 3 1

HB-ISBN: 978-93-5629-423-3
PB-ISBN: 978-93-5629-424-0
E-ISBN: 978-93-5629-425-7

Typeset in 11.5/15.7 Adobe Caslon Pro at
Manipal Technologies Limited, Manipal

Printed and bound at
Repro India Ltd.

HarperCollins *Publishers*, Macken House, 39/40 Mayor Street Upper, Dublin 1, D01 C9W8, Ireland

Contents

A Word from the Author

Impressions of what I have experienced, witnessed, heard and read about over the years, these stories are my word-pictures of Tamil society. While it is true that it is anger and exasperation and sheer dismay at the condition of this society that made me write, I do not wish to project my ideals or value system, to teach or to preach through these stories, but simply to show things as they are. I am a writer, not an orator. Like a playwright, a writer must remain in the wings and never voice himself. Importance should be given to the sense of time and place in short stories, without even a shadow of the author's presence. Creativeness comes out of an indescribable silence that occurs very rarely. I wrote each word, each sentence with trepidation, as if I were writing for the very first time. Each story has taught me something. To try to put new perceptions into words, to explore and to strive to reach ever newer boundaries in the world of expression – that is the practice of writing. A writer is the disciple of the Magician who is Language itself. The Tamil language has grown richly over the last two thousand years, and writing in such a language makes one alert and tends to quell the ego.

My thanks to HarperCollins and to the Tamil Nadu Textbook Corporation for publishing this work. To Vasantha Surya for translating it with intense care, and to Mini Krishnan for ensuring the quality of this whole enterprise, my warm affection.

– Imayam

Introduction

Imayam's 'True Stories'

'Write what you see, not what you want to see.'

These words of Jatin Anand, a journalist witnessing the present COVID-19 pile-up of calamities, are a timely pointer to the bridge between fact and fiction, over which Imayam takes his readers. Not one egregious comment does this writer make on the way things 'should be'; his focus is on the way things are, both in the material and in the psychological world. As the editor of these translations, Mini Krishnan, has said, 'What is unsaid in Imayam's stories speaks of the dynamism of both language and experience.'

Selecting from these stories those which I hoped I could translate with all their nuances into English, I was reminded of what A.K. Ramanujan enjoined me to do, back in the 1990s. A major Indian English poet himself, he told me that writing in English was okay, it was all very well – but what was happening to life, language, and literature in

India in our lifetimes demanded something more of any Indian writer, in any language: 'Translate!' he said.

The reformist ferment which leavened the freedom struggle and culminated in the formation of a new nation-state with an egalitarian constitution had by then created a by-product in Tamil Nadu in the form of a rationalist movement, with two ambitious goals: to strip away not only superstition and obscurantism from the collective psyche of Tamils but also caste-based discrimination and misogyny. The Self-Respect Movement (Suya Mariyaadhai Iyakkam) set in motion by Periyar Ramasamy Nayakar aimed at strengthening the humanistic components of the Tamil linguistic and cultural identity. The ripples set off by that tidal wave of modernist thought have not, however, washed away dams of cultural conditioning. Deep within the consciousness, the twin currents of class and gender still largely flow unimpeded, through entrenched channels of entitlement that determine a person's worldly circumstances. The argument of 'identity', however, has often tended to reinforce ethnic, religious and caste markers here, as elsewhere in India.

Yet, although Imayam's stories bring the reader up against these formidable currents, they also record the effort made by each of his protagonists to resist, if not actually override, structures of power and entitlement. It is this energy that vibrates in his writing. Set for the most part in the small towns and villages of Cuddalore district, around the temple town of Vriddhaachalam, these stories not only describe the aspirational agonies of men and women in

Tamil Nadu but throw light on the plight of many others elsewhere in India.

One story that struck me at once was 'Bus to Aaladi'. Here is a male writer who is tuned in to the flesh-and-blood reality of being a woman in today's India. And yet, there is not the slightest tinge of voyeurism or tear-jerking sentimentalism. Not a traditional name in Tamil Nadu, the name Priyanka evokes the persona of a prominent Indian woman would-be leader, scion of the Nehru family, and that of a Bollywood actress who has made her mark in Tamil cinema. This Priyanka asserts her right to a seat in a mofussil bus – and also the right to reserve one for a woman who teaches in her home village. 'Yearning' and 'Payback Time' also offer sharp insights into certain facts of women's lives.

But it is not only misogyny that compels Imayam's attention. 'The Pulse of Life' has its finger on the collateral damage caused by a skewed vision of 'growth' and 'development'. Written in 2008, it presciently described, in miniature, the threat to agriculture as a way of life, which resulted in an unprecedented farmers' movement in 2020 that resonated strongly in many parts of India. Imayam makes candid comments on political life, as an insider in Tamil politics himself, in 'One of Ours'. The phenomenon of widespread alienation that has often been glossed over in the chest-thumping assertion of regional cultures is described in all its starkness in 'A True Story' and 'Missing Persons'. Both his male and his female characters rack their brains and harden their hearts to make workable deals with the socio-psychological forces that not only prevent their upward mobility but too often seek to divest them of their self-respect as human beings. They stage their existential protests as individuals, rather than as self-conscious participants in processes of social change. It is not revolution that they envisage or even desire. What they want is only to survive, to live and to thrive, but the future they yearn for has not yet been born, and all too often its foetal heartbeat seems faint.

The perspective in Imayam's fiction is not one merely of pathos. Nor does it leave one with the taste of ashes. This winner of the Sahitya Akademi Award (2020) imparts a bracing tartness to common speech. Scorning literary artifice, his prose bristles with the idiom of the Tamil that is spoken today, a free-and-easy blend of regional dialects and modern lingo, sprinkled with 'Tamlish'. The effect is hair-raising, no less, as he brings to life his instantly recognizable characters and the situations in which they find themselves. The reader is stung – and tickled – by his sense of the absurd.

As in 'An Order from the Sky', you walk away, sure of the way ahead, like a worshipper who has received the go-ahead from the highest quarters.

As the translator, I am happy that this selection of Imayam's stories will reach schools and colleges, as part of an initiative taken by the Tamil Nadu Textbook and Educational Services. Mini Krishnan as Consulting Editor has consistently promoted the translation of quality literature.

– Vasantha Surya

An Order from the Sky

AND OTHER STORIES

An Order from the Sky

UPON A CEMENT DAIS WAS a god, who sat on a horse and faced east. Judging by the looks of him, it was Muniyasaami.

A man came and stood before this idol, brought his hands together in a kumbidu[1] and unhurriedly set about preparing for worship. He was dark-skinned, streaming with sweat from his walk to the spot. Not bothering to wipe it off, he set his bag down on the ground, took out a sheet of newspaper and spread it out. Next, he brought out a paper cone of roasted gram and a bunch of bananas, into one of which he poked an incense stick. Then, two quarter bottles of brandy, a tin of cigarettes, some limes, camphor, a coconut, flowers, betel leaf and areca nut – he set out all these items for a ceremonial offering. He placed the camphor at the feet of the god's horse, set it alight and waved it three times around the deity. Lighting the incense stick that he had pushed into a banana, he stuck a lime into

1 Kumbidu: Hands folded in respectful greeting – a namaskaar often accompanied by a partial or a whole prostration.

the trident standing near the god. Breaking four bananas, skin and all, into two pieces each, he smeared them all with vermillion and turmeric, and set them out. Then he threw himself straight down on the ground, in obeisance.

Rising up, he picked up pieces of the lime, pressed them reverently to his eyes and flung them, one after the other, in all four directions. Strewing a handful of roasted gram upon the horse and its rider, he scattered the rest in the four directions. Opening one of the bottles, he sprinkled the brandy all around the god's dais, as if it were water, and spattered some of it upon the horse. Stripping the peels off four more bananas, he mashed them up together into a dough, and made four balls. These he tossed towards the east, the west, the north and the south. Gathering a handful of the sacred ash and kumkumam[2] that lay at the horse's feet, he liberally bedaubed himself on the forehead, and prostrated himself again, and stood up.

He scanned the four directions. Seven or eight vanni[3] trees stood around, singly and in twos, and one neem[4] tree.

---

2 Kumkumam: A vermillion powder made from the root of the turmeric (manjal, haldi) plant and held to be auspicious.

3 Vanni: The Indian mesquite, *Prosopis cineraria*. This scrubland tree, haloed in myth, and found in temples, is valued for its medicinal properties. It is not to be confused with the seemai karuvelan, *Prosopis juliflora*, which was brought from Mexico in the mid-nineteenth century and has overrun large tracts of fertile land.

4 Neem: A tree common in India, with medicinal uses.

A quarter or a half mile away were groves of casuarina and fields of maize, but around the open-air altar there was nothing but stony ground. A barren stretch, with not even goats or cattle to be seen.

He turned towards the god, folded his hands together, and muttered under his breath, as though sharing a secret: 'Today is Maasi Magam.[5] They'll be bringing out the temple chariot. I have to do my work there. That's why I've come here, to ask you for your permission. If you give the command, I'll go there. If you don't, I'll go back home.'

The man looked around the shrine. No one was about. Nothing – not a crow, not one sparrow. He could see nothing moving at all…

Except the wind.

'Shall I go to work today, or not?' he whispered to the god. 'Give the command. Unless the gecko arrives and gives me a sign, I won't go. And then, too, it must not call from my left – that's the shit-wiping hand. If I treat *that* as a lucky omen, the job I'm on is just doomed. Won't see the light! That lizard must call from the right side, near the hand I eat with. Otherwise, it won't work,

---

5 Maasi Magam: A festival day dedicated to the ancestors (pitrs), who are worshipped in the morning, and to the evening worship of Siva, who is borne on a chariot through the streets. In Vriddhaachalam, thousands throng to take part in the temple procession of Siva (Vriddhagireeswarar or pazhamalai naadhar).

do you understand? The job won't get done. It'll get dark soon. Hurry up! Let me have the sign.'

Having spoken, the man sat down on the ground. Inch by inch, his measuring gaze swept over the dais, the horse, the god. He peered closely around himself, ears cocked to catch the click-cluck of any lizard that might be about. For five or ten minutes he remained seated right there.

Not even the flapping of a grasshopper's wings could be heard.

He looked westwards. The sun seemed about to set. A scowl now came over his face. 'Two miles I have to walk to catch the bus! Then after getting down, it's half an hour more to where the festival is going on!'

It looked like he was angry with the god, as he went on, 'If I leave late from here itself, will the job be done? By that time won't the crowd have disappeared? Suppose there's no crowd left over there, should I just go roaming around and come back empty-handed? … Why don't you give me an answer, instead of just squatting there? Tell me: do I win, or do I lose? If nothing is going to happen, why should I come and gape at your face any more?'

He got up and began to walk around the platform, looking keenly at the ground, at the horse, at the god – everywhere. There was no trace of a lizard anywhere about. Was there a sound coming from anywhere at all? He listened carefully. Not one person was anywhere to be seen.

Again, he looked towards the west. In a little while the sun would disappear. Striding up to the god, he addressed him indignantly: 'Quarter bottles! Cigarettes! Limes and fruits – everything you need I have brought here! I've made the offering! Done every damn blessed thing! Still you are not giving me a sign? I've got to get my hands on some stuff! I need one whole armful! And whatever I get, half of it I'll bring here to you – trident, upper cloth, a chicken, another quarter. I have promised all that, no? Then what more d'you want? Why aren't you giving me a sign, why're you making me late? Last Friday when I went to the shandhai[6] at Veppur, I could catch only some poor wretch at that market … But if I worry about poor wretches, how will I myself get food to eat? Will my belly eat mud? … I thought what I caught was worth a pavun,[7] but when I tried to sell it, the fellow told me it was worn out, all spoilt. "It's only weighing three-quarter pavun," he told me. In spite of that, when I got my hands on the cash, didn't I bring you an offering the next day itself?'

He paused to listen for the click-cluck of a lizard…

Frustrated, he turned to the god once again, scolding, 'Without a clear sign, it's wrong for me to go – don't you know that?' He walked off towards the neem tree and stood there awhile … No, no sign of a good omen there, either. He went to the vanni tree to the north of the neem and waited there beneath it. What he wanted didn't happen there, either. Balked, he returned and confronted the god.

---

6 Shandhai: A weekly market.

7 Pavun: Pound – a measure of gold.

'Okay, don't give me the order if that's what you want! Po![8] What happened the time before last? D'you remember what you did then? Only one chain I got, but I thought, how fat like my finger it is. And it turned out to be fake! Nothing but "covering"! For that shiny fake thing, so much beating I got, so many kicks! Ei, you hairy lout! Were you the one who got those whacks and kicks? Such a big crowd collected and beat me up just for that thing! It was only after the jeweller came and said it's not gold at all, it's only gilt, that they let me go alive. Otherwise, police and court would have sent me to jail for a whole month.

'And it was just inside the big temple that it happened. She's fat, she's old, it'll be easy to cut her chain – that's what I thought. But that old hag shouted louder than anybody – "He's cut my chain! Catch him! Catch him, da!" – yelling so loud, the coconut-shop fellow came running and cornered me. "Everybody come! Everybody come! Run!" that old woman screeched till a mob gathered there. Right in the sight of god, that whole crowd that had gone there – to worship! – those holy-holy folks didn't care about the sinfulness of what they were doing. How they thrashed me! How I howled and wailed! Those men, and even women – all of them hit me! Spat right in my face. They didn't care to find out if it was true, if there was any justice in it.'

Tears gushed from the man's eyes. Wiping them away with the back of his hand, he spoke in a low, constricted

8 Po: Go.

voice, 'Even today the pain is there, from the beating I got that day. You couldn't save me from that crowd then. So why should you be my family deity if you can't do anything at all for me? "Sky hero" it seems! Which hairy-bum fellow gave you that name of yours? Each and every fellow in the crowd was thinking, "Nobody is as good as me, I am the best, the most righteous person in the world!" as he was beating me up … But in this world, who is good? "I don't tell lies! I don't do crooked things! I don't go after what belongs to the next man, I don't even touch it!" No such great-and-good man has ever been born who can say that…

'… So, that was my bad-luck time … I didn't have your support. I didn't have your blessing. That's why I got caught. In my twenties, I could run so fast even the wind couldn't catch me. Not even a hare could catch up. Now I can't run, I'm old. But *you* – *you* could have given my legs the power to run like lightning! And then why would I have got caught?

'… Here I am again – after all those blows and kicks. Standing right in front of you. And you are not even giving me a good-luck sign! How many times have you eaten my offerings and sent me roaming around, only to come back empty-handed? All those times, did I ever come back and curse you? That day at the big temple, it was you who got me caught! You only! Can I bear the blows of the whole town, the way I could at one time? And you – are you an outsider to me? A foreigner, a stranger? Ei, you're my family god. You know me very well. I'm the man who always turns up, festival day after festival day, to make an offering to you, right? To this altar of yours, I brought my three sons. To have their heads shaved, their ears pierced – and names given to them. What's more, my own mother has given me your name only! "Aakaasam!" Sky! When I say my name at the police station, and at the court, they all laugh! But I speak proudly about you to everybody. Have I ever said anything bad about you? I have named my eldest son "Aakaash", and everybody says it is a grand name! At least for that, now give me a signal, da, you thieving fellow!' the man finished.

Taking out a beedi from a fold at his waist, he lit it up and sucked in the smoke, as he inspected his surroundings, listening intently … Peeved that his prayer was not being granted, he seized one of the bottles, opened it, poured the brandy into his palm, and splashed it on the horse and on the god.

'This temper tantrum – come off it now at least!' he told the god heatedly. 'Give me the command, da!' He took another look around, but his eyes did not alight on any lizard. 'Nowadays every fellow is using *this* medicine as manure, *that* medicine as pest killer. All the bugs and worms in all the fields they've killed off. So where will any lizard come from, then?'

He looked towards the west. The sun had set, and darkness was spreading itself in a thin layer over everything. Now he was angrier than ever. 'Can't you see it's getting later and later, da?' he snapped furiously as he strode round and round the god's platform, until he sat down again, fed up. There he sat, his head hanging in despair, for a little while. And then – who knows what got into him? – he burst out:

'You…! What kind of god are you anyway?'

As though confronting an adversary, he said, 'Are you trying to test me? Today, after all these years? You won't give me the command? Have I ever set off to do a thieving job without getting your consent? You've made a name for yourself as the god of thieves, no? Aren't you the family saami for all thieves? If you suddenly turn over a new leaf and decide to be a respectable saami, what will I do? A luckless wretch, that's what I am – there's no other job I know. Am I asking you, "Make me an MLA, make me an MP! A minister! Make me rich as Kuberan!"[9] All I'm saying is don't let me get caught there, in that place where I'm going to steal what I can. Is that a big crime? A sin? Am I going to steal so that I can build a two-storey house? To buy a car? A bungalow? To buy rich, well-watered land? Or am I off to rob so I can get a string of diamonds for my wife's waist?

'Just for some damn food, I'm going to cut a chain from some woman's neck – enough to live on for one day. Well, say, for one month, maybe two months, it'll be enough to get along on … When I have any cash in my hand, do I

9 MLA: Member of the Legislative Assembly. MP: Member of Parliament. Kuberan: The god of wealth.

ever go out to rob? If my mother and father had earned enough and kept it for me, would I go and cut anybody's taali? That's a holy wedding chain tied in the presence of god! A baby still feeding on mother's milk – would I ever cut off that baby's waist chain?'

... Was that a lizard clucking close by? He stopped speaking and peered around. Could it be the long-awaited omen, the auspicious sign? Had the command come at last? Motionless, and full of doubt, he sat there listening. Not a rustle, not even of the wind.

... He felt very bitter. Glaring threateningly at the god, he cried out, 'Give me the order! Or tell me you can't do it. I'll pull out all the tridents stuck in this ground and sell them in the scrap-iron shop and buy rice and dal. Family god, bum hair! I couldn't care less, don't you know that? I'm that kind of man! Think about it – what happens when I get drunk? I just stop bothering about family god and all that – you know?' As he spoke, his voice sank, until it sounded as if he were talking to himself.

'Are these like the olden days, when sorghum and paddy were harvested, when we plucked white pumpkins and red pumpkins and brought them home to eat? Nowadays, every fellow is growing only cotton. Or planting eucalyptus trees. At the most, they'll plant sugarcane. If they can't do that, they'll sell off the land to fellows who'll cut it up into plots for building this and that. What sort of crop can you harvest from that land? What will you bring home to cook and eat? Stealing chicken, stealing goats or cows, stealing cable wires from a motor shed – I've tried all that, but none of it was enough to buy food even for one week.

'As if that's not bad enough, I'm a fellow from right here. So they can catch me easily. And can I run a household when I'm called a thief? Nowadays in the village, there isn't one chicken wandering around that you can steal! In village after village, they're setting up sheds and breeding broiler chickens. As for you – *you* don't see how times have changed. How every village and town has changed. That's why they've gone and set you up here in this good-for-nothing patch of barren land. They haven't even given you a roof over your head.

'If you're a god with any kind of brain you would know all this, but you're just a drunk. That's why you bless anyone who offers you booze. Nowadays, when fellows go out robbing, they go in a motor car, they go from town to town and rent out rooms. To tell you the truth, they even steal from inside temples. They break the collection box! Some of the bolder fellows steal the idols of the gods and goddesses and sell them off!

'Me – do I do such things? Vriddhaachalam, Neyveli, Thittakkudi, Pennaadam, Ulundhurpettai – I go to all these places, but only when my hands are completely bare … Because for all the trouble I take, half of it goes waste. Half of what I get is "covering" – all fake! Gilt! What I spend on offerings for you is sheer waste! Miserable! The ones who wear gold and diamonds come and go about everywhere in cars – rich bitches! The ones who go to the shandhai, and walk on the roads, carrying their yellow cloth bags to buy vegetables – they wear "covering" jewels! Such customers will only be wearing gilt jewellery, no? If it's in the daytime, you can tell if it's gold or gilt, and then cut a woman's chain. But how can you see that in the dark? And night is the only time you can grab a chain and yank it off, no? But even when I get only a "covering" jewel, do I ever deny you your share? When have I ever shortchanged you?'

He thought he heard something, and looked around to see if anybody was around the shrine. No, nobody had turned up. There were no goats, no cattle, no crows, no sparrows, not even kites flying above. Nothing at all … Not a swish of air among the trees…

Then how was it that he had heard something? Again, he peered this way and that. Having made sure no one was about, he resumed talking to the god.

'Remember when I went to Neyveli? I got a good, rich fistful of stuff. And I bought a trident for you, I came and planted it right here. That wedding in Vriddhaachalam – where I snatched a chain – I went straight to the potter right there in that town and got an earthen horse for you to ride, for when you go hunting. Two–three times I've bought fine, gold-bordered upper cloths and draped them round you. Year after year I kill a chicken for you … do pujai three times daily, with all these offerings! You took it all! You ate it all up, and now, you won't give me the thing I need! A go-ahead sign to do what I have to do!

'... Okay, don't give it then, po! This dirty hairy me – this body's used to going hungry. But how'll it be for you – to go hungry?'

Lighting up a beedi, he blew out the fumes, his eyes in search of a lizard. There was no trace of one anywhere around. Pulling the beedi out of his mouth, he flung it down and rubbed it out. 'Why are you playing with me this way today like you've never done before? What's this game of yours? This ordeal! Why are you putting me through all this, and not even giving me a sign! I need to get my hands on something!

'... Not cell phones, though. These days I don't steal those. They're worth nothing. Cost has gone down to just a thousand ... Go through all the trouble, get trampled and kicked to steal it, and when I give it in the shop the fellow says he'll give only a hundred for it – or fifty!' He smiled wryly. 'Who'll give more than that for a stolen article? Stolen thing itself means rock-bottom price, no? So, I don't touch cell phones now – you know that.'

Driven by a sudden onrush of energy, he quickly lit himself another beedi and scanned the western sky. The very next moment, his face darkened. His voice thickening, the words tumbled out. 'No use blaming you, da! I should blame that woman – the one who gave birth to me. *She* is the one who taught me all this godawful business.

That murungai[10] tree next door – when it was dark, she told me to quietly go break off the drumsticks without anybody finding out ... *She* sent me into other people's gardens to dig up their sour greens while she kept watch on the path. *She* told me to go pluck their millet and bring it ... Big red pumpkins and white pumpkins – she got me to cut them off somebody else's vines and lug them home. Groundnuts growing in who-knows-whose fields – *she* told me to dig them up – and to pick brinjal and ladyfinger ... *She* was the one who told me to pluck tamarind pods from trees in other people's yards...

'And on the bus, she got me to say I was younger than I was, so she didn't have to buy a ticket for me, and then how she quarrelled with the conductor! But when I went to do coolie work, she'd tell me to say I was older than I was, so she could get a higher wage for me ... She's the one who taught me how to talk smart ... To say one thing and mean another, and switch words around. What-all bad things that awful woman taught me to do, damn her!

'... Because her chappal straps might wear away, she would carry them around all day – that Unnamalai. I'm the child she gave birth to, no? Same Unnamalai used to go to you for everything. So I do it, too – I keep going round and round you only. Do I go to a different saami every month,

10 Murungai: A common tree with dangling seedpods, which are used for making the typical Tamil Nadu sambaar. The leaves are also edible.

like others do? Do I go to a different temple every month? One-and-only saami, that's you! It's why I come to you only! And what do you do, da? You won't come out with one good word for me! One lucky omen! You won't give me that go-ahead…

'First time I ever went out to do a job, I stole eggs. And it was to you that I brought that first egg I stole. To *you* I gave it! That time, when I stole those big pots and pans, I lit incense, waved burning camphor around you, I broke a coconut for you. Every time I stole a goat or a cow, I brought you a share of the curry…

'Even now that I've started stealing jewels and all, I've never let you down. I've been giving what's due to you. So many jewels and trinkets around these days, like never before … But never mind all that now – don't waste time! Give me your order, you low-caste brat, you!' he exclaimed, and hurled himself face down upon the earth. Arms raised high, hands folded in a kumbidu, he lay there awhile…

'Don't think bad of me,' he moaned under his breath. 'As though the world has never seen anyone like me before! As if I'm the only one who is praying to you to bring ruin on somebody. Is there anybody who comes to you asking you for a mind that doesn't wish harm on somebody? A mind that doesn't covet another man's wealth … doesn't lust after his wife … doesn't envy anybody he sees? Does anyone ever plead with you to let him remain a beggar forever? "Let me always live in a hut with a roof of thatch!" – which fellow ever asked you for that? Where's he?

'… I have children. Little ones. They're just in the eighth and ninth classes. Once they start earning their own food, why would I go and steal? Is this some great collector's job or teacher's job that I have got to do? I steal just to fill the stomach. Why is that a crime? Now, are you still going to keep on sitting there without giving me any sign? As if in this whole world I am the only man who's robbing and stealing…!'

As he finished speaking, he thought he heard a lizard call. That, too, it had clucked from the right side. With a jerk, he looked up towards his right … Seized by a conviction that a lizard had indeed uttered an auspicious click-cluck, he sprang up exultantly. Making a kumbidu to the saami, he laughed, 'That'll be all, da!'

'Wait!' he said, suddenly. 'Let's just see if it's a lucky sign or not – heads or tails? Flower or leaf? Then I'll know the job won't turn out sour. It'll be nice and ripe! And I can boldly go ahead…' As he spoke, he bent and picked up a fistful of tiny areca-nut-sized pebbles. Holding them between his palms, he made a kumbidu to the saami. Then he shook them up three or four times, threw them on the ground, and sat down beside them. With growing excitement, he placed them in pairs, next to each other, and as the uncounted pile decreased in size, his agitation increased, his fingers trembled, and he began to perspire a little. When he had counted out the last pair and he saw that there was only one left over, his face brightened and he gave a laugh. Handling it delicately as if it were a piece of gold, he tucked the last pebble safely into his waist-knot.

'Every once in a while, you go crazy and send me roaming round and round for no good reason! You make me wait and wait … But sometimes you bring me a good catch! This time, too, the omen has spoken. Now this stone has given me a flower! Without your support, and without your say-so, I would never ever take one step anywhere! You know that, don't you?' he declared.

Getting up, he went to the neem tree and stripped off a handful of leaves from a branch. Then he came back and sat down as before, in the same spot. Pair by pair, he set out the leaves … What it was that got into his mind just then is hard to say, but he clasped his hands together once again in a fervent kumbidu and prayed, 'Don't let it be anything but flower! Don't let me down, da! I won't be able to go and do the job, then!' He finished arranging the leaves in twos.

When he had counted out the last pair, he saw there was just one leaf left. Tears stood in his eyes. With utmost reverence, he picked up that last leaf and tucked it away safely at his waist. Rising to his feet, he raised his folded hands high.

'You're a powerful saami, da. It's not for no reason that I make my kumbidu to you, isn't that so?' he asked, as he backed off from the cement dais, hands still clasped together, and made three circumambulations. Gathering the sacred ash strewn near the feet of the horse, he anointed himself on the brow, saying, 'This work I'm off to do – when everything goes right and the job is finished, I'll be here tomorrow morning.'

He tramped off in the direction of the footpath. It was dark. Yet his feet clearly saw that path. They sprang eagerly forward, like the paws of an animal out on a hunt.

Bus to Aaladi

'JUST MOVE UP A LITTLE,' said the woman from Vadakkiruppu.

'That's someone's seat. They'll come now,' said Priyanka.

'When they come, I'll get up. Now move up.'

'They've gone to the shop. Be back now.'

'Is this bus your family property or what?'

'It's the government's.'

'Then what's the problem? Move up.'

'It's someone's seat, they'll be coming – how many times do I have to tell you? Find another seat.'

'Let them come. You move up. Or move out of the way!' The woman spoke with some force. She was from the cluster of huts to the north of Priyanka's own village.

Priyanka was sitting in a space meant for two people. A handbag lay on the seat next to the window. When the northerner told her to move, she had at once taken hold of the bar above the seat in front with both hands. Only if she removed her arms could anyone go past her. The woman tried to push away those arms. It was no use. Priyanka wasn't loosening her grip even a little.

'You're going to which place?' demanded the woman.

'Aaladi.' Priyanka was curt.

'All the way to Vadakkiruppu I have to go! Can't keep on standing so long. In this whole crowd it's only you who's just four stops from your place, isn't it? So why can't you shift a bit and sit over there?' said the woman.

'Is there no other place in the bus?'

'If there was, why would I come and hang on you?'

The Vadakkiruppu woman's angry question fell on deaf ears. Deliberately looking away from her, Priyanka stared out of the bus. Her eyes searched for Teacher. She was the one who had asked her to keep her seat, and left her handbag on it. People were crowding towards the bus from all directions and milling around waiting to get in. No sign of Teacher. Besides the Vadakkiruppu woman, eight or nine others had already enquired, 'Anybody coming?' 'Anyone coming?' Who knew how many more would ask? Enough of it, Priyanka thought. Teacher had better come soon...

It was always only after the eighth of the month that she got her period, but this time it came sooner. If she'd known, she would have stayed home. It was only after two that afternoon that it happened. At once she had gone to the boss and told him she had to go home in a hurry.

'What for?' he kept asking. Seemed like a hundred times he asked that question.

'Just like that, saar,' she said, glossing over it. After much pleading, this boss of the Xerox shop where she worked said, 'Go at six o'clock.'

She could barely contain the fury she felt. It was only at nine every night that he ever let her leave. Knowing what the man was like, she rarely took a day off. When she did have to go home early, she didn't usually inform him beforehand. It was only because she had a problem today that she had asked to be allowed to go home. Even so, he had delayed it by four whole hours … For some reason, this month there was more bleeding. Maybe it was because she had been standing continuously, she thought.

The woman from Vadakkiruppu set down the two bags she had been carrying and pushed them behind Priyanka's feet. One tilted forward and fell on Priyanka's foot. Abruptly pulling back her leg and shoving the bag away, she demanded, 'You'll bring your bags here and put them down only on top of my feet, is it?' Glowering at her, the woman retorted, 'Why are you kicking the bag with your foot?' and put the bag back where it had been.

Just then, a woman who had got on from the back entrance looked about for a seat. People were standing in a row and holding on to the overhead bar. At last, her eyes fell on the seat next to Priyanka's. Jostling and pushing, shouting, 'Move, 'nga![1] Make way!' and stamping on

---

1 'nga: A short form of the second person plural pronoun, expressive of respect.

numerous feet, she reached the spot after a formidable struggle. 'Is anybody coming?' she demanded urgently.

Priyanka nodded a 'yes' but did not open her mouth to speak. Nor did she look at the woman.

'Can I sit until they come?' the woman beseeched. 'I just can't stand here! Such a tight squeeze! Head is going round and round.' But Priyanka kept gazing outside the window as if she had nothing to do with what the woman was saying.

Her eyes searched among the people swarming back and forth. Not a sign of the teacher who had left her handbag on the window seat. Her temper rose. How many more people must she fob off? And that too, in the condition she was in? It burned her up just to think about it.

'No respect for age, no sense of what's right!' the woman declared. Then she asked abruptly, 'Are you married?'

'Why're you asking?'

'Just like that.'

'What for d'you want to know that? What are you going to do? '

'Just to ask you when you're going to invite me to your marriage feast!' As though she knew what she was insinuating, Priyanka sharply averted her face.

At that, the Vadakkiruppu woman added, 'Just look at that face! Would this little pet ever invite the whole town for a meal? See if that happens, or it turns out the way I am telling you!'

Wretched period, plus a headache, and now this! Already in a torment, Priyanka lost her temper. She said fiercely, 'So what if I don't get married! No need for you to roam about looking for a bridegroom for me!'

'Each and every word of yours is like a coconut being cracked open! Why do you talk like that?' The Vadakkiruppu woman confronting Priyanka could not contain her rage. Twisting her face in a grimace of contempt, she went on, 'Just now only she has got on this bus, and see what a fancy act she puts on! How'll she act if she really owned the bus!' Hardly had she finished when Priyanka cut in angrily, 'What do you mean, "fancy act"? Ever since you came, I've been watching how *you* act. Talking as though *you're* very great! Supposing you had taken this seat before me, and I asked you for it, would you ever have given it to me?'

'Yes, I would,' said the Vadakkiruppu woman proudly.

'One look at her, and you'll see how true that is!' jeered Priyanka.

'What do you see, here under this saree?' said the Vadakkiruppu woman provocatively.

'What do I care what is showing? Just don't push me, stay back. You are keeping on pushing and shoving – just like these men, these dogs!' fumed Priyanka. She went on in an exasperated, fed-up tone, 'That teacher who gave me her bag and told me to keep her seat, who knows where she's gone and got lost! I myself am in a bad state. A huge headache it's giving me, and yet I'm forced to quarrel with all the devils in town and listen to their talk.'

At once, the Vadakkiruppu woman pounced: 'Watch your tongue! Who are you calling a devil?'

'Why would I call you a devil? Here you go talking away, with no idea what state I am in.' As she spoke, she was consumed by worry about whether there was a bloodstain on the seat. She was very angry with her boss. If it had been a day like any other, she would have been the first to say, 'Sit down,' and yield her seat to any old woman, or one carrying an infant. She couldn't do it today. If she stood up, something awkward might happen, and then what would she do? Beset by anxiety, she sat there wondering when the bus would leave the terminus and begin its journey, and when she would at last reach home.

'You said somebody is coming, but nobody has come yet. Supposing I sit there until they come? Will it cost you a lot of money or what? Is that why you are sitting there blocking that seat? The way you're acting and talking, it looks as though you've dropped down from the sky or something.'

'You're coming from the sky, is it? Born and brought up there?'

'No.'

'Then what's all this about? Stop laying down the law, and keep your mouth shut,' burst out Priyanka. Vexed with her own predicament, she was saying a little too much. After all, she badly needed to hurry home. More than anyone else…

'Who are you to tell me to shut my mouth?' demanded the Vadakkiruppu woman. Then, as though she had just remembered, 'Oh, you're from Aaladi, isn't it? So that is why you are like this! A person is just like their home town.'

'What do you know about Aaladi?' With Priyanka's retort being countered by the woman's derisive remarks about Aaladi, the quarrel escalated and gathered strength. Coarse words began to be hurled. Neither of them seemed to be concerned that the bus was full of people.

Watching them, a man in a black shirt in the seat ahead put in a word of advice: 'Why are you two fighting about saving a seat for who knows who?'

'And which village headman are you?'

'Okay, okay,' muttered the man. Not a word came from him after that.

From a stout, dark fellow in the next seat came an angry question: 'Can't anybody ask why you are making *your* fight into a town fight? Everyone is just roaming around looking for some worthless fight in this place! Full of drunken fellows! How many people with children are standing here, can't you see? If you move a little, what is going to happen? As if you've got the title deed to this government bus, you are keeping your bag there. How many people don't even have a place to stand, can't you see?'

With equal vehemence, not stopping to think at all, Priyanka shot back, 'You are the headman of which village? Who called you to hold a panchayat meeting here?'

'Can't one speak up for justice?'

Like a slap on the face came Priyanka's rejoinder: 'Are you the only one who knows anything about justice? Big panchayat head you are for whole country or what?' The man now launched a verbal assault with the Vadakkiruppu woman joining in. But not even by the thickness of a single thread did Priyanka's grip slacken. She took on both of them single-handed.

Those ahead heard the ruckus and were turning to look. Not the conductor, though. Seated right behind the driver, he was busy tearing off tickets and handing them out. That many could not find space even to stand in the crush, that a fight was going on in the back of the bus, that many were getting abusive as they demanded, 'When's this damn bus going to start? There isn't any air to breathe here!' – none of it seemed to affect him as he went about his work. From time to time, out of sheer force of habit, he came out with, 'Move on inside. Go inside.'

'What d'you mean "go inside"! No place even to stand here! To go inside we'll have to climb up on people's heads … One ticket to Paalakolla,' said a woman, handing the cash to the conductor. 'There is so much noise and fighting going on back there. Can't you just give a shout and quieten them?'

'Same rowdy fight goes on every day in this seven o'clock single.[2] You are seeing it only one time. Daily

2 Single: A single-decker bus.

one hundred times I am seeing the same thing. It would be good if they arrange another bus for this time slot. But which fellow will make that happen? If somebody misses this bus, finished. No other bus there will be for the next two hours … Please move up, Amma. Daily they are sending up so many rockets to find out all sorts of things! One more town bus they will not provide.' As he spoke, the conductor shoved his way past two or three passengers a foot or so ahead and stood there announcing, 'Ticket, ticket!'

Just then, a woman clambered in clutching three large bags. As she forged ahead, thrusting aside some people and pulling away others from her path, the conductor remonstrated: 'Why are you bringing so many bags at such a time, Amma, when there's no place even for a person to stand?'

'So! A person must travel in one bus, and their baggage must travel in another?' As though her words had not entered his ears, the conductor continued to shout, 'Ticket! Ticket!'

'Get into the bus after six o'clock, and it'll be full of booze smell!' complained the woman who had earlier spoken to the conductor about his peacekeeping duty. Making her way forward and intoning 'Please move! Please move a little!' she spotted the seat next to Priyanka. Urgently, as though that seat was waiting just for her to arrive and claim it, she barged past ten or twenty people, treading on the feet of several. At the sight of the bag lying on the seat, her expression altered. Pushing aside the woman from Vadakkiruppu, she addressed Priyanka.

'Just move up a little!'

'There's someone coming,' Priyanka said. Her face was set.

'I'm carrying three bags! I can't keep standing! Sweat smell is making me faint!' the woman protested.

'Just now only I have finished one fight. And now you also have come! Stand back, don't touch … There is somebody coming,' snapped Priyanka. A man sitting opposite remarked, 'Just to give a seat in a bus she is showing off so much, how big she'd be if she could hand out MLA or MP seats!'

He had hardly closed his mouth, when a terrible rage came over Priyanka – who knew where from? Utterly beside herself, she shot back: 'Go catch any MLA seat or minister's seat! Am I stopping you?'

It looked like the man was about to get quite angry, too. 'Ever since I came, I have been seeing you. How you are going on and on talking as if you are some very, very big thing! People like you will become okay only when we call the conductor.'

'You call the conductor, or call the collector himself. I'll see who comes and what they can do!' challenged Priyanka.

'Tomorrow you'll have to go through my town in this bus, right? Then I will get you!' said the man.

'With that face? Like a dirty leaf licked by a dog? *You* are going to get *me*? Tell me when and where I should come. Just try whatever you can!' Not tiring in the least, she let fly her challenges.

'One look at her is enough – it's plain to see!' commented the man drily, upon which Priyanka started to shout. 'What is it that's so plain to see, 'ya? Show some respect, some decency here! Or *you* won't get any respect. You've lost all sense of shame! Something or other is so plain to see, he's saying!'

It was only after one or two people scolded, 'Why open your mouth and pick a fight with a woman?' that the man finally shut up. But Priyanka was still smarting, thinking of how terrible it was that everybody was quarrelling with her today of all days, when she couldn't come out with what really was bothering her. Which was that, if she stood up, it would become really obvious. If people noticed, it would be so shameful. That was what worried her, and that was why she had made up her mind not to shift from her seat, no matter how many people tried to make her do it. Nor would she cut back on any words to keep them off ... She would have to be very careful getting down from the bus. Checking for any smell, she worried that the women nearby would guess from that alone what it was.

At that moment, another woman climbed in from the back entrance, sweating profusely. Something had mightily incensed this middle-aged casual worker returning from a construction site. 'Bloody damn bus! Get on it, and every time it is the same old nuisance!' she shouted. 'As if they have never before seen any bloody female, every one of these dogs will come and dash and rub against me!' Nobody seemed to have heard her at all, so loud was the music being spewed out by the bus's speakers.

'Ticket, ticket!' said the conductor, as he approached Priyanka.

'Aaladi,' she told him, handing over the fare.

At that, a youth standing on one of the steps from the entrance enquired, 'When are you going to start the bus? Can't you see it's already seven o'clock?' That set off a muttering among others standing on the steps and inside the bus. 'When is this bus going to leave, anyway?' and 'Are they going to start it at all?'

As though he hadn't let any of it enter his ears, the conductor called out, 'Climb up, please, climb in!'

'We may climb up or climb in, just let that be! When are you going to start moving this bus?' one fellow wanted to know.

'Driver's gone to drink tea. Soon as he comes, he'll start the bus. You just get in, don't talk about law and all.'

'He's taking one whole week to drink tea or what? Every time you get in this damn bus, it's the same problem. We never know when they'll move it,' the man said bitterly. The conductor said nothing in reply, but went on asking, 'Ticket, ticket?' Complaints that the bus was not moving did not appear to have entered his ears. The jabbing and jostling and pushing that was going on around him, the bags that blocked the way, all the little cloth bundles –

he worried about none of these and went on handing out tickets.

That was when the teacher who had left her bag with Priyanka turned up. Equal to two persons in bulk, she thrust herself past the five people on the steps and others standing in her way. By the time she got to Priyanka, she was out of breath. Hurriedly seating herself, she wiped off the sweat streaming from her face and neck.

'What a huge crowd in that shop! Almost lost my life before I could buy a little coffee powder. I thought, let me recharge my cell. But there was an even bigger crowd over there. In any ordinary shop for rice or provisions there will never be so many, many people! What sort of town, what sort of country is this!' she cried. Then, turning towards Priyanka, she asked, 'Why such a crowd today in this bus? By the time I got in, they made a chutney out of me!'

'Daily it is like this only. Morning when it comes from the village to the town, more than fifty people will be riding on top of the bus.' Priyanka's tone was offhand, as though it meant nothing to her.

'Such trouble I went through, climbing up the steps and getting in, I might as well have walked to town!'

'Travel in the town bus day after day and then only you will know. One moment you are dying, next moment you are alive … it goes on and on. Ride a bus every day! Then only you will know what it is like,' remarked Priyanka. Then she noticed that the teacher was looking closely at her cell phone.

'Your phone is a costly one?' she enquired.

'Yes.'

'You came only just now. Why couldn't you have come earlier? A huge fight took place. Why, this was a battleground!' said the Vadakkiruppu woman. The teacher was baffled: what was the woman talking about, and why was she telling her all this?

'What business is it of yours, when madam comes and when she goes?' Priyanka said fierily.

'Too rude and bossy you are for a woman! Just a female.'

'Are you the one who fed me rice and brought me up?'

'No!'

'Then? Just shut up.'

'O Siva Siva! Never heard such talk in my time!' the Vadakkiruppu woman burst out, turning to glare at a fellow jabbing into her side. Six or seven schoolgirls returning from evening tuition classes were being stuffed into the bus by those getting in behind them – like onions and tomatoes crammed in a mixie jar.

'Can't breathe inside, sweat smell is tearing out my guts, no place to put the feet. No way for my hands to reach the bar. When the bus moves, it'll shake so much my insides will come outside. How will I ever reach my village? From town to village, they send only such tin-box buses!' wailed the Vadakkiruppu woman to the owner of the three bags. Even a bedbug wouldn't find a hiding place inside the bus, but unconcerned with all this a youth was poking at his cell phone in search of who knows what.

‘Are you working anywhere, ’mma?’ asked the teacher.

‘I work in a Xerox shop,’ answered Priyanka. After a while, quite of her own accord, although the teacher had not spoken a word more, she confided, ‘My period came, all of a sudden. Afternoon itself I explained and asked for permission. But that dog let me off only now. While walking, it has increased. I am worried that it will come on the seat. That is why I didn’t get up at all. A big fight it became! When will I ever get home, I am thinking.’

‘Is that so?’ the teacher said, distantly. Neither in her face nor in her tone was there anything out of the ordinary.

The driver got into the bus. Jubilant yells of ‘Right! Right! Let’s go!’ came from the more than ten young fellows standing on the front and back steps, forestalling his usual shouts. The bus started to move.

‘Was there a problem keeping my seat?’ asked the teacher.

‘No problem at all. Don’t say anything, Teacher, let it be.’

‘Tell the truth.’

‘Getting out of the house itself is a problem. Will getting into the town bus be anything less than a problem? That, too, for a female!’

‘So, keeping a seat for me became problem for you?’

‘You are the teacher who works in our village. You have newly come. Won’t I hold a seat for you?’

'I thought I would get back quickly, but it got late at the cell-phone shop.'

'Hunh! You call this a problem? In our village there are people who get into fights to catch a seat in the bus and end up going all the way to court.'

'Really?' asked the teacher, astonished.

'In this bus, what-all love stories are going on! If you saw that, then what will you say? Just look at those four-five fellows standing there, squeezing those schoolgirls.'

'What you are saying, it is all so new to me!' The teacher spoke as though she were an innocent young girl who knew nothing of the world.

'It isn't new and it isn't old, daily it is happening – same story,' Priyanka told her. On a sudden impulse, as though she had just noticed, she whispered, 'Teacher, why are you wearing so many jewels when you are travelling in a bus? Some fellow will just snatch it and go off! These days they don't leave alone any female, even somebody who is not wearing any jewels.'

Alarm spreading over her face, the teacher turned to breathe in some air through the window. Just then, the Vadakkiruppu woman snapped at the man next to her, 'I am here! A person is standing here! Don't you know that?'

'It's only for a little time, no? Just quietly keep on standing, 'mma! If there is any space, won't I go and stand somewhere else? Why should I bang against you? Is it some holy, holy blessing I am wanting or what?'

The bus had travelled only a little past the town. With every lurch, the Vadakkiruppu woman kept falling over Priyanka, as if on purpose, and kept being glared at in return. Feeling something pressing into her, Priyanka turned to see a man, fully drunk, bending over her. Once more his hand fell on her shoulder. Not only that – she felt a distinct light pressure. When she turned to look, his hand swiftly grabbed the overhead bar. Again, when she turned away, it descended to press against her shoulder. Priyanka tried to put up with it. Tried to rein in her fury. Again and again, the hand kept pressing her shoulder. It did not stop.

Rising with a jerk, Priyanka shouted, 'Are you the only man in the whole world? I've been watching for a long time. Where are you putting your hand? It is only in the bus that you have to show that you are a man, is it? Show off your heroism in the place where it belongs! Show it off to me, and I'll cut it all off!'

'You say I touched you? Where?' the man countered.

'Shut your mouth! Do you have no other place in the world to put your hand inside?' shrieked Priyanka like a wild thing.

'Why are you screaming, 'mma?' the man asked, and then all hell broke loose.

'Hit him, da! He's been doing it to me too! How long should I bear it?' The moment the Vadakkiruppu woman came out with this, Priyanka forgot to worry about blood staining and wetting the place where she had been sitting.

She dealt the man a violent push. Immediately, the Vadakkiruppu gave him another.

'Pushing a man, are you? Which village are you two from?' shouted the man. Together they pounced on him. It was hard to tell whose tongue was doing the most work.

But the teacher was paying no attention to this fight going on right next to her. She was busy checking her cell phone: had the money paid resulted in its being charged or not?

'Ticket, ticket,' intoned the conductor. The loudspeaker was belting out a film song, as the bus drove through the darkness.

'Ayyo, my purse is gone!' a girl screamed, and broke into sobs.

'Kuravankuppam! Stop!' shouted a passenger.

Unaffected by any of the noise around him, the conductor continued his chant: 'Ticket, ticket.'

A True Story

'WHERE'S THE VALLALAAR DESTITUTES' HOME here?' Selvam asked the auto driver.

'D'you know the Government Hospital?' the auto driver asked him, in turn.

'Yes, I know.'

'Go west, straight past the Government Hospital. It's there, the place you're looking for.'

'Can the auto go there?'

'Sixty rupees it'll be. Get in, please, let's go,' said the auto driver.

'Okay, and I'll give you ten rupees extra.'

To Leelavati, who was looking on, he said, 'Come get in, let's go,' and began to climb into the auto without waiting to hear what she had to say.

'We'll walk.'

Pausing in mid-climb, he turned to her, protesting, 'What are you saying, Amma? Doesn't matter how much it costs. We'll reach there sooner by auto.' He got in and sat down in the auto.

'Are we going to a wedding or something? Do we have to hurry and reach before the auspicious time for tying the taali[1] gets over? What I'm going on is my last journey, isn't it? It's my time to leave home and go off to spend my last days in the forest … To get lost, and die there.'

Selvam's face looked stricken. He got out of the auto at once and came and stood by her side. 'It's very hot, Amma,' he said.

'Why should we reach so early? What are we going to do there?'

'We're only going to make enquiries there, isn't it? We aren't going to stay there, no? Come. Let's go in the auto,' he entreated.

'Why should I go so early? Are you so eager for me to go to the cremation ground?'

The way she put the question aroused his anger. It also drained him of the energy to speak another word. To avoid looking at her, he turned his gaze on the auto and its driver.

'We are going to walk there!' Leelavati spoke defiantly, as though confronting an attacker.

'Can't you understand why I'm saying it? It's because it'll be hard to walk all the way.'

'If you're in such a hurry, just go back to the house. I will walk! I'll find out everything by myself. If you come with me, they won't take me in. If I go by myself, I'll say I have nobody, I'm destitute. They'll believe me.'

---

1 Taali: Marriage thread.

His face flushing an angry red, Selvam turned away. Staring at the street, he said, 'If I say one thing, you put some other meaning to it.'

The auto driver, who had been glancing back and forth at Leelavati and Selvam all this time, now said, 'Want auto or not?' Instead of answering his question, Leelavati asked: 'Will they admit anyone into the Home? Will they ask for money – and ask about caste?'

The auto driver gave her a searching look from top to toe. Then he said. 'It's free. No need to pay any money. Just have to be poor and have nobody.' His tone was detached.

'Won't they take somebody who has a family?'

'No, they won't,' he told her. Once again, he demanded, 'Want auto or not?'

'I *am* without anybody! Will they take me?'

'Go and find out,' the auto driver advised her, and turned to Selvam, asking once again, 'Want auto or not?' Since Selvam did not open his mouth to respond, he abruptly drove his auto four or five yards off and stopped it there, looking out for a likely passenger.

Leelavati felt suddenly deflated. Anxiety seized her that the Home might not take her in. She was also very annoyed with the auto driver. 'More than having to pay out one's cash these days, it's having to listen to people talking like this that's really hard,' she muttered. One or two blunt words was all he had spoken, before driving off. Should she go up to him and ask once again? She thought about it. How could she ask, with Selvam standing next to her?

A bus came roaring up just then, close enough to knock her down. Alarmed, she stepped back just in time. 'Come this side, Amma!' Selvam called out.

'Come! Let's go,' she told him.

'In this hot sun how will you walk all the way, leaning on your stick? There's so much traffic. Let's take the auto, Amma,' he pleaded.

'Just tell me the way, I'll go by myself,' she said resolutely, her face averted.

Selvam gave himself a sharp smack on the forehead in sheer frustration, 'You don't listen to what anybody says! That's just why you're now going to a place where you shouldn't be going at all.'

'You just tell me the way, that's all.'

'It's fate! No one can change this!' Selvam moaned bitterly, glaring at Leelavati.

'Those who die early have done good deeds in their previous life. I'm not one of them, I've not done any good deeds.'

'What are you saying, standing out here! Amma, this is a bus stop!' protested Selvam, much mortified.

'That place I'm going to – I don't know what they're going to tell me. That itself is boiling in my head. All right, let's go. Whatever happens, let it happen. There's no law, is there – that only what *I* want must happen? I don't have any god who will take my side – that's what.' Her eyes were on the Annapurni Hotel opposite as she spoke.

'Amma...'

'If you're coming, just come. Otherwise just go!' she told him, and began to walk off at the same speed at which she had spoken.

'Not that way, this way!' Smacking himself exasperatedly once again on the forehead, Selvam pointed in another direction. When she set off, he trailed her, watching her hobble along leaning on her cane. It made him feel uneasy – the sight of her leaning forward and jerking up her waist with every step she took, bending a leg in a kind of curve, then stretching it out. It was the only way she could walk, but anyone watching her could not help but stare. The thought came to him that not just people who knew them but anyone on the road might be cursing him for forcing a lame old woman to walk. He was furious with Leelavati: what would all those passers-by be thinking of him?

That it shamed him didn't seem to bother Leelavati at all. There she was, limping and tottering on and on, as if she'd gone crazy … To look at her, one would think she knew exactly where she was headed. 'Why won't she do as she's told? What terrible thing is going to happen if we go by auto? How stubborn she is, the old hag!' he muttered, teeth clenched.

Leelavati's obduracy baffled Selvam, she seemed like another woman. For three days she had not eaten. To not one person had she spoken a single word. The only thing she kept saying, intoning it like a mantra, was: 'I'm going to the Destitutes' Home.' Asked for a reason, she would say nothing. After begging and pleading with her, Selvam got the neighbours to come and speak to her. Even people on the street came in and tried to make her see reason. But she would listen to no one. 'So stubborn, at such an age? So then, let her go and find out for herself! For one week, let her try it out. Only then she'll know what's the value of a home. When she's throwing a tantrum like this, worse than any child, what else to do? Growing old means brain is getting rotten. Much more than children, it is these old people who are a big bother to take care of.' Without exception, that was what every single person finally declared, fed up of trying and failing to talk sense into her … Seeing no way out, Selvam too had finally consented to take her.

'Eat!' he had implored her, before they left the next morning, but she would not budge an inch. Distressed that she had not eaten even in the morning, he hastened to her and said, 'Let's eat something at least before leaving. Okay, you haven't eaten at home, but at least take something at the shop. How will they take you in as soon as you reach there, Amma? Who knows when you'll get food? It's three days since you've eaten!' he said, his voice breaking.

'I'm not hungry.'

'Listen to me, Amma!'

'If I die like that, very good!' she announced, cutting him short.

Selvam persisted, 'At least have coffee.'

'Coffee on an empty stomach will turn my guts inside out. I don't want it.'

'Tender-coconut man is standing just here, shall I buy one?'

'No need.'

'With your own son why are you being so adamant? Amma, listen to what I'm saying!' He wanted, somehow or other, to make Leelavati eat.

'It's so hot. Let's go. Who knows what they're going to say over there? Seems they take in only people who have nobody.'

'Why are you talking like that, so sharp? Come this side. Car fellow will run you down.'

'Nothing like that is happening! Each fellow driving a car is thinking why the hell should I bother to run her down? They're all getting out of the way, the dogs!'

'Don't go on saying whatever you feel like. Look! "Come-and-Eat" it says on that board! That's a hotel. Come, let's go eat a couple of idlis. Don't be angry, just listen.'

'I don't want it! So now they've started giving hotels such names, is it? Some devil has got into them!' she said, hobbling on even faster than before. The way she was carrying on would drive him mad, Selvam felt. He tried to ignore her and keep his eyes on the traffic. But nothing would hold his attention. Again and again his glance turned to her, and he felt the same rage. He felt sad, too. But more angry than sad … It was awkward, walking along with her. Unable to subdue his rage, he demanded, 'Are you going to your own house or what? And d'you think you're going to get something to eat as soon as you get there? Are we going to the house of someone from the family? Somebody known to us?'

'From now on, I'm going to live in the forest. I'm going towards the cremation ground.'

'Don't make me angry!' he yelled. The next moment he lowered his voice: 'I haven't done anything wrong! You are the one who is insisting on going to the Destitutes' Home, aren't you? All these years, have I ever talked back to you? Have I ever scolded you? Used bad words?'

'Why are you talking, here in the street, about what goes on at home?' There was no agitation in her voice. It did not sound like the voice of a woman who had not eaten for three days. Each word she spoke sounded as though she had rehearsed it many times in her mind.

It was Selvam who was confused and fumbling for words. Two contrary thoughts were jostling in his brain: that it was no bad thing if Leelavati was put into the Destitutes' Home; and another thought – that she must not be left there. Would they or would they not admit her? Would they refuse her on the grounds that she had a son? As though suddenly overtaken by emotion, he hurried to come up alongside as she walked on. 'Won't you please understand me, Amma?' he begged.

'If you are feeling ashamed, you go back. I will find the way and go there myself. We must be halfway there, already, isn't it?'

'Is that what I have been saying? What are you talking about?' he shouted angrily.

'If you come with me, there will be a problem. Don't come and say, "This is my mother." Say, "This is a woman I know, somebody on our street." Only then they'll admit me.'

'Will you just shut up or not?' he said, glaring at her. 'Is there no limit to what you say? … It's all my fate, written on my forehead. I'm born as your son, and just look at what I am suffering … Better to just die,' he muttered to himself.

'We wanted it, that's why you were born. You didn't ask for it.' Tears appeared in Leelavati's eyes.

'Why are you saying such words? Was it I who told you to go to the Destitutes' Home? You're the one who's cantankerous. So hell-bent on going there!'

His head felt as though it would crack open, he was so angry. If he had been at home, he would have put up a huge fight, he'd have roared like a wild beast! Unable to bring himself to strike Leelavati herself, he would have grabbed hold of his children instead and thrashed them. He would have thrown things around and smashed them, made a huge ruckus. But how could he do such things on the open street? Looking from shop to shop on either side of the street, he walked along. His mind was on fire, and nothing that his eyes rested on could quench his anger. 'Why was I ever born? That's what I'm feeling now!' Selvam thought bitterly.

It was becoming difficult for him to walk on, but Leelavati was trudging ahead, hauling her feet forward one after the other. The traffic and the people on the road, the heat and the pungent, bitter sweat – nothing mattered to her. It was not so much the road in front of her that she was looking at, as something else that she clearly saw in her mind, so purposeful and swift was her walk. When a scooter or a bus or a car approached, it was not she who moved away, or stepped aside. Selvam was utterly amazed, he just did not know what force it was that made her walk like that.

At the Government Hospital, Leelavati came to a halt and Selvam too, with her. Each gave the other a look, but neither spoke. They just stood there as though two lifelong enemies had chanced to meet. Seeing Selvam standing there with his mouth shut, Leelavati finally asked, 'You know the place?'

'Have to find out,' he answered tersely. Enquiring at the medical shop nearby, he returned to announce, 'Seems it's at the end of the next street.' He spoke as though he was giving directions to some passer-by.

'Which way?'

'This way.'

Leelavati set off in the direction he was pointing. He came up alongside, and they walked in silence for a while before he said to her, as though imparting a secret, 'Don't get angry. Even now it's not too late. We can go back home. You've fought with her so many times, have I ever said anything? Just because of a quarrel with a daughter-in-law, would anybody go off to a place for homeless people? So many times you've quarrelled with her, but have I ever asked why? How can I even eat, Amma, if you are not there?' he asked, almost in tears.

'I'm not angry with anybody, I'm not sad. When I've already left the house, how can I go back? With what face can I return?'

'It's your house, Amma.'

'Wrong. It is not my house, it's your wife's house. Your house. Your ma-in-law's people's house.'

'Why do you talk like that? Divide people up? All right, so she is an outsider. Am I also one?' Selvam's eyes were brimming.

'How can one live in a house where nobody talks to anybody? Even when it was empty, that house used to talk to me, but now that house doesn't speak to me. That's why I came out. Now all sorts of people come and go.'

'What do you mean, Amma? I don't understand. Is Kalamani doing something wrong? Is she a bad character?'

'I didn't say that.' Leelavati stopped walking and gave Selvam a peculiar look. Her eyes were brimming.

'What wrong thing did I do? What mistake did my children do? You're leaving without even seeing them! Fights between mothers-in-law and daughters-in-law go on in every house in the world, no? Is it something new that is happening? Or is ours the only house where it happens? You are old now. Why not adjust? Tolerate a little?'

'What should I tolerate?' Sparks fit to burn Selvam up flew from Leelavati's eyes. She gritted her teeth. 'So! I must "tolerate" it when your wife goes loitering around town, is that it? Look at the fancy name he's given her, that father of hers – Kalamani! A gem of art, it seems. Gem of a thief, he should have called her. That father of hers is to blame for everything.'

'What are you saying, Amma!' Selvam asked piteously.

'Don't prod my tongue and make me say things. Let me go my way. That is what is good for you and your children.'

'You don't like me, okay! You don't like my wife. You don't like her family, okay. What about your grandchildren? Don't you even think of them?'

'It's all because of those two little devils that I've been sitting in that house for so many years.'

'Why not stay on for their sake now, too?'

'From now on, I will not stay in that house. Why should a pottachi[2] have a cell phone of her own? How long does a female creature need to talk on a cell phone, every day?' demanded Leelavati, and began to walk off.

'Is my wife doing something wrong? Are you suspecting her? Her people keep coming and going, and she

---

2 Pottachi: A scornful way to refer to a female.

gives them money. Are you talking about that? Tell me if she's doing any wrong thing, I'll cut her down.'

Leelavati stopped and gave him a look. 'Money! Is that important to me?'

'Tell me, then, what is your problem?' Selvam persisted and blocked her way.

'What's this you're doing? On the street!'

'Tell me the reason.'

'*I* don't have any problem.'

'Is this your final decision?'

Leelavati did not pause to think it over even a little. 'Yes!' she said, cutting the matter short with one stroke. Thrusting aside Selvam's arms, she began to walk on.

'You pushed Appa around! Made him do whatever you wanted … Me, too, you've been pushing around. Always you talk too much. This week it's gone beyond all limits.'

Leelavati stopped. 'I pushed your father around? I pushed you around?' she demanded tearfully. Opening her mouth wide, she wailed out loud, as she had never done before. 'A real wife tied by marriage – that's what I've been. A mother who's cooked and dished out your food for thirty–forty years, who's washed the shit off your clothes! So, I'm a woman for sleeping with, for waking up with – what is worth more than that!' she shrieked, enraged. 'And you – you're the child born in the few minutes your father got up to piss – for whose sake he went and hanged himself and died!' She trembled from head to foot, both hands clenching her cane.

Unnerved by her words and her tears, Selvam tried to placate her. 'What I am talking about is one thing, and you are thinking it's about something else. Whatever I say is going all wrong! What I am suffering, stuck between two women! Much better to just swallow poison and die. It's all my fate!' He gave himself yet another smack on the head. 'Just stop, Amma, let's talk about this before we go on.'

Leelavati continued to walk, regardless of his pleas … At last, she came to a stop in front of the Vallalaar Destitutes' Home and looked up at the building … A big place, with a broad entrance, like a marriage hall … Should she go in at once, or should she find someone and make enquiries before stepping in? Undecided, she stood there under the hot sun for a while. Then she moved to the shade of a neem tree, watching to see if anyone was coming out. Selvam stood nearby, as though next to a person whom he did not know. Leelavati avoided looking at him.

A girl of about ten came out.

'Eh, pappa, come here,' Leelavati called to her.

'What?'

'Just come here, 'mma.'

'What?' the child asked again, as she came up to Leelavati.

'Are you a child from this place?'

'Yes.'

'Can anybody join here? Will they take them in?'

'Don't know.'

'Who to meet, if we want to join?'

'Anna.'

'Which big brother?'

'Ilayaraaja Anna.'

'Who is that?'

'Owner.'

'Is he there?'

'Mm.'

'Will you take me there, please, 'mma?'

'I have to go to the shop.' With her eyes fixed on Leelavati, the child turned and began to walk away. A feeling of dread arose in Leelavati – What would the man inside be like? Would he admit her? If he didn't, what should she do? Her gaze spun around wildly in all directions – southwards and north, eastwards and towards the west – before it stopped at Selvam.

He was reading the sign on the building: Vallalaar Destitutes' Home.

'Will you go and find out?'

'No, Amma!' Tears stood in Selvam's eyes, and he turned to hide them.

Heaving herself forward, Leelavati stepped into the building. First there was a large hall. Beyond that, away to the north, was a room, and on the wall near it a large portrait of Vallalaar. A brass oil lamp stood beneath, with a flaming wick. From somewhere came the sound of a cassette softly playing 'Great, blessed light, mercy most rare and great…' Two girls, around six or seven years old, could be seen sitting and writing at the southern end of the hall.

Something made them raise their heads to stare in wide-eyed silence at Leelavati as she stood leaning on her cane.

One of them, a girl dressed in a long green paavaadai, got up and ran into the room towards the north. Leelavati called out, but the girl paid no attention. In a short while, the child emerged along with a middle-aged man, and as soon as she set eyes on him, Leelavati greeted him with folded palms as though she knew who he was.

'Whom do you want to see, 'mma?'

'You only, saar.'

'What, me?'

'Mm.'

'About what?'

'Just like that, saar.'

He had taken in Leelavati's appearance and her words, together with the way she looked at him, and instantly understood why she wanted to see him. Yet he asked her as if he had no idea of it: 'What do you want, 'mma, tell me?'

Speech failed Leelavati. Not a drop remained of the courage with which she had left the house and arrived in front of the building. Not only had all the moisture on her tongue utterly dried up, but her mouth was refusing to open. No words came, but tears flowed freely, with no obstruction whatsoever.

'Do you want to see me? Or do you want to meet anyone staying here?'

Leelavati did not know what to say, and how to say it. Nothing remained of the words she had used at home, of the boldness she had shown on the way. She wept. Ilayaraaja was unmoved by the sight. He had seen many women like her. Time and time again he had seen them weep, and he had had enough.

'Was it me you came to see?' he repeated.

Speechlessly, Leelavati jerked her head, as if to say yes.

'I have to go out now. What is the matter, please tell me?'

Just then, Selvam came in. He looked at Ilayaraaja and greeted him with a vanakkam.[3]

'Vanakkam. Welcome.'

'Saar is Ilayaraaja?'

'Yes, that's me.'

'You are the person who runs this institution?'

'Yes.'

'This is my mother, saar,' Selvam said, indicating his mother.

'Oh, is it so?'

'I need to talk to you a little, saar.'

'On what subject?'

'Just like that, saar. Nothing much.' Selvam's voice sank. He tried to avoid Ilayaraaja's eyes.

'Are you coming to give us some donation? For a birthday? Or wedding day? Some memorial?'

'Nothing like that, saar.'

---

3 Vanakkam: A term of respectful greeting, meaning a bow, the same as the namaste or the namaskaar of North India.

'Then?'

'Last week, they had some news on local TV, about this home for destitutes. Ever since she saw it, my mother has been insisting, "I will go there, I'll get admitted there." And here she's come.' Selvam's voice resounded with rancour and bitterness.

'That programme was to give people a chance to contribute. Some publicity. But not one donation has come! Only you have come!' Ilayaraaja said with a laugh.

'I will give what I can, saar,' said Selvam eagerly.

'If you do that, it will be a great service. It is with great difficulty that I am running this place for the last thirteen years.'

'Thirteen years?'

'Yes, that's right.'

Selvam fell silent. Leelavati did not speak either. Nor did Ilayaraaja. As he stood there gazing around the hall, Leelavati suddenly fell at his feet and brought her palms together in supplication. Selvam's heart seemed about to stop at the very sight. A quiver of fury went through his body.

'Get up, 'mma.' That was all that Ilayaraaja said, and in an ordinary tone of voice. With an inscrutable expression on his face, he looked them both up and down. Finally, he said, 'Please come inside,' and walked towards his office room. The two of them followed him in and seated themselves on a wooden bench opposite his chair.

For a while, no one spoke. 'It will be adding to all your good deeds if you take me in,' Leelavati said at last, her hands raised in a kumbidu.

'Why are you crying for everything? Why do so many kumbidus?' asked Ilayaraaja, sounding faintly irritated. Then, changing his tone, he explained: 'We run this place for people who have got nobody. But you have a son, don't you?'

'I've got everything, and yet I have nothing.' Leelavati's voice was full of bitterness, and her eyes full of tears.

'Please try to understand what I am saying. Once you begin to admit people with money, and people with children, everybody will start doing this kind of wrong thing. And I don't have the resources to run the place on that scale,' Ilayaraaja said with a smile.

'I don't have a house, and I don't have a husband.'

'What happened?'

'It's eight years since he died. I should have also died right then. When you get old, you shouldn't stay alive. That, too, with a broken back.' Tears stood in her eyes.

'What is wrong with your back? You can't walk properly?'

'It is very hard for me to walk. My hip got twisted when I was climbing on the bus – I slipped on the step. For six months I was lying in Korimedu Hospital. No operation at this age, they told me. Use a cane as far as possible and pull on somehow or other for the rest of your life, they told me, and sent me away.' Leelavati's head was bent, her body shook with sobs.

To change the subject, Ilayaraaja asked Selvam, 'What do you do, saar?'

'I'm a clerk in a government school.'

'Not bad … Your son has a government job! Do you really want me to take you in as a destitute? You really should not come to places like these, 'mma.'

'My heart has gone dead.'

'What are you saying, 'mma?' asked Ilayaraaja, startled.

'Please let me stay here, 'nga – somehow! You will be blessed, the parents who bore you will be blessed…' Again she wept. Again she raised her hands, made yet another kumbidu.

'Admitting is not the problem. Some people come here, like you, after a fight at home. After a week, their temper comes down. Then they make a big fuss, saying, "We have to go back!" In all these thirteen years, is there any story I haven't heard? Just go home quietly, 'mma!' he said, with a chuckle.

'Even when they have got tiny little babies, some people hang themselves and die, others with two–three young children go off and jump into the fire and kill themselves. How many die saying, "Mother-in-law fought with me! Husband quarrelled!" How many youngsters die after failing an exam? But I don't have the heart to die like all those young people. I don't know how to hate the world. Not to have the heart for it – that's so shameful!'

'What is this you are saying, 'mma!' Ilayaraaja remonstrated.

'I don't want to live. Can't die.'

As though it had just occurred to him, he asked, 'When did you eat last?'

'Three days back,' Selvam told him.

'My god!' Alarmed, Ilayaraaja turned to Leelavati. 'Will you eat, 'mma?' he asked her. And then, not addressing either of them directly, he declared, 'Food itself is the world! How can there be anything without that?'

'Admit me, please, saami. I don't want food.'

'If you declare that you are a destitute, there is no question of not admitting you, I'll take you in at once. Was there a fight in your house?'

'No, nothing like that.'

Noting her grimace, Ilayaraaja turned to Selvam. 'Are you her own son?'

'Yes.'

'How many others?'

'I'm the only one.'

Ilayaraaja fell silent, gazing closely at them.

'Your mother is in great mental confusion,' he said at last, wearily. 'Take her home. After one week has gone by, everything will become all right.'

'No, saami!' Leelavati cried out with folded hands. At that very sight, Selvam felt like running away. Beside himself with anger, he shouted, 'Will you keep quiet for a while?'

'I'm an old woman about to die – why do I need a mouth?'

Looking at her with loathing, Selvam gnashed his teeth. He struck himself on the forehead. 'Let her do what she wants, saar. I'll send you whatever money you say, every month!' he said disgustedly.

'It is not for money that I run this place!' Ilayaraaja at once cut him short.

'I'm not saying that you are running this place for money, saar!' came Selvam's rejoinder in a broken voice. After a long pause, and apparently having thought about it, he said, 'If I listen to my mother, my wife tells me, "Okay, just listen only to your mother!" If I listen to my wife, "You better listen only to your wife!" that's what my mother tells me. For a whole year something has been going on between my mother and my wife, I can't find out what it is. I feel as if I am going mad!' Tears fell as he spoke.

He blew his nose and went on: 'All because I was given my job on compassionate grounds, not a single fellow in the office has any respect for me! All the work falls on my head. Sixty people work in that school. I can't stand still even for one minute. Even on Saturday and Sunday there's work. Giving out salaries, dismissing people, distributing GPF[4] amounts, granting medical leave – so much work! Whether the teachers are actually teaching and taking the classes, I don't know, but they are always wanting to find out which

4 GPF: General Provident Fund.

bank gives what sort of loans, and applying for them. And for all that sort of thing, I am the one who must write the applications! As if that is not enough, every day I'm asked by the government to provide data! How can one single clerk do it all? I don't know computer typing, so I have to run outside to get it done all the time. Should I do my job or watch the fighting in the house?' Selvam was weeping softly. Nothing was said for a while. Though Ilayaraaja saw that Leelavati's eyes, too, were blurred, he did not speak.

A boy of about five or six years ran in, calling out, 'Anna!' Gathering him into his lap, Ilayaraaja asked, 'What is it, kanna? What do you want? Tell me, dear!' Having petted and fondled him for a few moments, he set him down and sent him off, saying, 'Run! Go and play!'

Then, on his own, he explained: 'Somebody left him behind the hospital building and went off, it was not even ten hours after his birth. I picked him up and I'm bringing him up. It's Sunday today. So that's why they are all here. Other days they are in school.'

'So, you give them education also?'

'Yes. But only in the government schools. Not only because there's no alternative, but also because we shouldn't support the private schools.' Ilayaraaja tried to smile, but failed.

'That's amazing, saar!' Selvam said admiringly. A conversation then followed between him and Ilayaraaja to which Leelavati paid no attention.

She was busy muttering to herself: 'Leaving a child after giving birth to it, right on the road – what kind of heart is that? A heart of stone, that's what! Why give birth to a child that's not wanted? People's minds go off in all sorts of directions! In this world, whom can you call a real woman? A mother?'

'Why has the child's head been shaved, saar? All the children in the hall have shaved heads,' Selvam ventured to ask.

'We shave the heads of all those children who can't bathe themselves. It becomes easier to bathe them, then. They won't get lice or catch cold. And we don't have to bother with haircuts. It's the old people who live here who take care of these children.' Ilayaraaja smiled. Then, as though he had just remembered her, he abruptly turned to Leelavati and said, 'Tell me, 'mma.'

'Let me stay here. Even in the house I am all alone. Son and daughter-in-law being there makes no difference, it is like being in a house with no people in it. How can I live in a house where nobody talks to anybody? My heart is all burnt up! If my husband were there, why would I need to come here? Why did the wretched chandaalan[5] hang himself, anyway?' Leelavati sobbed.

'Didn't he die because of illness?'

'No.'

---

5 Chandaalan: Chandal – the 'lowest' caste among the so-called untouchables. Also used as a term of opprobrium.

'Then how did he die?'

Selvam did not speak. Nor did Leelavati. They sat there with their heads bowed.

'Was he in bad pain? Something that he couldn't bear? That made him hang himself?'

Selvam said nothing.

'If you don't feel like talking about it, just let it be. A man died. He's no longer here. That's all,' Ilayaraaja said, wearily.

'I'll tell you if you admit me.'

'What is this, 'mma? So you're laying down conditions and all, is it?' He broke into laughter. 'Right, I'll admit you. Now tell me!' Another laugh.

She looked at Selvam. He was staring at the framed photographs hanging on the walls.

'OA – that's what my husband was. Office assistant in a government school. He did quite a lot to get our son educated, but who knows what was written on the fellow's forehead – nothing that he read ever went in. Went to college, wrote exam after exam, year after year – couldn't pass even one … We don't have land or property or anything. Don't even have a house. There was nothing but that OA job. That brought in the food. We people used to working outside in the fields now depended on this government job. My husband was so worried about our son getting used to town life. Getting older and older. And he began to worry about another thing – our son was getting past the age for marriage … How the idea came into his head I don't know, but before he retired, he hanged himself.'

Leelavati stuffed her mouth with the end of her saree, trying in vain to suppress the sobs that shook her body. After a few minutes, Ilayaraaja asked, 'How old was he?'

'Fifty-nine and a half.'

'Everybody retires at fifty-eight, isn't that so?'

'OA, watchman – it's sixty for them.'

'Is that so? I didn't know that. But why would a man in a government job hang himself?'

Selvam did not have a reply. But his mother did: 'To get his son a job. That's why he hanged himself.'

She had stopped weeping. Ilayaraaja was dumbstruck. 'What are you saying, 'mma?' he brought out after a moment.

'Because he died in service, his son would get a job. On "compassionate grounds". As his heir. That's why he hanged himself.'

'Seems so strange to me – shocking!' exclaimed Ilayaraaja. 'A world where people leave children out on the street – children born to them. Where people hang themselves ... Hard to believe all this. Now government has a cradle-baby scheme. Every day, two or three babies are thrown on the open road or in garbage bins. And every day some old person or other is left on the street...'

He followed his musings with a question: 'Did he get the job?'

Leelavati did not answer.

'After three years,' said Selvam reluctantly.

'That's not bad!'

'Three years I spent, running around trying to get the job!' Selvam said aggrievedly. 'Up and down I went, didn't leave out even a single office. Spent so much money also!'

'Right … but what if they had got to know it was for that reason that he hanged himself? They wouldn't have given you the job, would they?'

'This is the first time I am opening my mouth to talk about it, after eight years,' Leelavati suddenly announced. 'When I saw the note he wrote before he died, I threw it in the fire!' she sobbed.

'What was written in the note?'

'*I am an old man of sixty. What am I going to do with my life, now? If I die, my son will get a job on compassionate grounds, as my heir. On the strength of that job, and that money, some man will give him his daughter in marriage. Is this the olden time, when a man gives his daughter to a man on the strength of his character? No! When anybody gives their daughter away, it's the man's job, his money that is trusted. It was only for my son that I held on to my life so far, and I will let it go, now, for him. I have no regrets. You go and somehow get that job for him. Get him married. Don't tell anybody about how I died.* This is what he had written in that note.'

Leelavati now spoke calmly. She had controlled her tears. But having listened to her in silence, Selvam now burst out: 'Don't tell lies, Amma! You never kept quiet about this! Didn't you keep telling me whenever you got angry, "It is only because my husband died that you got a job!'"

'So! I am the only one who talks, and you and your wife are oh-so-quiet, is it?'

'I am your son, I can put up with whatever you say. After all, my wife is an outsider, isn't she? How can she put up with your talk?'

'Oh, is that so?' began Leelavati in a strange tone. And then fury overcame her. 'Out of my husband's hard work, doesn't she also eat? Shouldn't there be some thought of that? Can't you see it? But did you two ever keep any new-moon fast for him? Do the memorial rite in the month of Maasi? One measure of rice, a raw banana, a single handful of agathi greens – have you ever made that offering to the priest? I am the one to go and do all that, isn't it? And if I ask about it, I'm told I'm a quarrelsome woman who doesn't want her daughter-in-law to live! Right? You yourself say your mother doesn't like you to laugh and talk with your own wife!'

'Don't shout, Amma. You don't understand what it's all about. All the mothers and fathers in the world are living only for their children. Earning for their sake. Here you are talking as though you two were very special people, very great! As if you've lived and brought me up only for my sake.'

Leelavati shrieked, her wrath surfacing from who knew where: 'My husband and I are not special people, okay?

You and your wife alone are oh-so-great. And your mother-in-law's people are also very great!'

'Why are you screaming, Amma?'

'I'm not screaming! And I'm not coming to your house any more. Let me go! But just one thing – keep an eye on your wife. Once honour is lost, there will be no use living any more.'

'What? I don't understand…' demanded Selvam.

She was cornered, there was no way of getting out of the situation. Hurriedly she muttered, 'I didn't mean it, I was in a bad mood … somehow, the words came out. Just drop it, don't talk about it.' At the sight of his woebegone face, she tried to change the subject: 'Whenever your children fall ill, don't you pick them up and go running to the doctor? How many days have I been lying right there, wherever I fell down, and you never asked what happened or how it happened?'

'Haven't I been taking care of you?' he asked pathetically.

'Very fine care you took!' she said cuttingly, jerking her face away.

She was driving him mad with anger … Striving to hide it, Selvam started to talk with Ilayaraaja.

'Do those who give money get any special treatment here, saar?'

'No, we don't do that sort of thing. Sixty-eight old people stay here. Four of them cannot walk at all. We have seventy-six children – from newborn infants to sixteen-year-olds. We make no difference between them. Six people here are pensioners. They also get the same facilities. Morning, idlis. Afternoon, rice, sambaar. Night, idli or dosai or something like that. No non-veg.'

'Do those who get a pension give you anything, saar?' asked Selvam eagerly.

'I don't ask for it myself. If they themselves give something, we don't say no. Even if they give anything, it's never more than four or five hundred.' Ilayaraaja's smile made light of it. Then he added, 'You needn't give money just for your mother. You can help others also. You need not limit your help only to those whom you personally know. You can help by giving money, or anything – rice, pulses, provisions, dhotis, towels, sarees, bed sheets – you can donate even soap. We will take anything you give. For thirteen years I have been struggling to keep this place running. I don't wish to turn it into a business or a trade.'

'Definitely I will do whatever I can, saar!' Selvam assured him. A measure of clarity had come over his face after a long while. He said, as though he had just then considered the matter, 'It must take a lot of heart to run a home for people who've got nothing and no one, saar.'

'When I started it, I set it up in just one shed, under a thatched roof. At that time there were only three of us. It's our own land – my own house. So there's been no problem. Two more buildings are behind this one. They're all full.' Ilayaraaja smiled wryly.

'Really!'

'At home, everyone scolds me. In the whole town they say I don't know how to get on in the world. It was just something that I felt in my mind. I was eager, to begin with, but now I'm having a terrible struggle. At that time, I was twenty-five years old. I have a little land. It's the paddy from there that's running this thing. Somehow or other, for thirteen years I've been able to run it. Whenever I think about it, I feel quite amazed.'

He continued after a pause, in a very tired tone. 'Every once in a while, one or two people will give a thousand or five hundred. Or they'll take on the expense of providing a meal. That's only those who haven't forgotten their mothers and fathers, who want to remember them. But usually, it is only on their own birthdays that people bring biscuits or fruit. So many people nowadays celebrate birthdays and wedding days … It's like a new disease in Tamil Nadu. Of course, I'm happy they do it!' He grinned.

'That's true, saar.'

'And then there are those who abandon their mothers and fathers on the road. And those who cast off their own children. If there's such a thing as a world, it has to have all these strange things going on, right?'

Selvam was silent.

'That orphan child who just came here – can I see her?' Leelavati asked.

'I'll call her,' nodded Ilayaraaja, and continued, 'You are in a government job, getting a good salary. Your mother gets a pension. Don't do what people who have no money even for food are doing. I am not saying this just because of the food. You have been given the name of "Selvam" – "wealth". For this lady, you are Wealth. It's not just any old name that's been given to you. It is a *good* name.'

Having come out with this, Ilayaraaja gave Selvam a penetrating look, and resumed: 'These days, there is a new trend in our country – a sort of fashion. When people want to attend weddings and festivals, or go to temples, they leave their old people in hospitals. It's a thriving business now … And many elderly foreigners are coming here on medical tours. They stay for as long as six months sometimes. It's cheap to live here, compared to other countries. So, because they can't keep old people at home with them, they send them off on these tours. Some do it, of course, to show off their money. So now there's a lot of cash circulating in this country. More homes for the aged have also been coming up.' He spoke calmly, without emotion.

Selvam began to feel uncomfortable. Offended, he protested, 'This is not *my* wish, it's my mother's wish, saar! *Her* stubbornness! There was no way out! So I came along with her. At least to satisfy her wish, let her stay for a week or ten days. If she changes her mind, I'll come and take her back.'

This time Ilayaraaja guffawed loudly. 'Are you leaving her in the house of family people? Relations? For her to spend a week with them? This is a destitutes' home, saar!' Selvam did not utter another word. Struck dumb, he sat there with his arms folded.

What Ilayaraaja said sent a thrill of fear through Leelavati. What was she going to do if he did not take her in? She had been determined to fight, no matter what. Once having left the house, how could she go back into that same house? Supposing she went back, in spite of it all, what would Kalamani say? How could she bear to listen to whatever she said? And even if she put up with her talk, how could she endure her objectionable behaviour? Her leaving the house for long hours, her endless talking and giggling with somebody on her cell phone – how could she go on watching all this? That it was some other man she was talking to, with whom she had a relationship, was something she could not talk about: there would be a huge fight. And supposing during that fight she said, "I don't want this husband!" and ran off? What would happen to Selvam? What would happen to the children? The more she thought about it, the more she felt she would go mad. Panic seized her.

'Let anything happen!' she thought. 'I mustn't be around to witness whatever it is.'

'I get two thousand monthly, I'll give you all of it,' she told Ilayaraaja beseechingly. 'All I want is a glass of water that's given without somebody making a face at me! At this age, what am I going to do with money? Let my husband's money be useful at least to get these children's hair cut! I'll stay right here, and I'll take care of the children. Keep me as an ayah! If I am with children, I won't feel time passing. If I can be of some help to children like these, I'll be doing something good in my last years. I'll be on my way to motcham![6] Freedom! At least for the sake of my next life, let me stay here!' she wailed, with her hands raised in a kumbidu.

Ilayaraaja gazed fixedly at her. It was unclear what was going on in his mind. 'Please don't cry,' he murmured, apparently to soothe her.

'I don't want any money. I just want to talk to somebody, I want to laugh, I want to cry! That's all I want. That is money for me, that is gold, that is food, saami.' Again, she folded her hands.

'When you have, right here, your own son born to you, it is wrong for you to speak like this. It's wrong also for me to take you in. This is all talk, spoken in anger and excitement. Not the truth.'

'If I had my husband with me, the one who tied a taali on my neck, why would I come here? Will even one hundred sons be equal to my husband?'

'Keep quiet, Amma,' Selvam shouted. 'You go on saying this again and again – as if nobody else in the world has a husband!'

'Oh yes – as a husband he wasn't very different from others in the world. But to you he was a father unlike any other father could be! He thought, "What am I going to do after I turn sixty years of age? Let my son have my job, get married, let him have children!" That's what your

---

6 Motcham: Moksha – eternal release.

father decided. So he hanged himself! Is there any father in the world who has done that, da?' she sobbed. 'You are the best husband, your wife is the best wife? Okay, let it be like that. Stay well, both of you. Am *I* going to stop you from being happy and well? It is only because I don't want you and your family to be ruined that I am weeping night and day. That is why I came out of the house, da. Am I a woman who thinks "Let my son die – my own son, born to me!" – how can I have such a thought?' Her tears flowed without cease.

'You're hiding something – keeping it all locked up. Break it open! I can't understand!'

'No need for you to understand anything! Nothing you have to know. Just leave me here and just go. Do this great service, that'll be enough for me, for having given birth to you.'

'Going on shouting and shouting, and shutting everyone else up!'

'Right! I'm shouting. My mind's gone bad, that's why … But weren't you given an education, like other children in the town? Why didn't you pass any exam? If you had passed and got a job, why would your father have killed himself? If you didn't have this job would your wife have held out her neck for you to tie the taali? Would that wretched fellow, that father of hers who couldn't even feed his family, have given his daughter to you?'

'D'you know where we are? What are you saying – here, in this place?' Selvam said between clenched teeth.

'Why can't people live together – that's what I don't understand. Even dogs live together. Cats, goats, cattle … but people can't do it. Strange…' Ilayaraaja smiled. 'What is your final decision?' he asked.

'I'll stay here. I'll give you the cash for it.'

'And what do *you* say, saar?'

'At least one of us should be happy, saar.'

'I don't understand.'

'For three years, my mother and my wife have been fighting off and on. But nowadays the fights are going on and on. They don't end. There's some kind of problem between them. And yet my wife is the woman my mother chose for me.'

'Oh yes!' Leelavati made a face, her lips twisting crookedly. 'A fine girl she is, all right. Pure gold – Thangam! That's the name she should have been given. That's the one thing missing in her.'

'A never-ending fight it is, between you two. Which one is going to die first?' Selvam muttered irately.

A ten-year-old girl ran in at that moment. 'What is it, 'mma?' asked Ilayaraaja.

'There's no water for the noon meal. Cook Akka said to tell you.'

'No water at all?'

'No water.'

'Power hasn't come back yet?'

'No.'

'How many times I keep telling them, "Fill up water when there is electricity!" But do they listen? And now daily there's a power cut for eight hours. What a government!' exclaimed Ilayaraaja in exasperation. 'You go now, I'm just coming,' he told the child. 'And tell the children to go play behind the building. Too much noise here.'

Having sent the girl away, he turned to Selvam. 'Tell me your decision. What shall we do?'

'Daily I am dying, saar! Can't stand it any more!'

'Tell me what you have decided.'

'Everybody has problems, saar, but money problems one can put up with.'

'Everybody? Whom do you mean by that? Whom do you mean by "everybody"?'

'My mother must have some peace!' said Selvam. 'So much she has done for me! I can't bear to see her suffering … For two–three days she has eaten nothing. Doesn't matter how much money it will take, saar, let her be peaceful! I will pay for it!'

'Looks like you have already made your decision,' Ilayaraaja said, smiling. 'But I am not running this place for money. Please understand that. If I had wanted to make money, I could have started a business, I could run a cloth shop, or an idli shop. Could have gone in for politics. My father was an old-time MLA, he's dead and gone. I didn't want anything like that. That's why I run a place like this, understand? If you had not turned up as her son, I would have asked no questions. I would have admitted her at once! There are four or five people who have told lies like that and got admitted.'

'Sorry saar! I didn't say that to give you any trouble. I am working nearby, in Thirumuttam. I live there. Not somewhere abroad. Whenever I want, I can come here in just two hours. How can I be without seeing the mother who has given me birth? My own mother, saar!' Selvam pleaded tearfully.

'Please calm down,' said Ilayaraaja, but Selvam was not about to listen. 'Tell me how much money I should send every month and I will give it, saar,' he repeated forcefully.

'It's up to you. You can give it. Or not give it. There is no compulsion. If a person like you gives money, it is a great help. It will come in useful to pay the electricity bill.'

Fearing that he would somehow further complicate the matter, Leelavati announced, 'I get two thousand. I will give that! You must not give even one single coin, understand? If you disobey me and give it, on that very same day I will die!'

Like a snake rearing up to strike, Selvam turned a venomous eye on her. But she was not looking at him. Glancing from one to the other, Ilayaraaja at last addressed Selvam: 'Please remain outside for a minute.' Giving him a puzzled look, Selvam reluctantly left the room.

Then, speaking to Leelavati as though to a babe in arms, Ilayaraaja said, 'You are not destitute. You get a pension of two thousand rupees every month. You can keep it and eat and stay peacefully in your house. That is the best for you.'

'I am not a person who likes to fight. I am not a person who gossips and spreads rumours all around town. You will not have any trouble from me. I'll sit where I'm told to sit, won't budge even one bit. And I'll do whatever work is given to me.'

'All that you are saying is okay…' Ilayaraaja started to say and stopped.

'You seem to be in some great mental agony,' he observed after a pause. 'Who is the cause of it, why is it there at all – that is not clear. Why you left the house is not known. For an old person to leave the house in a fit of temper is not right. If there is one problem at home, there will be one thousand problems outside, do you know that? Being alone – *that* is death.'

'It's not because of me that anyone has a problem. But I have a problem with myself. My backbone is broken, I don't have a husband, and I'm still living and not dying. That is the problem. I'm caught in that bunch of knots!' Leelavati covered her mouth with her hands and wept.

'All the old people in the world have got this same problem, it's nothing new. Because we don't realize that we possess nothing in this world, we have all these problems. This "you–me" competition – that's the problem. And then there's desire, there's the urge for power.'

'I cannot live in a house where there is a woman of bad character!'

'I don't understand.'

'Nothing … If you want to admit me, do it. Otherwise, just let it be. It's not that there is no way to die in this world, is there? It's just that I had a dying wish, and I thought let me ask for it here!' cried Leelavati.

She was afraid she had said too much to Selvam and to this outsider. How was it that something she had sworn to herself would never escape her lips even if she were about to die had suddenly slipped out? What should never be known outside, and why she had wanted to leave the house – must she come out with it just to get admitted to this place? No, she must never again open her mouth about it. Even if she were really going to die…

Kalamani! Never before had she ever been so angry with her as she was now. 'Look where I'm sitting right now! She's brought me to this!' she thought. How had the change taken place in Kalamani's behaviour, over this past year?

… It was when Selvam bought her a cell phone. That was when it had all started. How she talked, how she behaved, how she laughed, how she dressed, how she went out – everything had been turned upside down. Selvam only had to leave the house, and the very next instant she would start a conversation with who knows who on the cell phone. For half an hour at the very least, or a whole hour, she would be on the phone. If questioned, she would say, 'I was talking to my mother.' Or 'I was talking to my brother.' Announcing, 'I am going to take the children to school,' she wouldn't be back for an hour. Ten days ago, Kalamani and Leelavati had a huge fight because Kalamani had set off, all decked up, immediately after Selvam left for the office, and she had not come back till four in the afternoon.

Leelavati had finally spoken out: 'Where did you go? Why are you coming back so late? What you are doing – is it good for the family? Don't forget you have two children! If Selvam gets to know, do you know what will happen?'

Being slapped with a leather chappal – that's what Kalamani's answer felt like to Leelavati:

'Say it! Call me whatever you like! Is your son the god of love? The *only* handsome prince in the world? Whatever is cooked and placed before him, can he finish it off? Isn't he just a useless fellow who can only sniff and smell and go off? Set a fine, tasty dish in front of him, and he can't even bite into it!'

'If that's how it is, then how did you give birth to two children?'

'Just like you did … It just happened.'

'So…! You have two children. Don't forget that.'

'Only if you die will I have peace. When you go deep down into the earth – oh, when will that day ever come?' Even those words did not cause Leelavati as much anguish as what Kalamani had said earlier: *Isn't he just a useless fellow who can only sniff and smell and go off? Set a fine, tasty dish in front of him, and he can't even bite into it!* It felt to her like being pushed into a fire. Those words that Kalamani had spoken – what would happen if she told Selvam? If, some day, she ever had to come out with them, what would happen to the family? It was after having thought it over that Leelavati had made up her mind that she must not remain in the house. If she stayed on, she would not be able to endure what Leelavati was doing, and neither would she be able to tell Selvam about it. If she were driven to tell him, the family would be destroyed. And so, she had walked out.

… But now Ilayaraaja was asking her to tell him. 'No. I must not tell him even if I die,' she decided, and sat there with her mouth shut.

'What is it, 'mma, you are sitting there without saying anything?' demanded Ilayaraaja. Because she still sat silent, he got up, went to Selvam who was standing in the hall, and came back with him.

'So, what does my mother say?' said Selvam, grinning.

'She is under a lot of pressure, there's some great wound in her mind. Let her stay here for a few days. We'll see what happens after that.' Ilayaraaja spoke emotionlessly, like one uninvolved in the matter.

'That's good, saar. Let her have a change.'

'When do you want to come, 'mma?' enquired Ilayaraaja.

'I've already come. I'll just stay, that's all.'

'Good!' smiled Ilayaraaja. Then, turning to Selvam, he said, 'If you want to bring her anything you want her to have, please bring it.'

'What should I bring, Amma?' asked Selvam with great solicitude.

'I don't want anything at all. You go and see to your life. See to your family,' she told him sharply.

'Don't you want a change of clothes, or…?'

'No!' she snapped, stopping him short.

'She is very upset now. You go and come back later. We can talk then.' Then, to Leelavati he said, 'Come inside, I'll show you the other people, we'll see where to put you. You have to do your own work here and take care of yourself. For doing the cooking there is somebody, but not for anything else. You have to help with the cooking. And you must do the sweeping and cleaning. And look after the children.' Then, turning to include Selvam, he said, 'If I fall, you must pick me up. And if you fall, I must pick you up. That is why human beings live together. That is why we have relationships. Just keep that in mind, please … If this is the state of the world in two thousand and fourteen, how will it be in fifty more years? Just thinking about it is frightening!' he concluded and went out into the hall.

'Is this your fate, Amma? Is this what is written on your forehead?' Selvam said tearfully. But Leelavati was no longer weeping. Thrusting into his hands a small bundle she had tucked in at her waist, she walked quickly into the hall. Following her, Selvam tried to return the bundle to her, but she turned aside in disgust, telling him, 'It's something that should go to you.'

'Saar, you can leave now. Come tomorrow and we can talk. I have work to do,' Ilayaraaja announced.

'Tomorrow, or day after tomorrow, I will come and see you, saar,' Selvam said, and tried once again to return the bundle to Leelavati. When she walked off, he took his leave of Ilayaraaja with a vanakkam, and went out with a sour expression on his face.

He opened the bundle. Inside were a nose stud, ear studs, two rings … Thirty hundred-rupee notes … Selvam's face brightened. He sighed a great sigh, as though he had set down an enormous burden, and his mind felt light, as though he had escaped from a terrible danger. Cheerfully lighting himself a cigarette, he felt that the world held no more troubles in store for him. Humming a film tune, he set off for the bus stop.

Leelavati stood hidden behind the corner of the gate of the Destitutes' Home and watched him walk away. She was crying, but not only did he not notice her, he did not look back even once at the building.

The Pulse of Life

'SELL IT WHEN I'M DEAD.'

'Is the man from the Company going to be sitting around waiting for you to die?'

'So what? Let him go.'

'Can't you understand what I'm telling you?'

'I understand everything. Just push me into a hole and cover it up. Then go and sign.'

'Chhee! What sort of man are you?' exclaimed Ramasaami angrily. Gritting his teeth, he glared as though to burn up the old man who sat there, twisting strands of hay into rope for tying up the paddy sheaves. The more he scowled at his father, the more he felt himself burning instead. Striking himself on the brow in sheer frustration, he got up with a jerk and went to the back of the house. There, he lit a cigarette and brooded on how to get the old man to agree.

The old man peered after him, but all he could see was cigarette smoke. 'Why is this boy so stiff and stubborn? Standing on one leg just to get his way!' he asked himself.

A resolve followed: 'Whatever happens, the land must not be sold.' And then another question: 'How is Ramasaami to be pacified? He's got spoilt by the village people. No use blaming him either, the way the village is changing…'

Those who had lands adjoining the proposed national highway had become rich in a single month. A man from up north had come and bought up all their lands, saying he was going to put up a factory. Sites worth twenty, thirty thousand were being bought for one and two lakh. 'How can one man have so much money? Where is it all coming from?' marvelled the old man. 'But even if he offers me crores and crores of rupees, I won't sell. I can give up my life, but I won't give up the land. Doesn't it feed us, this Earth Goddess?' Returning from the back of the house, Ramasaami came and stood face to face with the old man as he had done before, waiting for him to open his mouth and speak. But the old man went on with his task of spinning rope, as though he had not seen him at all. Incensed as he was by his father's indifference, Ramasaami held himself in check. As calmly as he could make himself speak, he informed him that the land was about to lose its entire value. That there was no way around the problem but to dispose of their own land. But the old man still kept his mouth shut.

'If we don't sell our land now, before those who have lands all around our place sell theirs, we won't even be able to get there! Understand what I'm saying?' Ramasaami demanded with some asperity.

To that, the old man replied after a few moments, 'I can hear.' Ramasaami felt as though his head would crack open with sheer rage. How was he to bring the old man around? To whom would he listen? Thwarted, he let out a stream of abuses. There was not one person from the village whom he had not brought in to persuade his father over the past week. Not a word would the old man come out with, even when any of them talked to him for a whole hour – a whole day, even. Finally, he would shut the visitor up by saying, 'If you ask me to give up my life, what can I say? Tell him to sell it after I'm dead.'

Yesterday, as a last-ditch effort, Ramasaami had brought Muthayya from his two-storey bungalow. Muthayya was the big man there in the village. His word counted. Unable to refuse Ramasaami's request, he had come and spoken to the old man for two–three hours. He told him the good things that would happen if he sold the land, and the losses that would result if he did not sell it. Having patiently heard him out in full, all the old man said was:

'Dig out my eyes and make me blind … that's what you are all trying to do.'

'No, it's not like that at all!' protested Muthayya, making every effort to pacify and reassure him with all kinds of arguments. Fed up at last, he walked out, declaring in annoyance, 'I can't talk to a person who won't adjust to the times.' It bothered Ramasaami terribly that such a personage had left in anger ... If the old man paid no heed even to Muthayya, he was not likely to listen to anyone else from the village. What was to be done next? How could the old man, alone, of all the people in the village, fail to grasp such a thing?

Back from the fields with a headload of firewood, Rani dropped it – *poth!* – almost at the old man's feet. Without a word, she turned sharply and went into the house. Emerging a little while later, she asked, 'Didn't you eat this afternoon?' To which Ramasaami gave no reply except to yell, 'Go! Get away from here, di!'

'Why are you jumping on me and snapping?' she demanded, undeterred. Untying the bundle of firewood lying near the old man, she gathered together a few sticks and went back into the house. Having kindled the cook-fire, she came out again, asking, 'Where are the children? Don't see them around.'

'Who knows where they've disappeared? Let the devils go and get lost and die there – wherever it is!'

'Why are you talking like that about the children?'

'Go inside, di! You have no idea at all about what's going on here and what a man's going through.'

'If father and son are fighting, is it my fault? My children's fault?' Rani retorted. 'As if it's not enough that you're beating each other up, all for the sake of that worthless patch of land, why must you kill us also?' At this, the old man, who had kept his head lowered all this time, quickly looked up. He watched her disappear into the house. Then he turned his gaze to the street for a few moments, before going back to twisting the hay into rope.

Pacing restlessly between the house and the outer gate, Ramasaami could not bring himself to calm down, or to stay still in one place … *'Tomorrow's the last day. After that, we'll put up the wire fence. If you sell it after that, you'll have to pay for the wire fence.'* That was what the Company fellow had said, and it was the only thing that he could think of just now. Again and again, he heaved a sigh and wrung his hands.

Kamala came running in and asked, 'Has Amma come back, 'ppa?' Glowering at her, Ramasaami shouted, 'Where were you roaming around all this time?' Kamala stared, not knowing what to say to him. 'Evening is study time – don't you have the sense to know that? Should a chit of a girl be out roaming on the street? Where did you get such a habit?' he demanded.

Kamala couldn't say a word. All she could do was cry.

'What did I say now that you should cry? I can't open my mouth and ask, is it? Just for that you'll cry?' Ramasaami demanded, slapping her on the cheek. At that moment, the cow tied on the west wall of the house passed urine and some drops splattered on his foot. That was it: he started to hit out at all the cows in a blind rage.

Having watched for a few minutes without attempting to stop him, the old man turned his attention again to the work of twisting hay into rope.

When Selvaraj came running in from the direction of the temple, Ramasaami blocked his way and bellowed, 'Where were you gone all this time, da? Already at this age you are going to be the town stud bull, are you? Will you dare to go out without telling me again?' He began to beat him up.

Hearing the boy's screams, Rani came running. After a desperate struggle, she managed to free Selvaraj from Ramasaami's grasp and pull him to her side … at which Ramasaami rained a couple of blows down upon her.

'So this is the son you have given birth to, is he? That's why he's growing up to be just like you! What else can I expect?' He swore at her in whatever words sprang to his lips. Paying no heed, Rani stroked Selvaraj's bruised and swelling cheeks and back.

'Can't you see with your own eyes what-all drama that man is doing?' she wailed to the old man. 'Don't you know he beats the children every day! For one whole week – ten days! – he's not been turning up in the house for regular meals. Makes a huge racket, fit to break down the house. It's been going on in front of your eyes – don't you see it? Suppose you sell off that useless jungle-land, what is the terrible thing that's going to happen? Why not just get rid of it?' she demanded. The old man did not even look up at her. 'So…! You'll just go on squatting there like an owl, without opening your mouth. Let that man beat me and my children, let him just kill us!' she said to him bitterly.

When Ramasaami shouted, 'Just shut up and go, di!' she continued to address the old man: 'Yes or no, that's all you have to say, isn't it? It isn't five hundred kaanis,[1] or a thousand, no? As if we are getting our food from whatever grows on that ground?'

Wrath came over the old man, all of a sudden, from some obscure source. He raised his head and gave Rani a fierce look. 'That costly dowry land your daddy signed and gifted to you – you can tell your husband to sell *that* off if you want!' he declared with vehemence.

'And why should my father sign away any dowry land to me? For you and your son to sell off and eat, is it?'

'So! This is your father's land we are selling off – to buy and eat our rice and curry, is it? Have you forgotten you're the daughter of a man with nothing? Didn't even have a tattered bamboo winnow to blow the chaff from a handful of grain!'

'So why did you come running and falling over yourself just to marry me to your son – I'm the daughter of a man without even a torn winnowing basket to his name, isn't that so?'

'Lost my mind, what else? Ever since you set foot in this house, not a thing is left here. Nothing but ruination. Because of you, he's also become a useless good-for-nothing.'

---

1 Kaani: A measure of land, about 1.32 acres.

'So! In this house all the bad things have been happening only because of me? If that's what it is, then why did you keep this unlucky female all these years? Why didn't you send me back the very day I came?'

'If you'd gone back there, what would you have had to eat?' retorted the old man, just as Ramasaami snarled, 'Go back inside, di. On and on you're talking back.'

Ignoring him, Rani addressed the old man with a reply like a hard slap. 'Whatever I am eating here is same as what I'd have eaten there also.'

'Over there, for even salt and chillies they have to scrimp and scrounge. As if you don't know that!'

'So, what's so great about this place? What riches do you have here? Oh yes – as they say:

> In your treasure-chest here, we know there's a lot,
> But to mash up some greens, not even one pot!'

'Are you still going on and on, talking back? It's all my fault, telling him to bring a fox-hunting gypsy[2] woman here and tie a taali[3] on her.'

'No, it's all my fault for having held out my neck to a bull that does nothing but roam around the village.'

'So why are you still staying with that good-for-nothing bull? Why not just go to hell, where you belong?'

---

2 Gypsy: Refers to the Narikuravar nomadic gypsy tribe of Tamil Nadu, known for hunting foxes.

3 Taali: Marriage thread.

'Then give me back what I brought, and I'll walk off right now.'

'So what did you bring with you anyway? Was it a hundred or two hundred carts you unloaded here? Not even a broom to sweep the house with, don't you remember?'

'So! I came here just swinging my arms. Right? But wasn't it with whatever I brought with me that you got your three sisters married? They've been living on what I brought! If what I'm saying is a lie, then let their good luck as married women come to an end right now! Let their lives stop!'

Hardly had she finished speaking the words, than Ramasaami sprang on her with a roar. 'What did you say, di? Did you say my sisters should lose their men and stop living?' In a frenzy, he struck out at her, heedless of where the blows landed. One descended on her mouth as she tried to say something. It was only when Kamala and Selvaraj cried out in terror that he stopped. 'Go inside, di!' he yelled, with a final kick before he rushed out into the street towards the marketplace.

Having shrieked and wailed in agony, Rani at last wiped the blood spilling from her mouth and rubbed her swollen cheeks and back. With every word that sprang to her lips, she cursed Ramasaami and his father. 'Let me be born as a dog for ten births, never mind! But I must not be born a woman … Oh God, even if I am born a woman, I should never be married into this rotten household!'

Just then, the smell of something burning on the stove reached her. 'Ayyo, it's all gone!' she shrieked and hurried inside.

At the same speed as he had rushed to the end of the street, Ramasaami rushed back. Confronting the old man with a ferocious look, he stood there, gnashing his teeth. When the old man paid no attention at all to him, he stalked off in frustration and sat down on the thinnai.[4] Again, he could not sit still for more than a moment. Bounding up, he went to the water pot, plunged a dipper into it and drank. 'Why is there so much smoke, di?' he demanded. Rani gave no reply. Instead, she picked up a winnowing basket and flung it in the opposite direction. The smoke made Ramasaami cough repeatedly. Hurrying outside, he was followed by Selvaraj, who was also coughing. 'Where d'you think you're going, da? Get back inside the house,' he scolded, sending him back inside, rubbing his eyes.

At the far end of the street, a car drove up and came to a halt. Three or four men from the village as well as a couple of outsiders could be seen alighting from it. Some youngsters raced up, and some adults, too, were headed that way. The sight set Ramasaami quivering with rage from head to toe, and drove him to roar at his father as never before: 'Say what it's going to be!'

---

4 Thinnai: A platform right outside the front door, for people to sit on.

'Same thing only. Sell after I'm dead.'

'I'll get angry.'

'Sell whatever you've earned yourself, if there's anything like that.'

'You'll never improve!'

'What use is it now for me to improve?'

'Are you a man at all?' Ramasaami exploded. He stomped angrily around a few times, then darted out. Standing just outside the doorway, he called out 'Ei! Ei!' several times in quick succession. A few moments later, Rani appeared and demanded, 'So, what have you got for this "Ei"?' Having forgotten why he had summoned her, he rasped, 'It's all my fate. Written on my forehead! Otherwise, why should I be suffering like this with you?' He turned abruptly away.

Rani waited for him to say something more. When he remained silent, she prodded defiantly, 'Is it only *your* fate? Is it written on *your* forehead only? You called me, isn't it? What for? To hit me as if I'm a cow or something?'

'Oh! So that's why you came so quick, is it? Now just go do your work, di!' Not waiting for her reply, he walked off and plonked himself down on the rim of the water tank from which the cattle drank.

'Gone mad! Here I am, stuck in a mad crowd, oh god!' Rani groaned, as she went into the house.

To keep sitting in any one spot was impossible for Ramasaami, he felt it would drive him really mad. 'What sort of person is he? Nothing can make this old man budge!

How was he to be made to understand? Did he really not understand, or was he just pretending?' He felt baffled and infuriated all at once. 'Could it really be that he didn't realize how great the loss would be if the land were not sold at the right time? Was it him alone who felt bad about losing the land? Are we telling him to sell the land so that we can spend the money on worthless things? Something's got hold of the old man's mind, but he doesn't want to free himself…'

Once again, Ramasaami bounced up and began to stride towards the shop at the street corner. Murugesan came sauntering up. 'Have you got it done?' he enquired as he bought himself a cigarette and lit it up.

'This is our one and only chance, we have to make good use of it!' he declared. 'It's our lucky time – the Company fellow himself is coming here and dropping the money straight into our hands! Useless dry land that wouldn't go for thirty or even twenty thousand is fetching two and three lakh today. Before this, was there anyone in the village who ever set eyes on a whole lakh of rupees? Why can't that father of yours understand this?' Sucking in the smoke, Murugesan slowly blew it out and went on, 'They're going to build three–four roads also. Once that's done, the government will take all the land on both sides of the roads and pay a rock-bottom price. This is so much better. Now, because the roads are coming, the Company fellow is buying the land up fast.'

On and on he went in the same vein, with Ramasaami joining in to talk about who in the village had sold how much of their land, and at what price.

They stood talking for a long time, there at the corner shop, and when the old man got wind of it, his resolve not to sell the land firmed up even more. 'So he's dancing to that fellow's tune, is it? Got to stop them from meeting … but how?' Along with this worry came another one: what if he failed to have his way with the land? Something very wrong was about to happen. Worrying over it, his hands slackened and left off their work of twisting strands of hay into rope.

Parvati came in carrying a load of maize stalks and dropped it in front of the old man. 'Cut it up and throw it all to the cows,' she told him curtly. As though she had just been waiting for her to arrive, Rani began to cry out loud. Kamala and Selvaraj joined in with their wails. Shocked, Parvati asked what had happened, but Rani could not speak a single word. It was Kamala who told her about Ramasaami beating her and Selvaraj and Rani, too, and how Rani's lip had got torn by the blow he dealt her.

Outraged at the sight of their bruised and swollen wounds, Parvati pronounced, 'Father and son both have the same character, isn't it? They're killers! So then why did you open your mouth and talk to them, di? That, too, when I'm not around? He's beaten the children, the filthy rascal! Let him come, I'll put an end to it, once and for all.'

As she uttered the words, Ramasaami came in. At once she assailed him. 'What for did you hit the children, da? Hitting a female and tearing her mouth! Is that what a family man is supposed to do? What're you thinking in that mind of yours? You roam around all over town and come back to eat whenever you want – so it's all gone to your head, is it?'

As though he had heard nothing of what his mother was saying, Ramasaami announced, 'Tomorrow is the last day. Find out and tell me, once and for all – is your husband going to sign or not?'

Ignoring the question, Parvati declared to her son: 'From now on, you just touch and beat the children, or beat her, and that's it! It'll be up to me if that's going to be the last day you live or die. Go show off your power somewhere else, not around here!' She continued to abuse him in words he found so unbearable that he directed an angry kick at a pitcher lying on the floor. Then he stomped away and sat down on the thinnai.

'Didn't I tell you to cut up the cornstalks and feed the cows? Can't this rope-twisting be done later?' Parvati snapped at the old man. Fetching a knife, she began hacking the stalks into short pieces. 'Such a temper they've got, both father and son – it swells them right up to their arseholes. When it comes to something that needs to be done, they've got nothing,' she muttered.

Ramasaami turned threateningly to her, demanding, 'Are you going to do what I just said?' Without glancing at him, she countered, 'Is your father very, very far away or what? Isn't he sitting there, right there in front of your eyes? You ask him yourself. Why should I get in the middle, like a lawyer serving a summons!' Ramasaami looked daggers at her. Then he rose and gathered up the stalks she had cut up. Flinging them to the cattle, he sat down on the rim of the water tank.

'Don't you hear what he's asking? What goes for the whole town goes for us also. Are they going to make a special rule for us? When the whole town is running together, we've got to run with them! Can we start an opposition party? If we do that, won't the whole town spit on us?'

Parvati – was it really Parvati who spoke thus? The old man looked her up and down, as though he could not believe it. For a moment, he seemed about to say something. Then he returned to his task of twisting rope.

'That man won't die, and he won't let anyone else die either. Let everyone else in the town sell their land and build themselves two-storey houses and have a good life! We will only die here in this place, within these broken-down walls. All these years, this man has never budged from that field. So let him die there.'

The old man stopped twisting rope and looked steadily at Parvati. 'Do you know why your father gave you to me?' he asked.

'You know why! Because he had no sense of shame, what else?'

'Shut up, di. Filthy woman.'

'... As they say, a man can get away with anything!

> A good-for-nothing pauper
> Married a woman,
> along with her daughter.

'That's why that father of mine could drag me along and give me to you. It wasn't a rich man with a fleet of five–six boats who gave you his daughter, was it?'

'It wasn't like that, you stupid girl with a brainless father! In those days, in this whole town, my father was the only man who had eight kaanis of land. It was because he had faith in that land! Your father knew it'd feed you. That's why he gave you to me.'

'Maybe that fine man didn't know that only ragi and maize will grow on that shit land. It's just as they say:

> For a son-in-law who's a lump of mud,
> The wedding sweet will be made of dung.'

'It's all because of that ragi-and-maize-growing jungle-land that I am known here as a landlord with many kaanis.'

'If that's so, then you can just go and bury yourself in that jungle-land!'

Parvati's words shut him up. Like an electric shock came the staggering thought that his property was actually about to leave his hands. And yet, along with it came a renewed determination. To never let the land go.

Staring at the old man whose hands had ceased twisting the hay in his lap into rope, Ramasaami nagged him relentlessly: 'Say it! Yes or no!'

At last the old man protested, 'It's gold! Why are you going on and on, wanting to write it off?'

'Gold? What can you do with dry land that won't grow anything but ragi?'

'You can have food to eat.'

'Would any man in his senses talk to you? You just won't understand what's being said. That Company man's bought up all the fields around our land! He'll put up barbed-wire fences and compound walls! Soon, he'll purposely block off the way to our land. We won't be able to stop him! Once he's done that, we'll have no other choice but to go to him ourselves. Then we'll have to beg, "Take our land, please!" And then, of course, he'll only give the lowest price. Instead of that, if we give the land now, at least we'll get something! Money! Company man has got money! So whatever he says, whatever he does, that is what matters. In this whole country it's like that only. Hasn't everybody here gone running and falling over one another to give him their lands, except for you? With your own eyes you can see what is going on in the village. So then? And it's not that I'm crazy about selling the land! But the whole village is against us. They'd like to bring us down.'

'To everyone he says, yours is the last and only field left. That's how he's grabbed all the land.'

'Whatever it is, somehow or other he buys it. What's it to us? Are you going to sign tomorrow or not? Just say that.'

'Even a lizard won't live with you if you don't have a piece of land. Nobody will come near you. Will you ever get it again if it's given away now?'

'Isn't every fellow in the village giving his land? Nobody in the world owns such a grand piece of property as this scrub jungle, is it? It is dry jungle-land! Have you forgotten that?'

'Jungle-land … that's what it is. Who says so?

> A sugarcane piece may be crooked and lame,
> But doesn't it taste sweet, all the same?

'This jungle-land you're talking about is what I ran this household on for so many years. Only because of this same wild jungle-land your own children are growing.'

'So, if that land wasn't there, we'd have all died? Is that it?'

'We wouldn't have died. But would we be known as landed folks? Landlords? Only because we have that bit of land – land that yields a crop! – are there any comings and goings at all in this village. Otherwise, we'll have no barber or washerman – not even a roaming juggler or one of those stick-dancing fellows. Not even a wandering beggar would come here. You're saying this earth's no good. But even if this earth were pure gold, if it doesn't yield a crop even a crow won't turn up here. Or even a sparrow!'

'Are you growing crops for crows and sparrows?'

'For goats and cattle, crows and sparrows … for all of them.'

'What a fine fellow you are … Now stop telling tall tales and making fine speeches and just say what you're going to do.'

'If we sell off the land, what'll we do to feed our goats and cows?'

'There's nobody here to graze them, is there? So just drive those devils down to the shandhai[5] and sell them off.'

'So, just sell them all off and blow it away, like cigarette smoke? Don't want goats and cattle here, all you want is that Company?'

'Times are changing. You don't understand.'

'I understand everything. If the whole place is built up, what will we eat? Look out, they'll leave you stranded in the middle of the road!

> If you ride a clay horse
> you won't get across
> this river.

'If we give the land away, is it only the land that's gone? Goats, cattle, hens will go also. Bullock cart will go, too, even the tank for watering the cows won't be there. Seed paddy, seed grain, even the seed bin will go … And the bullocks, and the plough, the harness rope, the pestle for pounding the paddy, the mortar, the

---

5 Shandhai: A weekly market.

grinding stone and the mill – and many other things – they'll all go. Even the measures will all go – the padi and the vallam and the marakkaa … they won't be here any longer. Grain bin, spade, axe and sickle – none of them will be around in this house. Every single thing will be gone, and only you and I will be left. Only you, only I – can you call that a household? When everything is gone, what for should you and I be here any more? When a man has always slept in a house full of sacks and sacks of grain, how can he sleep in an empty house? Better to just die, da! Who will have respect for a house that's as empty as a barren woman? If household goods all go, honour goes too. Even if life departs, it doesn't matter, da! Our honour must not leave us. If you sell your honour for half a coin, you can't get it back even for a thousand coins, da! If even one person respects you in this town, is it because of your white vaitti? Your oh-so-fine white shirt? Why does the Company fellow come looking for you? You're a fine-looking tall fellow, but is it because of that? It's all because of that bit of jungle-land. If that jungle-land goes, what will you do?'

'Did you give me a fine big education? Just eighth class! He'll only give me a job that's suited to that, isn't it? It's a sweeping job.'

'Biggest job in the world! So, he grabs the land and gives you a sweeper's job? It's like giving a man food and then strangling him!'

'Can't win against this old man by talking,' remarked Parvati.

'How did you last all these years with this man, Amma?'

'By giving up all sense of shame and self-respect. How else?' Parvati shot back, as she gathered the cornstalks and threw them to the cows. Returning, she sat down and began to chop up the remaining stalks. Rani fetched the water used for washing rice and vegetables, and poured it out for the goats tied up in the eastern side of the house.

Selvaraj came out and sat near Parvati. Having watched her cut up the cornstalks, he picked up a few and went and fed them to the cows. Then he tried to slip out into the street, when Ramasaami stopped him with a hard knuckle-knock on the crown of his head. 'Where are you going now, da? When it's getting dark?'

Pulling the weeping boy into her lap, Parvati bawled out her son. 'Why are you hitting the boy for any reason that comes into your head, da? Will a child who wants to play sit still in one place just because you say so? If you're feeling so angry, just go and show it to that father of yours!'

'Kamala! Kamala!' Ramasaami hollered. The girl appeared, her round eyes darting nervously about. 'What's your mother doing?' he demanded. Before she could reply, he said bitterly, 'Let her do what she likes, that beggar's daughter. She's got her father's brain, what else? Right now, you go and get me some water.' Kamala hurried inside.

Almost at once, impelled by who knows what sudden thought, Ramasaami rushed out towards the corner shop, having forgotten that he had asked for water.

'Why are you arguing with a grown son who's married and has two children of his own? Isn't he only saying what is going on in the village? Today, when I went with the other women to cut down weeds in the fields, I asked them about it. Seems all those who have fields around our land have signed and sold them off.' In a bewildered tone, Parvati went on, 'But it's just some cash … what can they do with it? Looks like the whole village has come down with a deadly sickness … a curse.'

'What about Chinnasaami's field, to the south of ours? Has he also given it off?' the old man asked, astonished.

'Tomorrow's the last day … Seems the fellow signed it away day before yesterday.'

'Very good! It's like moths flying into a fire all on their own. To die…' muttered the old man. Leaving off his spinning he sat in a state of bafflement, brooding over what the village folk were doing. Was it right and proper?

Was this a foreboding? Was a calamity about to befall the whole village? Along with a gnawing fear that his land would change hands in that upheaval, his self-confidence began a downward slide. 'This is not right … People are going the wrong way!' he cried out, flailing his arms to chase away a straying cockerel that had emerged from the henhouse.

'Those who've got land by the side of the road are striking it rich – but only those,' Parvati was saying. 'Company man doesn't want to touch the fields beyond them. Who knows how he found this village, it's like it's been cursed by the devil … Now there is no house in the village without cash. All of a sudden, people who never had any money have got into new habits. Now they go and spill lots of cash in jewellery shops, clothing shops…'

Her comments on the goings-on in the village fell unheard on the old man's ears. Bereft of words, he sat there sunk in anxiety about what was going to happen to his land.

Ramasaami returned from the corner shop and sat on the wooden mortar near Parvati. Suddenly, as though he had just remembered, he asked, 'What's happening, 'mma?'

When his mother failed to reply, he repeated the question again, and yet again. 'Is he still stubbornly talking about all the wonderful crops growing on that land?' he demanded irately, at last.

At that, the old man raised his head and gave Ramasaami a scathing look. 'Nothing is coming from that land? Fifty, sixty sacks of paddy don't grow there every year? Groundnuts and gingelly, and maize and millet … don't they grow there? In the driest part of that land, doesn't tuvarai lentil grow? Don't jasmine bushes grow? What did we eat all these years, if that same land gave us nothing?'

'Whatever it grew, what's the use? How many multi-storeyed houses have you built?'

'Does the land yield a crop only for building houses? Not for us to eat food?'

'Eat? Is that all?'

'Then what else do you want from that land? What grew on it got three girls married. Till this day it is what grew on that jungle-land that has given them everything they have, good and bad ... It's because of what came from that land that *your* marriage could be fixed. Above everything else, it is that land that's made me grow, and you grow, and your children also ... It feeds us all. Doesn't a man need food? Even if there are a hundred people in this house, that jungle-land will feed all of them! But if what a fellow craves is a house with one hundred floors, or a fleet of fine ships, what can the land do about that?'

'You're going on and on saying, "It'll give food, it'll give food!" What about people who don't have any land – do they go hungry? Don't they also live?'

'*Landowner* – that is what they call me. That name, that respect will go, no?'

'Name-and-fame, huh! When there's no shame, what's the use of it?'

'So eager you are to sell that land. But have you seen what state it is in? The wall around the well has broken down, the yard on the south keeps getting flooded. Mud and slush, that's what it's become – but have you bothered yourself about that? That fellow who has land to the north of the tamarind grove has helped himself to four cartloads of earth from right there. And you! Not even once have you ever walked across that land, its whole length and breadth!

Not one step have you taken into that jungle-land, but here you are. All ready to put a price on it and sell it off.'

'What! Have I never gone to the land? Do the crops land up here in the house without my seeing to it?'

'Two months back, you and Karuppan's son had a fight. "I'm the only landlord in this village with ten kaanis of land, no man dares to pluck out my bum-hair!" you told him, with the whole village gathered there. You said that on the strength of what? This same land, no?'

'Do you think I want to sell off the land? All the fellows in the village are trying to make us bow down to the Company man … To topple us! If others were not selling, why would I talk about this at all? Won't I think about what we're going to eat once our jungle-land is sold off? Am I not also a man?'

'If we had a hundred, two hundred kaanis, we could have given them a bit from one corner. But there's no way for us to do anything like that. What we have is just a loincloth-sized scrap of earth. Shall we give it off and stand stark naked on the road, chanting "Narayana!" like some holy fellow? How will we run our lives?'

'Nowadays they're giving a kilo of rice for two rupees, aren't they?'

'If we go stand in line at the ration shop, won't we lose face? Won't our whole life become a joke for others? Our kith and kin will think we're not worth a single paisa! It's because of that land that we haven't sent our servants to buy vegetables and chillies and tamarind from the market. From now on, we'll have to give money for all those things … All right, when do we have to sell? After which harvest?'

'This harvest.'

'Oho, is that so?'

'Isn't he also a man? Doesn't he know?' cut in Parvati. 'He has a wife and children, won't he have a sense of responsibility? When every fellow in the village is getting together with every other fellow and all are falling over themselves, what can he do, all by himself? Isn't he telling you what's going on in the village?'

The old man appeared to have simmered down. 'So, we sell off the land…' he said.

Then he asked quietly, 'What are we going to do with the money?'

'We'll have to buy land somewhere else. Or set up a shop … or a tea stall … We'll have to live somehow … Survive,' said Ramasaami.

The old man let out a derisive laugh. 'Fine justice it is, da! First, we have to give away our land, then we have to go four–five miles deep into the jungle to look for some other land to buy! Is that it? And all that time that Company man will come and go, whizzing along on the new road, without feeling the least stress and strain! All this village cares about is that the Company man mustn't suffer any stress and strain, his body must feel no aches and pains! If we go deep into the jungle and buy land there, who will pay the registration charges? Even if we pay it, is it going to be like this land? Where can we get anything like it? It is the best land in the village!'

'We can set up a tea shop.'

'Must we wash the spit off some fellow's glass to just feed ourselves? Is that the kind of work that's suited to our caste? Our family? If a hundred fellows sell their land and all of them set up shops and tea stalls, who will go buy anything from there?'

Rani, who had just come out of the house to fetch some firewood, paused and gave the old man a baleful look. Then, as though choked by a gob of phlegm, she cleared her throat two or three times and spat noisily. As she turned to go back inside with the firewood, she snapped, 'Leave it, won't you? Are you the only one who has to sweat it out? If he dies, just haul this old man and bury him in that same jungle-land where his father's been buried. Then let him go round and round that jungle-land like a ghost.' The old man glared back at her.

Parvati finished cutting up the cornstalks and threw them to the cows, before she went into the house. Ramasaami followed her, only to come back in a few moments. As though sick of the sight of his father spinning rope as before, he set off once more in the direction of the shop.

'Why are you sitting there in the dark? Want some water to drink or something? Just lie down for a bit, and then start spinning again.' Exasperated by the old man's failure to respond, she groaned, 'Whole village goes one way, but he runs the other way … All alone. Shouldn't he understand the way of the world? Shouldn't he be aware of what is going on in the whole country?'

Then, as though she had just remembered, she announced, 'Grain has to be cut tomorrow. I'm going to see about getting workers for harvesting the grain.'

The old man gazed after her incredulously. Was it really Parvati who had just spoken? 'They're all getting together to pluck out my eyes!' he muttered, applying himself with renewed vigour to twisting the strands of hay into rope.

Moments later, a drunken youth came staggering along on the street. The comments of two women following him made the old man sit up and take notice.

'Look at that mother's pet! The boy can't even see where the ground is or where he's put his feet, he's just rolling and tumbling along…'

'All that money that the Company man is throwing around is turning this town upside down. Who knows what-all strange sights we're going to see from now on?'

The youth's identity was unclear in the darkness. Yet what the women were saying dismayed the old man. Maybe one day soon, his own son Ramasaami would be gossiped about likewise. As this thought hit him, he felt his pulse was about to stop. Not only was their wealth about to slip out of their hands, but also their good name. What was at stake was the family's reputation, its prestige. His fear that this might really happen made him even more determined not to sell the land, whatever happened.

… He remembered the hardships that his father and mother, and he himself, had gone through for the sake of this very land that was now being coveted by the Company.

Tears suddenly blurred his eyes. All that the old man's father had possessed at first was half a kaani of scrubland and a tiled hut. It was with that half kaani that he had slowly acquired ten kaanis. How he had struggled to get those ten kaanis was known only to God. Mornings, he would set off with his wife, roaming the scrubland, field after field, searching for cattle droppings to shape into dung pats for fuel. Evenings, he cut down and chopped firewood and sold it. Even on festivals like Deepavali and Pongal they could not stay at home. They never ate a decent curry with their boiled rice. Water was all they had to gulp it down with … When the old man was just eight years old, he used to go with his father and his mother to collect dung in the jungle pastures, and to cut firewood.

At age ten, he caught himself ten goats and took them out to graze. In five or six years, his own herd of goats took shape, and little by little, as his goats were sold, they bought patch after patch of land, and got a quarter kaani, then a half kaani. Struggling to pay the registration fee for a piece of land which had a well on it, and left with no other recourse, his father had said to his mother, 'Give me your taali. As soon as I lay the first brick for the well, I'll get you a new one.'

'Take my life, but just don't ask for my taali!' That was his mother's answer.

The quarrel that ensued separated his parents for a full six months. In the end, the taali did get sold, and it was with that money that his father paid the fee. Though he had said he would buy a new taali when he laid the first brick, that didn't happen. The old man's father had gone on instead to plant and sell crop after crop of groundnut, sesame, coriander, and many other grains. He made money, acquired field after field, but he never did buy his wife another taali. She died cursing him, and the memory of his mother's bitter curses brought a gush of tears, now, to the old man's eyes.

... When his father died, although he had had trouble finding money for the funeral rites, he didn't sell any of his land, or even take a loan on it. He just didn't have the heart to do it. Even to get his three daughters married, he had never sold or mortgaged any land. As recently as two years ago, he had purchased another half kaani. Since then, he had been putting in months of hard toil, with the idea of buying yet another quarter or half kaani with the proceeds of another two or three years' harvest.

Now, as though to turn to ashes this deep desire of his, the Company man had turned up in the village – as Yama, the god of death.

He had counted on his three daughters. They, he thought, would be formidable weapons that he could wield against the sale of the land. But they had utterly let him down. All of them had got together to trip him up and bring him down. 'How can we go against what Annan says?' they had protested. 'Isn't our brother more precious to us than any property? Doesn't Anna know what's right and what's wrong? Can we helpless females dare to give advice to a man?' And Rani, too, was dancing to Ramasaami's tune, with her pronouncements that the land must be sold. All of them, even Parvati, were justifying it by pointing to what the rest of the village was doing, and to what the neighbouring landowners were doing. They all insisted that what Ramasaami said was absolutely right. What effect could the old man's remonstrations have, when Ramasaami had openly made an astounding promise to his sisters:

'I'll buy you each a gold chain with the money!'

Shaken, the old man began to suspect that Ramasaami's wife Rani, and even his own wife Parvati, had been bought over likewise. 'What's to be gained by selling off crop-yielding land for buying gold trinkets to dangle from ears and neck? Will gold satisfy the stomach's hunger? Can you eat gold? What can you give a child that's crying for something to eat? But all of them are tilting in one and the same direction! So, maybe I'm the one who's doing something wrong?' he asked himself. 'They're lighting a bomb on this whole way of life, this livelihood that keeps the belly from shrivelling up, that gives us food to eat – why can't these people be damned forever?' He thought of all that was likely to happen, once the sale went through.

Little Kamala came out, saying, 'Amma is calling you to eat.'

'Go, dear, I'll come. First you eat,' he said, and sent her back. A little later, Rani herself came and said, 'Just because there's been a quarrel in the house, should anyone go to sleep without eating? Come, come and eat! Why show off your strength by refusing food? If you do this kind of thing, your son will also be just like you. Whole world won't be able to control him.' Having tried repeatedly to make the old man have his meal, she turned away defeated.

'How many times must she ask you? What terrible thing is going to happen if you just go and have a meal?' remonstrated Parvati. 'The older he gets, the harder to please he gets – acts like a fussy son-in-law,' she muttered. Then she raised her voice. 'How long are you going to remain in this stubborn mood? If you agree, sign the paper. If you don't, let it be! Who is going to hang you for it? Just for that are you going to let your stomach shrivel up and dry? Does the stomach know the land is going to be sold? Or does it know hunger?' she loudly demanded.

But he just sat there without uttering a word – looking bereft –

> … he's lost his zest for life,
> like a man who's lost his wife…

But there she was. Abusing and scolding him … but none of it seemed to irk him. His mind lay sunk in old memories. Disentangling himself from them seemed beyond him. Again and again, Parvati pleaded with him to come and eat. At last she turned away, saying bitterly, 'When his bum dries up, only then he'll get some sense!'

A while later, Kamala came out after having finished her meal. 'Come and eat, Thatha. Come, eat!' she entreated. When he continued to sit there without moving, she seized his hand and tried to pull him up. To put an end to her pestering, he told her, 'My stomach is not all right, 'mma. You go eat. Go to sleep, please, dear!'

Parvati had come out to see what the old man was doing, and was sitting on the thinnai and listening to all this. 'For forty-fifty years there was no tummy ache at all! How has it suddenly come now, today?' she taunted, and pronounced a curse: 'God, let him get a real stomach pain, please!' But nothing she said had any effect on the old man. His thoughts – his whole mind was on the field, there in the scrub jungle. 'After the age of ten, or eleven, was there any day that I didn't go to the field?' he was asking himself. Not one single day of that kind could he recall. Once he had started going regularly to the field, he had eaten both the morning and the noon meal there, out in the open. That was where he had spent festival days, too – even Pongal and Deepavali. To weddings and funerals and such family events, he would send Parvati. When his own attendance was unavoidable, he would hurry back almost as soon as he had arrived there. After any journey out of town, he would return, not straight to the house but straight to the field, and not one night had he ever spent away from home. Never had he ever grumbled about going to work in that rough terrain. Every morning when he reached the field, the first thing he did would be to take a look around the whole field, and every evening he would do the same thing before he left for home.

For this, he would be nagged every day by Parvati: 'No robber is going to carry off your wild jungle!' Her relentless needling could not make the old man give up this habit of vigilantly surveying his precious patch of scrubland, morning and evening.

... If the land were sold off, where would he go, where would he spend the whole day? How could he just sit and do no work, all day long? 'Doesn't the food that's eaten have to be digested? For that to happen, mustn't one do some work?' Such questions kept tormenting him.

Those who had lands alongside the road that was coming up had already sold them. What would the men in those families do with themselves now? How long would it last – that money that the Company man had given them? What would they do, after that, for their food? More than the men, it was the women who were eager to sell. Until then, they had sent their children to the shops with a quarter or a half measure of grain to buy salt or chillies, tamarind or cumin. From now on, what would they barter for such needs? When they wanted hair clips, collyrium to darken their eyes, ribbons and tassels and switches of false hair, and waist-strings, what would they give the wandering gypsy women who supplied them with such things? Their children took fistfuls of ragi, maize or paddy to the ice-cream vendor, to buy ices. What would they take to him now?

'A man who's had ten kaanis of land and a bullock cart, who's been harvesting fifty or sixty sacks of paddy, and seventy or eighty sacks of ragi and maize – must such a man do coolie work for a mere marakkaa?' He kept mumbling to himself – was he was going mad? 'But it's these people who are going mad! Company will only drug them with false dreams, it'll hoodwink them. Will it ever feed them? It's like that absurd story of the funeral feast in a poor paraiyan's[6] house ... about a paappaan[7] being given a gift of paddy! Which Brahmin priest would attend, much less conduct, a funeral ceremony in an outcaste house? Or be offered or receive such a gift? Is that ever possible!' he burst out, before sinking once again into his thoughts.

As long as he could remember, he had never wanted to go to the temple, or to a festival, or to any gala festivities. Or to lounge about at home. All he had ever wanted was to go to the field and work hard there. To get a bigger yield than others did. To prevent stray goats and cows from grazing on it, to see that rats did not get their teeth into the crop ... That was all. And until now, whatever he had desired had not been in vain. It was not only the land that was going now, nor just the work itself, but his desires, too, would come to an end. There would be nothing left to look forward to. To harvest the grain, then to plant another crop, to harvest that crop, and then to plant again: no more can I wait for it to happen. 'All I can wait for now is death,' he thought. He set down the rolls of rope that he had spun, and pushed the remaining bundles of paddy straw towards

---

6 Paraiyan: Outcaste, pariah.

7 Paappaan (or paarpaan): A Tamil term for Brahmins, particularly for priests, used derisively.

the mouths of the cattle. He stroked one of the cows. Then he went and sat on the thinnai. In a moment, he slumped and curled himself up.

'Don't you know it's getting late? Come, eat and go lie down! Must the light burn all night? Who'll pay the electricity bill? Whole town's gone all quiet!' Parvati continued to harangue him, but all her efforts were wasted on the old man, who lay inert, as though he were doing some rigorous penance. Wearing herself out, Parvati went on importuning him. 'Is this the time to show your toughness? As if you are a proud son-in-law who has to be begged again and again!' She tried reasoning with him, trying to reconcile him to what was about to happen. 'Whatever happens to the town happens to us also! That Company man has come here, like a devil – a curse from a former birth! Who can we blame for that? For that, who are you getting angry with? Before our own time comes to an end, who knows what-all we will have to see.' Having tried to reason with him and been defeated, she sprang up at last, demanding, 'D'you think you'll be the one who stops what's going on in the village? In the whole country?' She stalked off into the house.

When Ramasaami came back home, she emerged to berate him: 'Where were you gone for so long? Can't you come home at a decent time and eat your food and mind your own business? From sunrise I've been toiling in the field, and all night I have to stay awake for you men! Then how can this wretch of a woman get up again at sunrise and go to work in that jungle? Don't you men have the sense to feel all this? That man just goes on and on saying he'll single-handedly stop the flood that's about to drown this town, and then just lies there! And what is wrong with you? Only after this wretched worm of a woman has reached the burning ghat will father and son understand what's happening. Doesn't my body also feel pain? Is my body made of iron or what? Won't my arms and legs get worn out?' Parvati shouted.

Ramasaami sat down to his meal, and as he ate, he began to talk: 'Even now, I've been asking around, and everyone says selling the land is the right thing to do. But I still don't know what to do. All the land by the side of the road has been sold, except for three people who hadn't sold out till now. Two of them have just received the money, they'll sign tomorrow. What the Company man is going to do with so much land, who knows? But he's paying whatever price they ask. How one person can have so much money, how a company can run and pay wages after it's already spent so much on the land? A man who has so much cash – what is he like? Nobody knows, really.'

'Those people who're taking bags and bags of cash from him – what are they going to do with it?'

'They'll buy a house, with a door. And they'll buy things to eat – vegetables, meat…'

'How long will they be able to eat with that cash?'

'Don't know. Whole world is like that now … all the time eating, fucking…'

'Must buy a TV, first. Then a "vandi" to get around in … House has to be repaired. And then I have to buy gold chains for my sisters.'

'So, you're saying a plot of land that's yielding must be sold to build a house for sleeping! All right, is there nothing for me, da?'

'Why do you need any jewel, Amma? You're going to die anyway! Are you a young girl about to get married or something?' laughed Ramasaami. He went on with his meal, recounting the news in the village – who had sold their land, and for how much, in which households quarrels were taking place, about jewellery not being bought for the women out of the money received. He announced that, when the time came for signing, he would ask for a job. He blamed himself bitterly for not having studied more. Nobody in the other households with lands had studied very much. They were like him, he said mournfully. Half educated. The jobs available for those who had sold their land, he reported with anguish, were those of watchmen, peons, cleaners and sweepers, water-carriers, bell-ringers, door-openers, and the like.

As though he were all of a sudden overcome by emotion, he said, 'If those fellows who have lands all around ours hadn't sold theirs, we could also have kept ours. But now there's no other way out for us. They say the water and the land in our village is the best around, and that's why they are giving whatever price we ask. Just thinking about putting a signature on it makes my heart beat so hard.

But I can't refuse. What does it feel like when a cobra has got into a house? That's how this whole village feels now.' Ramasaami rose to wash his hands.

And then he asked, once again, 'Amma, what does Appa say now?'

'Go to the man and find out for yourself.'

'They've told us tomorrow is the last day. So tell him to just come quietly, put his signature and decently take the money. Otherwise what happened to Mookkan in South Street will happen to him also. His son dragged him along and forced him to sign.'

'What! What are you saying, da?'

'I'm telling you the truth! Is it for buying jewels for my wife and children that I want to sell the land?'

'Talk softly, da. He'll hear you.'

'Let him hear it! Good thing it'll be if he behaves himself. Then what Mookkan's son did to his father won't happen here.'

'Don't say anything!' Parvati signalled, covering her mouth with her hand before she rose hurriedly and went out, closing the front door behind her.

Left alone in the front yard, the old man could not hear what Parvati and Ramasaami were now saying to each other behind the door. But he had already fallen into a state of shock. All the seven vital pulses in his body seemed to have stopped. The life within him was being snuffed out.

'Don't let it happen again, the way it happened to Mookkan's father!'

Ramasaami's words scorched the old man like live coals. He felt them burning him to ashes. Was that what was going to happen to him? The instant the thought struck him, he stiffened and sat up. Everywhere he gazed there was darkness. Very soon, he could not bear to sit still. He got up and went out into the soundless street.

It was as though every household had emptied and every family had fled the village, so utterly devoid had it become of any movement. That sinister hush felt like a portent of the doom about to befall the whole village. Aimlessly, he walked out, went to the end of the street and then returned and lay down on the thinnai.

The minutes passed. He tried all sorts of things, he tossed and turned. It was not sleep that came to him but thoughts of past events, and he just could not free himself from them … One among those memories was of his father telling him, 'When I die, take me to my own field and bury me there.' He remembered how he had taken his father's body there, instead of to the cremation ground. How he had buried him, and planted a mango sapling on the heap of earth above the corpse. That mango tree had grown, and it had spread itself out over a quarter-kaani area. Thirty or forty sacks of fruit grew on it.

… When he died, he wanted to be buried in the shade of that tree … he must tell them this. For quite some time, the old man had been thinking of it, and wanting to announce that he wanted to have a lime, or a mango sapling, to be planted on his grave. That was his sole desire, the only thing he had ever craved all his life…

Would the Company fellow who purchased the land leave the mango tree alone? Would he ever allow him to be buried there, let alone have a sapling planted on the spot? His mouth went dry at the very thought. Little by little, all his hopes for the land began to drain away. 'Nothing did I ever value more, you low-born scoundrels! Not even my life! It must be someone here, some sinner's bad-luck time that's crashing down like a lightning bolt. On my head! It's my family that's going to suffer this terrible fate,' he muttered, sighing.

Once again, a restlessness came upon him, and once again he heaved himself up and went out into the street.

Roaring along, setting the whole street aquiver, came a motorcycle – Selvan's new acquisition. The sight of it hit the old man hard. Immediately he thought of Nallamuthu, who had retired from his teaching job hardly four months ago. Every single day, without fail, his son Selvan fought with him, demanding, 'Why are you putting your pension money in the bank? I'm your only son! Why aren't you giving it to me?' Nallamuthu knew his son, and that was why he had arranged to withdraw just a thousand or five hundred at a time to give to him.

One day, after yelling, 'Take it all out and hand it over to me!' Selvan hit him – with his slipper. His own father.

The very next day after this incident, Nallamuthu took out all his money from the bank, gave it to him, and left.

That was the last anyone ever saw of him in the village. For two days he did not return, and after the third day, it came to be known that he had drunk country liquor laced with poison, stretched himself out upon the Thozhudhoor river. Drowned.

'Doesn't feel any grief, that his father died … Drinks and goes zooming around in the middle of the night!' the old man said to himself … Tomorrow, if he did not sign, maybe what Mookkan's son and what Nallamuthu's son had done to their fathers would happen to him … Maybe Ramasaami would do the same thing to him. The old man fell to trembling, gripped by terror. He wandered out into the street again, wandered back, stood in the doorway and looked at the dark sky.

'Those men who set up companies and factories and lay roads … can't they go find themselves something else to do? Why come into my little ill-fated garden to pluck fruit for themselves? … If it was only half the land that's going, it wouldn't be so bad, but it's the whole of it that's being swallowed up. I've got no place to go to, no place to come from. They've made a cripple out of me! Broken me! Thrown me down! Why couldn't they just pluck out both my eyes?' he wailed out aloud. 'I never meddled with anybody, never got into anybody else's business. Never tried to snatch anyone else's property, never wanted anything that belonged to anybody! Never did harm to anyone. My land, and I – that's all that mattered to me. Then why are they meddling with me? What is the quarrel between them and me? Why are they robbing me of my property?' Groaning to himself, he turned this way and that, could not sit or stand in one place. The question 'What shall I do?' kept gnawing at him, tearing him apart. 'Like moneylenders collecting a debt, they've announced a date! Suppose I'm not here? What's going to happen? How many days can I run and hide, as if I'm running and hiding from a policeman with an arrest warrant? If I run, will the land remain as it is, without changing hands? What will they say in the village? Shall I become a sanyaasi and just give it all up?'

Considering this possibility, he felt a little hope and energy entering into him. But not even for a little while did that hope and energy last ... If he became a sanyaasi, wouldn't he have to beg for his food? 'But in all these years of life, I've never even eaten in somebody else's house ... my hands never needed to be washed after a meal anywhere but at home. Not a drop of plain cold water have I drunk in anybody's house, never has it even touched my lips and teeth,' he told himself. 'If I leave the house and go off on a pilgrimage, won't I have to beg for alms? Won't my life depend on it? It'll be like jumping into the fire because I'm afraid of the water in the well ... If that's the only way to keep alive, why not just kill myself?'

Brooding over it, a kind of clarity descended on him, and in a few moments his body felt a little more energetic. He went to the cows, and one by one he caressed and stroked each of them. He looked at the water trough, at the wooden pounding stick that lay nearby. Going to the goat shed, he gazed at each goat as if for the first time. Turning to the front door in a kind of daze, and about to knock on it, he paused and stood there. He felt like calling Kamala. But he didn't do it.

Picking up the bundle of paddy straw he had put aside that morning for twisting into rope, he noiselessly set off towards the field.

His jungle-land.

Sharada

Pushing and shoving his way through, Dhanavel climbed into the train and looked about for a seat. The number of passengers had increased, with many having got on at Tambaram, and several people were standing in the passage with no place to sit. 'Looks like I'll just have to keep standing till I reach home,' he said to himself.

'But it's a reserved coach,' he told himself the very next minute. 'How would there be any empty seat?' The passage was so crammed, he'd be lucky if he got space even to stand. A fresh worry arose: what if the ticket examiner shouted, *Why did you get into the reserved coach? Go to the unreserved coach!* 'Then there'll really be no place to put my feet!' he muttered to himself.

Taking out his handkerchief, he wiped his face and looked around. Towards the left stood two women and a man, and leaning against the washbasin stood a young girl typing something or the other on her cell phone. Near the coach entrance on the eastern side was a fat man, and he himself was in the gap between that individual and the toilet. Instead of standing there leaning against that toilet door, he thought, wouldn't it be better to just open it and stand inside? But there'd be people constantly wanting to come in … He decided against it.

Looking out, he saw that the train had left the platform. A faint breeze blew in, and he held his face up towards it to try and cool himself. Annoyingly, it was blocked off by the fat man's bulk.

'Paani! Vaater baatil!' shouted a water vendor who came by at that moment. He suddenly felt thirsty. Reaching in his shoulder bag for his own water bottle, he took just one sip before he put the cap back on and stuffed it inside, deciding it was enough. Leaning slightly against the toilet door, he began to gaze outside.

'You're from Pulloor, aren't you?'

It was a woman's voice.

He turned … Fifty, fifty-five she might have been … She was looking straight at him. Dhanavel glanced at her doubtfully. Was she addressing him?

'You're from Pulloor, no?' asked the woman again.

Wondering how it was that a woman about whom he knew nothing was asking him about his home town, Dhanavel answered in a low voice, 'Yes, 'nga.'

'Do you know who I am?'

In an instant, as though a light had been switched on in a dark house, Dhanavel realized who she was – the woman who stood before him, asking the question. A thrill ran through his body. In that sweltering heat, it suddenly felt as though he were lying on a bed of ice cubes.

He could not bring himself to look at her. Nor could he open his mouth and speak a single word. After a while, with some difficulty, he brought out a question:

'You are Sharada, aren't you?'

Her reply was just that unwavering gaze, until he asked, 'You are from Pennaadam, aren't you?'

'Name, village – so you do remember all that!' Sharada gave a soundless chuckle with an air of mystery. 'It's amazing,' she murmured.

Dhanavel strove to summon up a smile, but it utterly refused to show up.

'What?'

'Meeting you like this ... I saw you getting on at Tambaram. At once I recognized you. I thought you would come inside, but you stayed right here, outside. How to go up to you and speak to you, I was thinking. Then I thought, let me see if you yourself will come and talk to me. But I couldn't keep on just sitting there. I thought, what if I go and talk to him myself? After all, what can happen to me? Let me do it, I thought!' Sheer joy blossomed visibly on Sharada's face, even as she spoke.

Dhanavel tried to look at her face. He tried to say something, but he just could not. He tried to smile. That too wouldn't happen. All he could do was squirm with embarrassment like a shamefaced youth. Try as he might, he could not bring himself to look back at her.

'How is it you came here?'

'My HM[1] promotion file – I had to submit it at the office.'

'A teaching job, is it?'

'Mm.'

Where?'

'Kammaapuram.'

Sharada stood there, not knowing what to ask next. From the corner of her eye, she tried to see what he looked like. Having noticed them in conversation, the fat man who was standing by the entrance moved off towards the washbasin. Dhanavel edged forward by about a foot into the space thus vacated, and Sharada, too, shifted a little.

'Are you in any job?'

'Mm...'

'In which place?'

'Nallur.'

'That's quite nearby!' he almost said, but didn't. Trying to sneak a look at her, he felt awkward, and pretended to be looking instead at the people seated inside. On her own, as though she had seen through his act and decided to satisfy his curiosity, Sharada announced, 'I am not in the old job.

---

1 HM: A colloquially used abbreviation of the English term 'headmaster', like the terms CM for Chief Minister and PM for Prime Minister, both English words which have been absorbed into everyday Indian speech. Dhanavel is in line for promotion to a HM post.

I got promoted. I'm a senior supervisor now, for the noon-meal scheme…'[2]

'Really?' Dhanavel remarked. Groping for what to say next, he finally murmured, as though sharing a secret: 'You don't look the same as you did in 1985…' Sharada smiled a mysterious smile, as if to say she knew exactly why he was reminding her of 1985.

'It's so surprising…' he said softly.

'What is so surprising?'

'So much difference…!'

'I was a young girl then,' she said with a little smile. 'Now I'm an old woman.' He now clearly saw her nose stud with its red stone, and the three dots on her brow. Feigning to himself that he had not noticed them at all, he took in a glimpse of her delicate, sharp nose, and her broad forehead. They looked just as they were when she was young.

'Up to the tenth, I studied in the village itself. School was right opposite the house. I had never gone beyond two or three streets away. Went to the town only to the cinema – twice my father took us, in a bullock cart. First time I went anywhere was to your town … Nowadays, there isn't a single day that I don't ride on a bus.' Sharada fell silent for a while, and stared out of the moving train. In a tone devoid equally of bitterness and happiness, she remarked:

---

2 Noon-meal scheme: A free midday meal programme for children in government run and aided schools.

'Not even one single day goes by without me thinking: why did it ever happen that I went to *your* town to work!'

Now he looked a little more closely at her. That happiness on her face when she first asked, 'You're from Pulloor, isn't it?' – it was gone now. Feeling his eyes on her, Sharada straightened the saree over her breast and smoothed down the hair that was flying about in the wind.

An old woman came along with a big aluminium pot, selling packets of peanuts. 'Roast peanuts! Masala peanuts!' Shrivelled as she was, the woman's powerful bellow belied her appearance. Dhanavel and Sharada both turned, at one moment, to look at her. Sharada's arm brushed lightly against Dhanavel's for a split second as she made way for the peanut seller. To him, it felt like a bolt of lightning had shot through his whole body and suffused it, oddly enough, with an electrifying chill. He had never before felt anything like it.

'Sorry…' he stammered.

'What for?' she asked in a matter-of-fact way. To that, Dhanavel made no reply. Nor did he look at her face.

Sharada laughed drily. 'Daily I am coming and going in somebody or other's car or jeep! This body is not the same as that one which first came to your town. Now it's all dried up – just like a tamarind branch that's shed all its fruit.' Having said all this, Sharada turned her gaze longingly outside, as though searching for something she had lost.

At last, he could get a good look at her. Of not more than middle height, she wore ear studs with some whitish stones. Lying on her neck was a thin, thread-like chain. Her taali...[3]

He felt he had to say something.

'What does your saar do?' he ventured.

'We have got four kaanis[4] of land. Bullock cart, a cow. Water from a well right inside the house. Sheep for breeding. Tenant farmer to work on the land ... A boy was born ... A girl also – just one. Just one girl. Didn't have to go from house to house for food to eat. What more do you want than this? That is what my father kept on and on asking me. I didn't answer him. What answer could I give? I was only nineteen, after all, and I was married and I had two children already. And now I'm an old woman!' Sharada ended with a laugh.

Why were her eyes blurring, even as she laughed? Dhanavel tried to understand it, but avoided looking at her face, not wanting to appear too inquisitive. But did her husband have a job at all, or didn't he? He had no way of guessing.

'Eating. That's his job,' said Sharada. 'And playing cards ... and sleeping.' From the way her face twisted, it was clear that there was no meeting of minds between Sharada and her husband. Maybe he shouldn't have asked ... Now he found himself coming out with another question:

---

3 Taali: Marriage thread.

4 Kaani: A measure of land, about 1.32 acres.

'No other problem, no?'

'Family means there will be problems, no? Mine's a thirty-one-year-old story. How to tell it all in one word?' Sharada asked, in an ironic tone brimming with mockery. Dhanavel didn't know what to say to that. Her free and easy way of speaking confounded him. What sort of person was she really? She was coming out with so much … Her family life must be a mess of knots and tangles. The very next moment he thought, 'As if my family life is oh-so great!'

'Not a bad person – is he?' he ventured.

Her face swiftly changing expression, she hit back: 'Neem leaf will taste bitter only, no?'

That shut him up.

Sharada's eyes had moved from the view outside to a child sitting two or three rows down. Having gestured to her, she turned back and continued, 'Nowadays, when a marriage is being fixed, people can ask – 'What has maaple[5] studied? What's his job? Private company or government? How much salary? Show his bank statement!' People can get everything they want printed out in the matrimonial column, and then select a bride or a bridegroom. It's just like choosing what you want in a cloth store, but in those days, it was only whatever Appa and Amma said. And they gave their girl only after seeing how much land that family had. Wasn't that the way it was?'

5 Maaple: Maapillai – son-in-law. In this case, a would-be bridegroom.

It gave Dhanavel a shock. What a woman she was! How had she become capable of talking like that? 'Women! Can't get a word out of them, but once they start, they'll never stop,' he thought, bemused. That she had come up to him and asked, 'You're from Pulloor, isn't it?' and was now standing here so close to him, and coming out with ten answers to every one of his questions, as though she were chatting intimately with somebody she had known for a long, long time – was it really happening? This Sharada who stood here, near him – was she real? To talk normally, to smile without affectation, as naturally as she was doing – it was something he couldn't bring himself to believe, let alone match ... He couldn't even look her in the face, let alone speak and laugh as she was doing ... This shyness he was feeling – it must be what a newly-wed bride must go through...

He wanted very much to look at all of her, from head to foot. He tried, and couldn't do it.

'If you want, you can go and sit over there, in my seat, 'nga,' she offered.

'No, no need...' he said hurriedly.

Bouncing up from her seat inside just then, a little girl about four or five years old came running up to Sharada.

'What is it, 'mma? Paati is standing right here, I'll come! You just go sit down.' Ignoring Sharada's words, the child stood staring in turn at them both. 'I'm just talking to somebody I know, I'll come soon. You go sit down,

Sadhana,' repeated Sharada. Angrily, the child turned and stalked off to her seat.

'Wait, please. I'll just come,' Sharada said to Dhanavel and went to her grandchild. 'Are you hungry, 'mma? Want water? There are biscuits in the bag, take and eat,' she coaxed, but Sadhana sat there stiffly. Desperate to placate the girl, Sharada pressed a button on her cell phone and handed it to her.

'You just go on playing that game, keep sitting … I'll come soon,' she told her, and came back to Dhanavel.

'Who is that?' he asked.

'My elder daughter's second girl. I'm taking her with me for the summer holidays,' Sharada replied. After a pause, she continued, 'She's in Perambur.' Moving a little to make way for a man heading for the toilet, she said suddenly, as though it had just occurred to her, 'Your … She goes to work? Or stays at home?'

'She's a teacher.'

'How many children?'

'Two boys.'

'What are they doing?'

'Older one is doing engineering, younger one is studying in plus-two.'

'A late marriage, was it?'

'Got married only at thirty-three years.'

'Madam is good-looking?' she asked with a strange smile. Dhanavel understood at once what was going on in that mind of hers, and wanted to retort, 'At eighteen, who doesn't look good? Any young donkey will look very, very nice!' Stopping himself from coming out with it, he thought, 'Looks like that's all women do – each and every one's only work is to make some comment or other about some other woman…'

Watching him standing there in silence, Sharada probed further: 'Was she working along with you?'

'No, no,' he hastened to reply.

'So, all you had to do was to write a note to her? That's how you must have caught her, no?' The words pierced like needles poking him somewhere in the chest. His face sinking, Dhanavel stood there, trying not to look in her direction.

In a low tone, she asked, 'Do you still write?'

'No.'

'Why not?'

'Doesn't happen.'

'Is that the truth?'

'It's the truth. On my family deity Chelli Amman, I swear it!'

'How is it you felt like writing to me as soon as you saw me?'

Dhanavel hung his head. Breaking into a cold sweat, he tried to laugh it off, but it was no use. He pretended to be gazing at the seated passengers, and even that was beyond him. Consumed with shame and mortification, he didn't know where to look and what to do with his own face.

Sharada, however, was looking up at him without the least trace of hesitation or embarrassment.

Turning his gaze outside, he saw that the train had reached Chingleput railway station. 'Didn't you ever send any notes to anyone after that?' she asked Dhanavel teasingly.

'No.'

'That's a lie.'

'It's not a lie, I swear it.'

'So why did you write only to me?' she said, with a smile as dazzling as a young bride's.

Dhanavel couldn't answer at once. Questions, questions – why was she aiming them at him, one after the other? Putting him in such a quandary? She was laughing like a mischievous child. 'Tell me, 'nga!' she coaxed.

'You could have asked that when you got the note. What's the use of asking now?' Dhanavel demanded, as if to put her down, once and for all.

'How does it matter when I ask? What's the difference?'

'Don't know,' he muttered.

'Really?' crooned Sharada innocently, her voice taking on the timbre of a ten-year-old's. How was he to answer her question? He thought of saying, 'I wrote it because I didn't know anything about women. What a woman is.' Once again, he held himself back. Now, as he thought back over it, it not just astonished him, it shocked him that he had done such a thing. Ashamed as he was, he also felt like laughing.

Fixed on him, Sharada's eyes kept asking, 'Answer me, please!' Impotent to meet them, he writhed in inward agony.

It was in 1985 when he had just enrolled in the first year of a BSc course in Tiruchi Periyar College, that the Sri Lankan ethnic conflict broke out. Students were abandoning college to join in the protests against Premadasa. They were burning his effigies. All the colleges in Tiruchi were shut down, and Dhanavel went back home to his village.

A girl came to teach at the village nursery school and childcare centre which stood right across the road from his house. He didn't know which village she came from, he didn't know her name, he didn't know if she was already in love with anybody. He had no idea if she was a hot-tempered type or a meek-and-mild creature. Nor had he observed the contours of her face or spotted the mole on it. Or noted her complexion – was it dusky or fair? Did she have a nice nose? He had never stood close to her. Yet, once having caught a glimpse of her from a good way off, he felt he must write a love letter to her.

After that idea came to him, he was emboldened to sneak a look at her. That done, his only occupation was to remain sitting upon the thinnai[6] in the porch of his house, watching the comings and goings at the nursery

---

6 Thinnai: A platform right outside the front door, for people to sit on.

school opposite. It took him two or three days to note when she arrived, and when she set out to go home to her village. At nine thirty in the morning, she would turn up, and by two in the afternoon she would leave. In addition to keeping watch from his porch, he took to waiting at the bus stop for the Pazhaniappa bus which carried her to and from her place of work.

The cook who worked at the nursery, Dhanalakshmi, was a cousin of Dhanavel's. He discovered from her that the new teacher's name was Sharada, and that she had been employed to fill in for Susheela, who had taken maternity leave for a month. Once he knew her name and where she came from, Dhanavel could not sit quiet. Poetry streamed out of him like sweat from a man standing in blazing sunlight, and it didn't stop. And as he wrote, he never gave a thought to how it was turning out, or whether or not she would take the chit from him and read it. That occurred to him only after he had finished writing it. Should he give it to Dhanalakshmi to hand over to her? But Dhanalakshmi was related to him! She was from right here, this very village. Suppose she let it out not only in her own household but outside? Suppose the whole village came to know about it? The disgrace of it! Worry seized him.

And as he worried, poetry came to him. Standing, walking, lying down, it was all he thought about – morning, noon and night. He even forgot to eat. Only Sharada remained in his mind.

And poetry. She stood right at the core of it. How would he reach his poems to her?

Brooding ceaselessly, he drove himself into a feverish state. Would it be all right to give Dhanalakshmi a note, or should he just give it to Sharada himself? What if she went home the very next moment and told her parents? Or maybe she would tell Dhanalakshmi or Susheela? But what remained constant in his mind was that he must give Sharada the poems.

His father saw the light burning every night in Dhanavel's room till early in the morning, and thought his son was applying himself zealously to his studies. 'Why don't you study in the daytime, 'ppa? Studying at night means keeping the light on. Current charge will go up, no?' suggested his mother.

'What is more important – studies or current charge? I've married the daughter of a man who never learnt even the first two letters of the alphabet – that's my fault!' Dhanavel saw his father letting loose a stream of abuse on his mother over the issue of the electricity bill, but he did not trouble his head over it. He kept the light on all night till the early hours. Writing poems … on Sharada.

Some ten days went by, by which time Dhanavel's poetry had filled eight notebooks. At around eleven one morning, he was sitting on the porch wondering when Sharada would turn up. If she went into the aanganwaadi[7]

7 Aanganwaadi: A government run neighbourhood childcare centre.

at nine thirty, it would be two before she came out. All that time she would be stuck in there, like a grindstone in its hole.

Dhanalakshmi emerged and set off in the direction of the marketplace. Suddenly, Dhanavel dashed out in a fit of madness and entered the nursery. Taking out the note from his pocket, he set it down on the desk in front of Sharada and dashed out again. Going in, putting the note down in front of her, coming out again – it all happened at lightning speed, and was over in a minute.

When Dhanavel reached home, he found he just couldn't sit down anywhere, he was so restless. All that had been agitating him, until he had taken the note and deposited it in front of her, was that he must somehow do it. Now that the deed was done, what tormented him was the question, 'Why did I do it? What for?' No need to have done it at all, he felt, and cursed himself for being so hasty. Just sitting there, in his own house, he was terribly afraid that she might come and ask, 'Why did you give me that note?' What would he do? He ran out of the house in panic and went into the fields. It was only when he found himself there that he realized that whatever courage he had had at home had shrunk by less than half.

Sharada ... what did she do when she saw the note? After she opened and read it, would she have told Dhanalakshmi, or come to his house and confronted his parents with it: 'See what your boy has done! He's written me a note! Just read it, 'nga!' Maybe she went and told

Susheela all about it. Over and over came the thoughts, searing his brain till it seemed to be burnt dry.

Back home, he flung himself down in the shed, fretting over the fate of his note. It was only after it grew really dark that he went into the house. There was nothing unusual that he could spot in the way his parents looked and behaved. But it took him more than half an hour – almost an hour, actually – before he could breathe free … So, there was no problem here at home.

But would Dhanalakshmi have come to know of the note? As though to get to the bottom of it, he went towards her house, hovered around and paced this way and that, three or four times. On her way back from fetching water from the well in Perumal Kovil street, Dhanalakshmi asked, 'What is it, thambi?[8] What for are you coming here so late at night?'

'Nothing … I came just like that only,' he mumbled.

He could detect nothing out of the way in Dhanalakshmi's tone of enquiry – except for her smile. Was she smiling because she knew all about the note? Or was there really nothing special about it? He carried his befuddlement with him as he turned towards Susheela's house. She sat outside, chatting with someone.

'What brings you all the way here to us, thambi?'

---

8 Thambi: Younger brother. Also a term of endearment for a child – rather like 'little boy'.

'Nothing, I just came, that's all,' he said, trying to brush away the question.

'This is night-time – you'll get bitten by insects. Be careful,' warned Susheela, and it was only then that Dhanavel relaxed a little. So, she didn't know. Sharada hadn't told anybody about the note – that's what it looked like. Consoling himself with this belief, he went home.

'Come, eat, 'ppa!' his mother said several times. 'Stomach is paining,' he lied, and went to bed. Dhanalakshmi had not turned up at his house and told his parents, nor had she said anything about it to Susheela. Was it because he ran off into the jungle that she hadn't spoken to him? Maybe Dhanalakshmi was waiting to speak to him in the morning. Maybe she would start a fight. All night he lay awake worrying about it.

At nine fifteen the next morning, Sharada arrived by the Pazhaniappa bus and disappeared into the nursery for a whole hour. It was only then that he breathed normally – she hadn't come and asked him any questions at all. And yet his eyes would not stop looking for her and trying to spot her glancing in the direction of his house. But she didn't come out of the building at all. Not even to go to the toilet.

For two days, he did nothing. On the third day, a new problem arose in Dhanavel's mind. Would she think badly of him because he had stopped with a single note? Just one poem? He thought he would go mad thinking over it. At ten o'clock on the fourth morning, he hurried to the aanganwaadi, slipped inside, and placed another note on the table. That day, too, she didn't get him into trouble. And so, for several days in a row, he took to delivering his notes exactly the same way … A total of eight poems, that was all.

By that time, Sharada's month-long tenure as a substitute teacher came to an end. As for him, his college in Tiruchi had long since reopened. It had happened on the very next day after Sharada had arrived at the aanganwaadi. And now she was gone, and Susheela was back at her post.

When he came back to the village for the Deepavali holidays, he discovered from Dhanalakshmi that Sharada was working in Vaagaiyoor. The day before the festival, he set off for Vaagaiyoor and stood near the aanganwaadi there, waiting to set eyes on Sharada. Because she did not appear, he took his courage in both hands and went in. At the sight of him, Sharada sprang up from her chair in a fright. Without a word, he put down his note and left her. Out he went, to stand and wait beneath the tamarind tree opposite the aanganwaadi. She did not come out at all. Finally, he caught a bus back to his village.

He had written down the address of his college on the note he had given her. Every day he waited for a letter from her, and there was none at all, ever. At home for the Pongal holidays, he set off for Vaagaiyoor once more. They said Sharada had got married and had got a transfer to her own village. After that, he made no enquiries about her. Nor did any news of her reach him.

Today was the first time he was setting eyes on her, after that day in Vaagaiyoor…

'All of a sudden, you just came running in and put down that note on my desk – do you know how I felt? I sweated all over … up to the thighs…' Having said this, Sharada fell silent for a long while. Then she said, 'I didn't know what to do with the note you left. So I gave it to Susheela.'

'You gave it to her?' he said in unbelief and repeated the question. 'Did you give it to her?' What would Susheela have thought of him, he thought with consternation.

'Really? Is it true, what you're saying? That you gave it to her?' he asked again. Unaware of the turmoil in his mind, she responded with a question of her own:

'Whom else did I know in your village, whom else could I tell this thing to?'

'Did she read it?'

'How could she not have read it?'

The way she laughed, the way she spoke of this matter – Dhanavel did not like it at all. He couldn't bear that Susheela knew all about it. Who knows whom she had told it to in the village? Maybe she had told his father and mother too. She'd probably have made a filthy mess of it. The very thought of it made him turn away from Sharada and stare outside.

The train had come to a halt at Melmaruvathoor station. Only one person alighted, but three girls dressed in red uniform, two boys and a man got on. They did not go into the coach but just stood near the washbasin. With these new arrivals, the space became very cramped, and Dhanavel edged towards the steps at the entrance. Sharada moved a little closer to him.

'Did you give her just that one note? Or all of them?'

Her saree edge fluttered in the wind. Pulling it tight around herself and tucking it in, she said, 'All of them, of course.' Her tone was matter-of-fact.

'All gone, then!' Dhanavel exclaimed in shock.

'Every time you came and left a note, I would be sweating and my throat would be choked. When I looked at the note lying there on the table, what I saw was a snake coiled there. I couldn't read it. And I couldn't tear it up. Looking at it, I felt my chest throbbing, the way it feels to somebody who's about to step into a fire. But what I did wrong was to give all the eight notes to Susheela.'

At that moment came the sound of the train running across a bridge – much more than the ordinary sound it made running on the tracks. As though she had been waiting for the noise to subside, she murmured, 'Susheela was not such a good woman as I thought.' All that reached his ears through the lingering rattle were the words 'good woman'.

'Is that so?' he said in a tone of disinterest – as though he didn't care to know more about it.

'The day I had left your village and come home, that same day my father arrived. In his hands were all the notes that Susheela had given him,' she said in a choked voice.

Her eyes were moist. To prevent Dhanavel from noticing them, she bent her head. Pretending to wipe her face, she dried her eyes.

'Until I reached home, I didn't know what had happened. I found out only then that Susheela had given my father those notes.'

Her eyes blurring even more, she wiped them openly, no longer bothering to hide it. Twice she blew her nose strongly. As she wept, her face flushed red and her nostrils flared. She dabbed at her nose with the end of her saree. Sobbing quietly, she told him all about it. She looked like a small child.

'I had just come home, washed my face and sat down, when my father took the notes out of his pocket and dropped them before me. It felt like he was throwing them at my face! "Did I send you to work? Or did I send you to collect love letters?" That's what he asked me. "I never held out my hand to take any of those notes! I didn't read even a single one of them. And I never wrote and gave any note!" That's what I kept on telling him, but my father wouldn't hear a word of it. He was yelling and shouting as if the house was on fire. Next week itself, he fixed up a bridegroom for me.'

This time, her eyes did not cloud over with tears, nor were her nostrils flared. She didn't blow her nose. To hide what was in her mind, she stood there woodenly. Her eyes did not wander. Dhanavel thought of asking her what happened after that.

'What did you do with those notes, 'nga?'

'Did nothing.' Her answer was curt.

'You didn't tear them up?'

'No,' she said, with obvious reluctance.

'What did you do with those notes?' he asked once again.

'I have kept them.'

'Even now?'

'Yes.'

Dhanavel could not believe what she was saying. She must be lying, he thought. Not having the nerve to tell her, 'You are lying,' he asked hesitantly, 'Why didn't you just tear them up?'

'If I had read them at all, I would have torn them up!' Dhanavel just couldn't believe her. What lies she told, one after the other!

'What are you saying, 'nga?' He tried to sound not too eager to know.

'I was so furious that day, I just shoved them out of the way somewhere – those notes that my father threw down so angrily. Then I forgot all about them. I saw them only two years after that.'

As she spoke, she looked down. The people who had got on at Melmaruvathoor were all sitting on the floor, right in the middle of the passage.

She wanted to shout: 'No place even to stand here! If all of you people sit down, how can we stand here?'

Controlling herself, she went on, 'After my father died and his body was gone, I was the one who washed and cleaned down the whole house. Saw the notes lying under the wooden almirah when I was sweeping.' She came to an abrupt stop.

Why didn't she just tell the whole story in one go, Dhanavel thought exasperatedly, instead of letting it out in bits and pieces? 'Why didn't you just tear up the whole lot then itself?' he demanded.

To that, her answer was a sigh, something like a bored yawn. She drawled, 'Already there was so much rubbish in the house. So I thought, let this just stay right here.'

Mortified, Dhanavel mumbled, 'So, is it still there?'

'Yes, yes…' The way she said it, as though it meant nothing to her, left Dhanavel in a quandary about what to say next. With that drained away more than half the thrill that had swept over him at Tambaram, when she had come up and spoken to him…

As though he were teaching a lesson in moral science to a schoolchild, he intoned, 'Got married, had children, and *they* have children. Still you are keeping those notes! It's wrong, no?'

Before he had finished speaking came her answer – like a slap on the face. 'Writing a note to a young girl whom you had never seen or known before – was *that* right?'

Struck speechless, he realized at last how terribly angry she was. In a very low voice, as though he were speaking to himself, he murmured, 'It was wrong…' He paused, and as though to console her, ventured to say, 'I thought it would cause trouble – that's why I said that.'

'My trouble had already come to me, no? Like death it came, when I was only nineteen! After that, what more trouble could come?' she said wrathfully. Dhanavel listened in bewilderment. Why was she so angry? Where did it come from – this right she was asserting, talking to him like that?

She went on: 'It was all because of the notes you gave me that I was married off at nineteen. By twenty, a child was born. Because of you, for thirty-two years I am running a family, living with a drunkard! Only because of those notes my life got ruined, isn't that so?' It silenced him.

… For a moment. Then, trying to express support, he said, 'Should those notes have been kept at all, when they had caused trouble?' As though challenging a bitter enemy, she flared up, 'If I had read them, I would have torn them up!'

'Till now you haven't read them?'

'Why should I read them? Why should I even look at them when they've wrecked my whole life?'

'Just to see what was written in them, didn't you read them?'

'You'd have described me in oh-so fine ways, oh-so beautiful – is that it? What for should I go and read all that?' she said mockingly.

There was a pause. Then, Dhanavel said slowly, 'Suppose they fall into somebody's hands? What will happen?'

'But there's no name, no address on them, so what can happen to you?' she said harshly. He stared at her. What kind of a woman was she? Must be one of those rough-and-tough ones, he thought. But if she really was such a bold creature, why hadn't she spoken a word to him? Or written? When he gave the notes, she had never said a word at all. Not even to scold him or reject his offering.

'Why did I ever get on the train today, and that too, why am I in this very coach?' he cursed himself.

With a jerk, she averted her face … The exultation – when he had first seen her – had completely drained away. Asking questions like that and making him hang his head in shame – how is it I didn't know she was such a person? It made him feel wretched.

It was only now that he became aware of the ache in his feet. There was no way he could move them even a little. Next to him stood Sharada, and near her feet sat those who had got on at Melmaruvathoor. How long could they both stand there, without even a glance at each other? With the idea of making her return to her seat inside, he said, 'Please go and sit down, 'nga. Such a pity – you're standing here because of me.'

There was nothing rude in the way he spoke, but once again she erupted vehemently: 'Is it only today that I'm suffering because of you? Ever since I went to your village, that's what I've been going through!' And once again he shut up – for a while.

'I didn't do it on purpose,' he said meekly.

'I know that too!' she snapped, scowling.

'Anything I say turns out wrong,' he thought to himself wearily. The whole effort felt to him like hard labour. Pulling out a water bottle from his shoulder bag, he took a gulp.

'Would you like to drink some water?' he asked, trying to make polite conversation.

'Thirty-two years ago, you poured poison into my mouth! If you give me water now, will it weaken that poison?'

Dhanavel said nothing to that. He decided that not talking at all was best. What could he say, when each word of hers stung him like a scorpion? Sharada gave him a quizzical glance and then looked at her granddaughter sitting inside. That her feet hurt, too, was evident from the way she kept shifting them.

'Because of me you are also standing, 'nga, it's a pity. Go and sit down, 'nga. Your place is still empty.'

She neither spoke nor gave him another look.

'As soon as you go home, just throw them in the kitchen fire.' The suggestion had hardly left his lips when she interrupted, 'Those were the first letters I ever got. And the last. Why would I go and throw them in any fire?' she demanded.

He stood there wide-eyed, with no idea what to say to that. This cow – it kicks when I face it, and it kicks also when I turn my back…

'If your daughters come to know, it will be so shameful, won't it?'

'They know all about this. Both of them. "These notes are why I held my neck out for your father to tie a taali." That's what I told them. And they keep scolding me, "Amma! Why did you marry a drunkard? You've not only ruined your own life but our lives also!"'

That floored him completely. What was going on in that mind of hers anyway? He couldn't understand it at all. Like a whirling cyclone, she was battering him from all sides. There was no getting around her. He tried pleading, 'At least when you go home today, please tear up those notes!'

'Never! I will never tear them up as long as I live! And I'll never ever read them too!' she retorted in a stubborn frenzy. 'They destroyed my life, didn't they? Let them just be there till I die. They're all the joy I have ever had – and all the hell I've been through as well.' She paused a little, and then her fury returned. 'People like you will marry government employees and live a nice comfortable life. What sin did I commit that I had to marry a farmer and die every day? These days, a government teacher gets a lakh a month – can a farmer with twenty kaanis make a lakh in a whole year? Those days are gone, when people married off their daughters to fellows with property – with their own house, their own land. If I had married a man with a job, I would have got my girls educated! Got them married to government employees. Isn't it true that, today, just to feed themselves, my daughters are having to do miserable ordinary jobs?'

This time, it was his eyes that suddenly blurred. How could Sharada go on and on like this, hardly taking a breath in between words? It baffled him. 'Eh, Appa! Such a talker she is! Is this the same mouth that stayed locked thirty-two years ago? All the females in the whole world are the same!' he decided bitterly, with a sudden memory of his wife.

Trying to prod her a bit, Dhanavel remarked, 'You never spoke a single word at that time.'

She hit back. 'You also! You never spoke even one word to me!'

'I didn't know what to say.'

'And what about me? Would I have known what to say?'

Neither spoke for some minutes. The two of them had forgotten they were standing there, in a moving train. They both seemed to be listening closely to the noise of the train. And then, she began again:

'You'd run inside, just like a monkey, put down the note and go running back – leaving me sitting there scared and crying, afraid of what Aayamma the sweeper there in the aanganwaadi would think of me. And what about the people on the road, in the village? What would *they* think of me? Did *you* ever think of me going through all that, 'nga? And when that woman Susheela told me, "He's a good fellow." I believed her! I might as well have trusted that Aayamma. But those days, I myself knew nothing at all … The day I left your village, when my father and I were standing at the bus stop, I saw you hiding behind the tamarind tree … I thought you'd get into the same bus.'

'I was about to get in. But I didn't, because you were with your father.'

'If you had got on the bus with me that day, my whole life would have changed! If you hadn't gone to Susheela that last day and told her you were leaving town, my whole life would have changed forever! It's all because you left that Susheela turned up with the notes and gave them to my father. If you had not gone away, she wouldn't have done that. Do you know I was crying all the way back, in the bus?'

Dhanavel said nothing. He was looking outside the train. It came to a stop at Dindivanam, emptying itself of those who had got on at Melmaruvathoor. Greatly relieved that no new passengers had entered, Dhanavel relaxed and stretched his limbs. As the train began to move, Sharada's granddaughter Sadhana came out of the coach and gave him a distinctly unfriendly stare.

'What do you want, 'mma?' enquired Sharada. 'Want to eat a biscuit? Drink water?'

Paying no attention to her, the child stood there, stiff and silent.

'What is your name, 'mma?'

When Sadhana refused to speak, Sharada reached out and hugged her close to her legs. 'He's asking what is your name! Tell him!' Though she entreated her several times, Sadhana would not open her mouth.

'She can talk. Really! To her own Thatha, how she talks! Super!'

Sadhana glared from one to the other. Then she stomped off to her seat. Worried that the child was in a huff, Sharada hurried to her, telling Dhanavel, 'Wait, please, I'll just come.'

He felt suddenly very hot. As long as Sharada had been near him, he hadn't been aware of the heat and the sizzling wind. He felt very thirsty. Wiping away his sweat, he suddenly realized that, today of all days, he was not dressed at all very well, in a good pair of pants and a nice shirt. His hair fluttered in the wind. Half of it was gone – more than half, he thought, as he pushed it down. As he mopped his face again and again with his kerchief, his cell phone rang. It was his wife. 'Yes, yes,' Dhanavel told her. 'It's very crowded. All the way I've been standing. Don't know when we'll reach Vizhuppuram. Too much noise…' he was saying, as Sharada returned, 'I'll talk later.' He hung up in a hurry.

'Who was that? Someone from home?' Sharada asked.

Not answering, he leaned out gingerly from the entrance. The train was just entering Vizhuppuram station. Sharada also looked out. As though amazed at the sight of the board saying 'Vizhuppuram Junction', she exclaimed, 'Already Vizhuppuram has come? Didn't even feel time passing!'

That evoked a nod of agreement from him, though he still said nothing.

Just as the train drew to a stop, more than ten people on the platform surged forward, trying to get in. As five or six passengers hurried to get off, both Dhanavel and Sharada stood aside, making way for the back-and-forth movement. It was much hotter now than when the train was moving. In five minutes, his whole body was drenched in sweat. All he wanted now was for the train to move, as he wiped his face repeatedly with his kerchief and fanned himself with it. He saw that the toilet door had been left half open. 'Why don't people close it when they come out?' he muttered exasperatedly.

The girl who had been standing by the west-facing entrance and typing on her cell phone ever since he had got on at Tambaram … he saw with astonishment that she was still at it. A young girl got on with a basket of ripe guavas. Dhanavel shifted to one side. 'When will this train start moving?' exclaimed Sharada. As she wiped her neck with the edge of her saree, the train slowly began to move.

'Feels like I'm looking at somebody double the size of who I saw then.'

'Women are like that when they grow old.'

'Purple colour – brinjal. The saree you were wearing on the day you left.'

'Really?' she remarked. There was a pause. Then, as though she had thought things over, she turned to him and said accusingly, 'So, you do remember all that, isn't it? What my saree was like, what my waist was like? But you never thought of coming to see me!'

'You, too – you never came and talked to me in our village,' he countered. 'Even when I went to Vaagaiyoor, you didn't say anything! That note I gave you, there, in Vaagaiyoor – I wrote my hostel address on it. But you didn't write to me!' … A death blow – that's what I've given her now, he thought to himself. It'll shut her up.

'Why didn't you speak first? You're the man, no? Does any woman herself start such talk? Anywhere, in any country, does that happen?' Her indignant glare left him with no answer. Throwing a swift glance at Sadhana, she went on, 'Just one day before you came to Vaagaiyoor, they fixed up my marriage! That is why I didn't say anything.' For a moment, her face twisted.

'I didn't come and see you after that because they said you had got married.'

'So what? Is there a law that you can't come and see me because I'm married? At least you could have found out where I was. Not even twenty kilometres distance is there between your village and my village.'

'You could also have asked around and found out–' Dhanavel just about finished saying, when she quelled him by demanding: 'Will any woman go around asking about a man?'

But why was she in such a temper? He couldn't figure it out. She was really being much too hard on him for those notes he wrote so long ago.

Abruptly, as though she had just thought of it, she demanded, 'Was it you who gave me notes, or was it I who gave *you* notes?' Wrath seized her and her eyes brimmed over as she went on, 'At once I was married off! Otherwise, only after two or three years I would have got married – to a man with a proper job!'

'Why do you go on thinking of something or other and start crying, 'nga?'

'I'm not crying about something I am just *thinking* about! My life is gone! That is why I am crying!' With a jerk, she turned her face away from him.

That was when he really got a good look at her from the rear … 'That waist that I saw that very first day – where has it gone?' he murmured as though to himself … How did she manage to hear him, above the thud-thud of the train?

A soft laugh broke from her. 'So! It was not my *face* that made you write those notes, isn't that so?' Sharada asked. Dhanavel once again feigned interest in the view. 'Are you looking for someone outside? Some girl you can send notes to?' It was clear she wanted to goad him. All he could do was hang his head.

As the train gathered speed, Sharada's hair fluttered in the breeze. She caught it and tucked it up into a knot. 'Not one hair has turned white,' Dhanavel whispered.

'It's the only thing left to me. You can't stand my having this much even, is it?' she frowned, pretending anger. Then: 'Just two years ago, my elder daughter said to me, "You've become chief social worker now, and you'll be travelling out of town. Going to other places … Amma, you must dye your hair!" she told me. And she dyed it for me. Now I've got used to it. I can dye it myself now.' With a mischievous look at Dhanavel's hair, she suggested, 'Whole head has become white! You should do something – why not dye it?'

'I should do it,' agreed Dhanavel.

'But to dye it, shouldn't you have some hair at least? Your head is like a brass pot – so clean and smooth!' she declared and broke into loud laughter. It caused him some chagrin, though he managed to squirm out of it and act unfazed. But would she or wouldn't she stop going on and on about his hair? He set about changing the subject.

'Do your girls have waist-length hair like yours?'

'Both the wretches take after their father. Their braids are like rats' tails only. As for their father – anybody can count the hairs on his head, they are so few,' she chuckled, as though she had come out with some remarkable witticism.

'Your girls – what jobs do they have?'

'Those four kaanis of land – he spent them all on drink alone. Mine is the only job. It's just the aanganwaadi rice that's keeping us alive. When I started work, my salary was just one hundred rupees. I made them both study nursing – that was all I could afford. But they couldn't get government jobs. They're working in private hospitals, both of them. If I had made them go in for higher studies, they'd have got educated husbands ... Right up till now, not one rupee has he given for them. Nothing that he has earned by himself!' she wept, with Dhanavel standing silently by.

It was getting very crowded, here in the vestibule outside the coach. Several men, and women too, came streaming out towards the toilet and making their way back. Moving among them was a blind man, collecting alms and singing an old film song, *'No one has the Lord ever forsaken...'* A vendor went around with a laden tray, shouting, 'Masaal vadai!'

From the way she was wiping her face, it looked like Sharada was all done with her crying.

'Did you speak to me?' she asked.

'No.'

'Seemed like you called me...'

'Call you? But what should I call you? Should I say "madam"? Should I be formal and say "'nga" for everything – like "vaa'nga" or "po'nga" and all?'

'Why'd you have to call *me* "madam" and all?' she demanded with an air of familiarity, as though taking it for granted that she was entitled, somehow, to reprove him for being excessively formal. Dhanavel gave her a searching look. This whole manner of speaking – what was it supposed to mean?

Feeling his unswerving gaze upon her, Sharada spoke in hushed tones: 'Supposing this mind is just like ears and nose and mouth? Then there will be no problem. But mind is not like that! It is remembering! Only the mind can think again and again! It goes on thinking of the same thing.' Tears flowed from her eyes, though she did not heave and sob. With a final sniff, she declared, 'When I saw you – it was like the sea ... So much happiness ... Yes, I can say that's what it felt like. But two seas of sadness have also come along with it.'

'Why are you saying that, 'nga?' It was on the tip of his tongue, but he held it back.

'Thirunangai![9] Money for this thirunangai!' somebody shouted, dressed as a woman, moving briskly about collecting alms. Turning away sharply at the sight, Dhanavel looked resolutely out of the train. As for Sharada, she had the money ready in her hand. But not until the thirunangai had moved off into the distance did Dhanavel relax and look around.

'And then...?' he prompted, trying to get Sharada to finish what she had been saying. After peering worriedly at Sadhana, there inside the coach, she began once again: 'Do boys give love notes to the girls in your school?'

---

9 Thirunangai: Literally, 'respected lady'. A term for the transgender community adopted by M. Karunanidhi in 2006 at their request, as a corrective to the traditional discrimination suffered by them.

'It might be happening, I suppose. But so far, no such case has been reported to me. If it ever comes, at once I would issue a transfer certificate. Expel the student!'

'What if the teacher himself writes a love note?' she queried with a sly smile. Dhanavel hung his head, discomfited, and muttered, 'Another fifteen minutes and Vriddhaachalam will come. I'll get off.'

In a mechanical refrain, she mimicked, 'Next fifteen minutes Pennaadam will come, and *I* will get off!'

'Have you got a cell phone?'

'Is there anyone who doesn't have a cell phone nowadays?' she laughed.

'If there had been cell phones in those days, what would have happened?' Dhanavel was saying pensively, when she cut in, 'As if you would have talked to me, even if there were cell phones! All you did was write those notes of yours. And then you did nothing! But today's boys don't write notes, they send SMSs on their phones. That's how they carry on their love affairs. Do you know, they do it on video calls? This is not 1985, it is 2019! Do you understand that?' she demanded contemptuously.

Her jibe felt like a blow aimed at his chest. 'Can't go near her … She's a touch-me-not plant … Now she's a burning fire,' he thought in dismay.

'Will you tell me your cell phone number?' he asked cautiously.

'What for?' she retorted.

'Just like that only...' Embarrassed, he tried to brazen it out with a smile.

'So, you want to chat, do you? With an old woman?' she giggled, smoothing her saree coquettishly over herself. Like a bride, he thought...

'When can we meet?'

'Why should we meet? What I am thinking now is, why did I have to meet him at all? So much better it would be if this was just a dream.' Once again, she averted her face.

It took some time for her to look in his direction again.

'Please. Give me your cell number, 'nga. Or at least tell me when we can meet.'

'Didn't come and meet me when I was fresh and young. Now that I'm an old woman, what are you going to do, 'nga?'

'Looks like Vriddhaachalam,' Sharada said, as the train slowed down and came to a stop at the station.

'Tell me your number.'

'Train has stopped! Get down, 'nga. Your burning ground is waiting for you ... and my burning ground is waiting for me. Is that something you can change? Like a pot or a pan that can be got in exchange for torn clothes?' Sharada turned away, weeping.

Dhanavel got down and stood on the platform looking back towards her. She had gone to her granddaughter. He tried to see where she was sitting, but the train was already in motion once again. In the blink of an eye, the next coach replaced that one, and after that the next, and the next, until the last one, and then came the guard van. It had a red cross painted on its rear, and he watched it go and finally vanish in the distance.

An emptiness filled his eyes as he remained standing there, gazing after it.

Yearning

Nobody came to see Selvamani off at the railway station. To see off Kokila, however, her mother and father and her grandmother, too, had all turned up. There they were, with no smiles on their faces.

Kokila herself, though, was all smiles. She was with her husband – and that too, she was travelling on a train. That was enough to make her happy. Her face showed not the slightest sign of distress at the prospect of soon being parted from her mother. Exactly like Selvamani, she kept looking in the direction of the train's imminent approach.

Meanwhile, her grandmother Muthamma was talking to her, saying something to which Kokila kept nodding a 'yes'. As soon as the announcement was made of the train's arrival, Selvamani moved ahead, saying, 'I'll get in first.'

Her mother Poomaari handed Kokila her bags, saying, 'You went against whatever we told you and got married. Now you're going away! What is the man like? How will he treat you? And what's going to happen? About all that, we know nothing. Is Madras nearby or what, for you to run back fast if something happens? … So! Then you better not open your mouth. Say "mm" to everything. Not even one word you should speak. If a female creature wants to live out her life, she can't have such a thing as a mouth. Keep quiet! Act like you've got no tongue at all.'

As if to say, 'I can handle it!' Kokila gave a toss of her head.

As soon as the train arrived, Selvamani pushed and shoved his way in through the crowd to grab a seat, sat down, and called from the window, 'Come quick, get in. Seat'll go!' Kokila climbed in, as Muthamma called after her, 'Keep a smiling face always, like you are now.' Poomaari was weeping. 'Careful,' said her father, as the train moved. Kokila came and sat down next to Selvamani.

'Careful, put the bag under your feet and push it in. Or it'll be gone.'

'Do people steal inside the train?' enquired Kokila.

'Thieves are all over the place.'

'I didn't know…' she said, eying the people who sat opposite them, and those with no seats who were standing in the corridor. In that jam-packed, jostling huddle, some had clambered up to sit on the luggage rack overhead.

'Why are they sitting up there?'

'Because they didn't get any other place. If I didn't rush in and get us these seats, we would also be just standing … Careful with the bags … How many d'you have?'

'Five.'

'So many bags? What for?'

'Things for the house … small-small things only.'

'–' He had nothing to say to that.

Hardly had half an hour gone by when he nodded off to sleep. Kokila was looking out of the window when she felt his head sinking down upon her shoulder … How could he sleep like this, putting his head on her shoulder, with people watching from all sides, thought Kokila, shocked … No, she just couldn't let it happen … Yet she was nervous, she couldn't bring herself to wake him up. Maybe if she shifted a little bit, he would wake up … That didn't work the way she thought it would. All he did was stir and make himself more comfortable. 'This is awful! Too much, really…!' she thought, looking down at that head of his, resting on her shoulder…

'Already it looks hard as rock, as if nothing will sprout from it. So what's this barren patch going to be like afterwards?' Muthamma had exclaimed, staring at Selvamani's head during the girl-viewing ceremony. Remembering it brought a smile. 'Old woman's got a big mouth, really!' Kokila murmured to herself.

When he came to see her at the girl-viewing, Selvamani had brought along only his father and mother. He was no relation of hers. Nor was he from a neighbouring village. They had got to hear about Kokila from the newly married girl in the house opposite the Mariamman temple – Thangamma, who had just arrived in the village. As for Kokila's family, everyone was delighted to hear of a prospective bridegroom, somebody who was actually asking for her as a bride, a 'wedding boy' who would actually land up in the house.

When they actually set eyes on him, a disgusted 'Chhee!' was what they spat out.

Besides Kokila, three others had been born to her parents. All girls. Not one of them had got married. Each would-be son-in-law who came asking for a bride asked also for a necklace, a ring, a steel almirah, a TV. No wedding had as yet taken place in that family, for they had no property other than the house with a tiled roof in which they lived. It took the labour of four or five in that household to make just enough to fill their bellies. Whenever a couple of hundred happened to be left over after that expense, one or the other of them would fall ill – as though to defy the very idea of any money remaining unspent.

It was because Kokila's mother and father had wanted a son that they had produced these children, one after the other. That all of them would turn out to be girls was not what they had thought would happen. 'We've got no property or anything! Why were these children born?' was what they now asked themselves.

Since they had not managed to marry off even one of their girls, Selvamani's father and mother thought, when they arrived, that all they had to do was to ask. Yet that is not what happened. Without actually saying they would not give their daughter, Kokila's parents brought out all sorts of excuses, including saying, 'Her horoscope is not okay, there is some unlucky thing in it. So we have to give her to a son-in-law who also has that same thing in his horoscope.'

Selvamani's mother and father would have none of it. Finally, Kokila's parents came out with it: 'We have only the girl. Nothing else. We don't even have enough money to buy clothes for the wedding.'

To which the groom's mother rejoined, 'You don't have to do anything. Just send the girl in the saree she is wearing. Wedding and all, *we* will arrange! And we won't let it out that you didn't give anything. Even before we came to ask for your girl, we knew how it was with you.'

Kokila's parents could say nothing more. It was Muthamma who said, with some force, 'Even if you do everything for the wedding, we have to do our share. Otherwise we'll lose respect! But it will take one year more for some money to reach us. So the marriage has to wait till then.'

'No need for you to spend even one paisa. Just send the girl. You just come and sit in the marriage pavilion and have a meal and go, that's all you have to do!' said the groom's mother.

That stung Muthamma into shattering all pretence of propriety: 'Even before the wedding, this wedding boy's head is looking just like a scrubbed brass pot – turned upside down and put out to dry! What more is there to say?'

Seizing on Muthamma's words as a great compliment, the groom's mother declared, 'This is our special family baldness! See my husband? He was just like this even at my girl-viewing ceremony. And didn't I marry him? And didn't I have children? Didn't I run a household? If you had seen my father-in-law's head, how you would have laughed! Like polished glass it was! Even a fully shaved head wouldn't be so clean!' she chuckled.

Nobody in Kokila's family laughed. Her face fell. To hide her discomfiture, she said brightly, 'See my head? At even this age, see how my hair is! So long, like a whip!' She turned her head to show off her hair. When no one responded to that either, she remarked, 'The hair on the head is not what we eat, is it? Boy has got education! And government job!'

No one said anything.

'On the way here, my son saw your girl. From that moment itself he has made up his mind. He says if he gets married at all, it will be only to this girl,' announced the groom's mother, although nobody was asking her anything at all.

'When did he get the job?'

'In two thousand ten.'

'What was his age when he got the job?'

When she realized why Muthamma was asking her all this, the mother said, 'Just twenty-eight,' instead of coming out with 'thirty-three'. Though Muthamma stuck out her lower lip in disbelief, she kept her mouth shut. Which drove the mother to declare, 'He said, "Doesn't matter about my age, I will only marry after I get a government job!" That was what he held on to. So it has taken couple of years extra. Anyway, who cares about age and all that these days? Job or no job? That's what they all want to know … Not a private company job. *That* they don't want … In the horoscope also there is nothing wrong. You can take a look at it, 'nga, if you want.'

'If we want, right? *Only* if we want this, we'll have to take a look at the horoscope, no?' remarked Muthamma. There was no mistaking her meaning.

'Don't just be thinking, "Boy is so big-built, so dark!" All that is from my side of the family.'

'How many children? Does he have any sisters and brothers?'

'He is our one and only son.'

'Seems like you thought, since the family is like this, we better stop with just one child!' jeered Muthamma. The groom's mother's face fell. Poomaari gave her mother-in-law a nudge to shut her up.

'It's only until they have a child that they'll be wedding girl, wedding boy. After that, they'll just be old man, old woman … We will think it over and let you know,' said Kokila's father.

'You don't seem to know about this world. It is not a small thing to get a groom with a job. Already he is earning ten thousand. It will go higher and higher!'

'Can you eat cash? Rupee notes? Will they come walking with you? Will they sit and laugh and talk with you?' snapped Muthamma.

'If your girl marries our boy, she won't have to work in the fields. Or do coolie work! She can sit in the house. Three times daily she can eat hot food. She won't have to be out in the sun all day. No need to come out of the house at all! Face powder won't get wiped off with sweat! As the wife of a man with a job, she'll get such respect … How many more years must your girls be sitting here, each with a bare neck and no taali?'[1]

Kokila's family began to feel there was truth in all that the boy's mother was getting at. Not one of the four girls had had such good fortune as marriage come their way. Here was a man with a job, asking for Kokila…

Despite all this, and though they were being assured that all expenses would be paid by the other party, Kokila's people did not want her to be given to Selvamani. A shapeless kozhukkattai[2] – that's what he looked like. And not one made of rice, but of bullshit! How could they give Kokila to him? What would people in the village say? Even if there was no wedding at all, it wasn't so bad. Even if she ran away with somebody whose looks she liked, it would be better than giving her to Selvamani. Muthamma was resolutely against it. It was because she was afraid that her son and daughter-in-law might change their minds and agree to this alliance that she was being so crushingly rude to the groom's mother.

---

1 Taali: Marriage thread.

2 Kozhukkattai: Stuffed rice dumpling.

As for Selvamani, he just sat there as though he had nothing to do with what was happening around him.

'You may go now,' said Kokila's father. 'We will ask the girl and let you know.'

'It's only one year since he joined duty. He can't take leave and come and go just like that. Yes or no? Best if you tell us now itself.'

'It's all right, 'mma, let them ask and tell us later. Let's go now,' Selvamani urged her. His mother ignored him and went on, 'We asked all about your family in the village. Don't you have to start giving out exit tickets for your girls, one by one? How can you go on keeping them in the house and spoiling them all their lives?'

That enraged Muthamma. 'My granddaughters aren't unsaleable goods! When the right time comes, they'll go off into the wide world – some other country, or some other city! You talk as if bridegrooms are yet to be born for them! Such a face-colour! Such features! Rows and rows of bridegrooms will come and stand here!' she declared. Her tone was loud and clear.

Selvamani got up. 'Please ask the girl and tell us. We will leave now.'

'What is there to say later? Who will jump into a well that hasn't any water? Just wait, I will ask and tell you right now.'

With that, Muthamma went off inside the house. Having told Kokila all that had been happening, she ended by saying, 'Come, you can say it to them yourself! Rub coal on their faces and send them off!'

'I'll marry him, Aayaa.'

Muthamma felt as though Kokila had just smacked her right across the face with a fistful of black soot. 'What! What are you saying, di?'

'Tell them to fix the date. Go.'

'It doesn't matter if he has nothing to feed you even! Hasn't he got to be at least fit to look at, di?'

'No need.'

'What's happened to your eyes? Gone blind or what? Lost your mind? He looks old enough to have had at least four kids. An old man almost, di! And that's not all! He looks just like a roasted pig.'

'Let it be. What is it to you? I like him.'

'What! It's like they all say! A female brain's a wretched thing, it'll swallow even shit!'

'I am the one who's going to live with him, no?'

'Chhee! Shut up, di! Here you are, like a fresh fruit – a sweet banana! Are you saying you should be married off to that burnt-black pot? Wait, wait, I'll call that father of yours, he'll spit on his face!' exclaimed Muthamma.

Her father and mother got the very same reply from Kokila that she had given her grandmother. They stood there, speechless.

'Isn't there anybody else? Some fellow who doesn't have enough to eat, just like us? That mouth, that belly – can't bear the sight … So black! Here I am, an old woman who's about to die, and even I can't stand him. Here you are, like a golden statue, and you say you like him?'

'Mm.'

'What else does he have, except for a job? Nothing! Don't be in a hurry. What does it matter if you're getting a little older? Much better to marry when the body is stronger and fatter.'

'Someone who's already born on this earth must be there, just for you, no? You won't have to wait for someone yet to be born!'

'Don't decide on this just because the other girls have to get married,' Kokila's parents joined Muthamma in rejecting this would-be son-in-law.

'Just get it all fixed up.' That was what she said.

Muthamma cajoled, pleadingly, 'Look at the son she's given birth to – a rotten pumpkin! My son also had a child – a tender coconut shoot…! But just being born is not enough – she's got to listen! Just listen to me!'

'Don't talk rubbish!' Kokila snapped. 'Get away! I'm the one who's going to live with him, no?'

'Oho, is that so? Instead of marrying this man, why don't you just catch hold of some other fellow and run off with him? I myself will send you both on your way. This one's no match at all for you – nothing, not even his face!'

'Just keep your mouth shut, will you? At least one girl has to leave, no? If we ever made money and saved it up, only then we could have talked about making a "good match" and not making a "wrong match" and such things

… You and your big mouth! All you've ever grown is that tongue. Don't you let it make a mess of something good that is going to happen at last!' Poomaari glared at her mother-in-law. 'How long can we keep these wretched girls in the house? They're talking about us in the whole village!' she sobbed.

'You be quiet, 'mma…' said Kokila's father. 'Let's send them off for now, we'll talk about all that later.' Returning to the prospective in-laws, he sent them away, saying, 'Please come after two days. We'll tell you then.'

Though Kokila's father and mother could not come to a decision, Muthamma kept tutoring all of them on one lesson: that this would-be groom must be rejected. 'A bright, glowing lamp – that's what your face is like!' she crooned to Kokila. 'Is he fit for you? Even a really old woman whose eyesight is all gone will say, "I won't marry him!"' But Muthamma's lesson did not hit home.

Kokila's father and mother were now convinced that it was high time that at least one of their girls shed her virginity. Above every other consideration was the fact that the man had a job. That led them to hope that he would help get the other girls married off, one by one. And towering above even that prospect was that, at the very least, one 'ticket' would now be leaving the house.

Promptly, as agreed, Selvamani's father and mother turned up on the third day. When Kokila's father announced, 'The girl has agreed. You must arrange the wedding in a temple, we will all come empty-handed,' the answer came right away, 'Just bring the girl. We will take care of everything. What is money, what is cash, 'nga? All we want is for people in town to say, "Nobody has such a fine daughter-in-law!"'

Eight days later, they came to settle on the date. On the tenth day after that, the taali was tied. Six days later, here they were, about to get on the train … Kokila was amazed at how it had all happened … Even on the way to the railway station, Muthamma had blabbered on and on about it: 'Ayyo, di, why did you say no to heroes and kings and marry this fellow who looks like a burnt-out dried-up tamarind tree?' Kokila had not deigned to answer. Not only her father and mother and her sisters, but all the village girls, too, had wanted to know what had made her consent to this marriage. She wouldn't tell them. It was a secret she could not reveal. If she came out with it, they would make fun of her.

… It had to do with … emptying the bowels and bladder.

'What! Is that such a big thing – how one shits and pisses?' That's what they would all ask her.

Ever since Kokila had attained puberty, families with marriageable sons had been turning up to ask her to be their daughter-in-law. As many as four families in this very village, and seven more from other towns, turned up. All their sons had finished eighth class or tenth class, all were at least ten years younger than Selvamani. Tall, well-grown youths they were, too. And among them was the one from Aathoor. He was actually good-looking, well-grown and really tall. He looked just right for Kokila. 'I'm going to marry Kokila!' he declared. 'Doesn't matter if she has no money, no jewels!' he said, and he came again and again. Everyone in her family liked him – except for Kokila. They tried to compel her, but she was adamant in her refusal.

The reason for it was that he was from Aathoor – which was exactly like all the other villages her other suitors were from. Whoever she married among them, she would have to live in a place just like her own village.

And there, too, she would have to empty her bowels and pass water in the same old way. Out in the open. And she hated doing that. She did not like it at all.

That was why she had insisted on marrying Selvamani – ugly as he was. He had some education and a job, and he lived there in Madras, on his own. It must be a place where she could shit and piss without anyone knowing when and where she did it. And so Kokila said yes. She never asked a single question about him before or after that, although her relations all wanted to know everything about her bridegroom and asked a thousand questions.

It was all because of her mother. When Kokila attained puberty, her mother stuck close to her and went along with her as if she were a watchman. Whenever she went out after dark to empty her bowels or pass water, there her mother would be standing. Not even just a little way off, but right there, in front of her. It had been different earlier, before she'd come of age. Then she had sat together in a circle or in a row, with her sisters and other village girls. They did their shit-and-piss jobs together, each choosing her spot, and each one doing it when they felt it coming. Not only did she do it with the village girls, she would even squat with her mother and get the job over and done with. If she felt it coming during the rest of the day and just had to go, the women who lived next door or opposite would take her out. There was never any problem until then. She was just like all the other little girls in the village.

And then it happened. She 'grew up'. The morning after she was given the cleansing head bath, Poomaari took her out and stood just two feet away waiting for Kokila to empty her bowels and pass water … While Kokila swatted at the mosquitoes trying to sit on her thighs, Poomaari chased away the pigs that circled around her.

'Go home,' Kokila said. But Poomaari paid no attention. 'You'll be bitten by insects in the dark, hurry! Get up,' she urged.

'People are around, no? I'll come, you go home first!' Kokila tried telling her several times.

'So much wind, so dark it is … you'll catch something. What is it to you if I stand here? Get up soon! If it doesn't come, just push … Grunt!'

Anger rising in her, Kokila averted her face and looked eastward … Three girls were squatting together, and they were chatting too. Crouched like them, just ten feet away from her, were two other girls who were also chit-chatting about something or the other. Being roused from sleep and brought here, with Poomaari standing right in front of her – it was all very new, and she was furious with her mother for waking her up so early, at sunrise.

And this job she had come to do – it wasn't getting done either.

'How long are you going to be squatting?' nagged Poomaari. She shooed the pigs swarming around Kokila: 'Thhoo! Thhoo!' Hearing her mother cursing those who reared those pigs in filthy language, Kokila began to ask herself a question: Why was there not one house in the whole village equipped to deal with the emptying of bowels and bladders?

There must be at least five or six hundred houses in the village. Among them all, there was only one that had a bathroom – the house that Chettiar had built only two years earlier. Over a thousand women and girls lived in the village, and of them four or five hundred were from well-to-do houses. A couple of hundred of them were from households that were struggling even for food to eat. Didn't any of them wonder why they had to come out and crouch like this – on the roadside? As she brooded over it, it slipped from her mind – the thing she had come outside to do … When Poomaari demanded, 'How long are you going to be sitting there?' Kokila got up without finishing the job.

On the way home, she asked, 'Amma, why don't we get a bathroom, like the one Chettiar has had built behind his house?'

'Tell your father to build one! As if I am saying no to it … Can't see any way of even getting rice to eat…'

'To squat like that, in a crowd! Feels so shameful…'

'This is new for you, you've just come to that age. So that is how it will feel, but you'll get used to it. It'll be okay … Don't you see so many women sitting in a row like that? This is how they do it in the whole town. In the whole world! Anyone who's born a female has to go and do it out in the open. Why will it be different, just for you? Are you special or what?' Poomaari went on, as they walked. Ten or twenty feet ahead, she stopped to talk to Poongaavanam, who was squatting there with her daughter. 'So, at sunrise today where will you go for work? Whose house are you going to?' she enquired. Sitting there, swishing the stick in her hand to scare off the pigs, Poongaavanam kept up her end of the conversation, answering each query. Kokila hung back and stopped a little further away.

From that day onwards, right until today, the very same absurd drama had been taking place. Every morning, it was either Poomaari or one of Kokila's sisters who would accompany her on her early morning excursion. When all four of them had come of age, Poomaari gave each of them a length of cane and sent them off, saying, 'All of you go together, di!' If it happened that Kokila had to 'go' at an awkward time, in bright daylight, Poomaari would say, 'One of you go with her!' Getting up and going outside every single day, even before dawn, with her mother or her sisters, clutching a cane in her hand, finding herself a place to sit with other women in a row or in a circle, rising and averting her face when any man happened to pass by … standing there with bent head until he had gone out of sight … and then sitting crouched again, till her bowels had emptied and she had passed water.

Kokila made up her mind.

She must marry only a man who lived in the city.

That was the reason for her spurning every suitor who had turned up so far. And why she was heedless of not only whatever the members of her own family but anything anyone else in the village had to say about her resolve to marry Selvamani. Thinking over it now, it seemed strange … How could women and girls regardless of their ages – little children and old hags, too – sit there and chat while they shat? Yet that's what they all did. Each of them seemed to think there was no other chance for them to converse on everything – from the meal they were going to cook that day, to the quarrels in the house, to whatever embittered their minds – right up to the conflicts between mothers-in-law and daughters-in-law. And they did not talk in low tones either. On and on they'd be talking, as they shooed away the pigs and cursed those who reared them. Standing around and talking even when they had finished, they would draw into conversation not only those who were just arriving, but those who were about to leave after having done their jobs. And they wouldn't forget to revile those who had already left their shit and piss lying there, on the footpath.

'Dirty creatures. Couldn't they do it in a corner? Look at how they've shat right in the middle of the road! Those guts of theirs should just be slashed off…' It was not only early in the morning, but even well into the morning that women passed that way, spitting and cursing those who had gone before them.

If some man happened to come there in a hurry when any woman was still squatting there, they'd curse, 'Shameless ass! Look at the way she sits, not even caring that a man is coming!' … The words that came out were quite something to hear. It was much worse in the rainy season than in summer. The entire stretch would be a filthy swamp. There was always a drizzle. You couldn't go off to find a private spot away from the roadside because the marsh teemed with insects and worms, snakes and lizards. It was right in the middle of the path that you had to sit … And all along the way you had to really watch your step … Even if you took care to select your spot, you would remain within earshot of croaking frogs and buzzing beetles.

And yet, the talkative ones would go on yakety-yakking with those who came along, those they met on the way, and those who sat opposite them. This led to huge fights in several households. 'Why so long in the shit-jungle?' mothers would demand of daughters, mothers-in-law of their daughters-in-law. 'Who were you fooling around with, instead of getting back after a quick shit? Were you yapping away with some dog on the way?'

And often, there was cause for their suspicions. Using the excuse of having to 'go', girls would set off to meet boys they liked, there in the jungle. The shit-jungle. That was the place for young girls and boys to meet. And it was the practice to keep a vigilant watch on girls who had come of age when they set off for their 'ablutions'.

Kokila knew which girls met which boys in such a way … It made her laugh in scorn. Compared with such undignified goings-on in the shit-jungle, her marriage to Selvamani was much better, she thought. She remembered Muthamma declaring, on her wedding day: 'It's the fruit of your penance, di! You got your way!'

All these thoughts of bowels and bladders made Kokila want to pass urine. She hesitated to tell Selvamani about it and tried to control the urge for some time. Reaching a stage when she really could not bear to hold back any longer, and with great embarrassment, she woke Selvamani up and said, 'I need to go … to the … garden.'

It astonished her that he woke up at once, just as he had gone to sleep at once.

'All right, go,' he said.

'All by myself? A woman like me? Go alone, in this big crowd?'

'Okay, come along then,' said Selvamani, getting up.

'Move a bit, 'nga. Out of the way, move!' Pushing forward, Selvamani got them all to clear the way for her as she followed him – those that stood in the passage, those that sat ahead of them. Just as though she were still in the wedding hall, a bride approaching the groom for the exchange of garlands. New saree and blouse, arms crammed up to the elbows with glass bangles, hair piled high with flowers, face smeared with turmeric, and a new yellow taali string on her neck. New ear studs, new nose ring, and on her feet, anklets – everything proclaimed the fact that she was just married … A bride. Their eyes swooped on her, buzzed and sniffed around her like flies…

Both the toilets were locked from the inside, she found, after trying to push them open. Someone was inside each. Though she was just about a foot away from both those doors, he stood even closer to them. 'Come close!' he urged, and got her to stand against the door of one of them. There were more than ten men standing there already, next to those toilet doors, blocking the entire passage between the two entrances to the train … An inch, or two inches – that was the gap in which she stood. Never had she ever been so close to so many men before. And that too, waiting for a toilet door to open! Awful – the shame she felt … it made her squirm.

And it was at just that moment that Selvamani chose to tell her that he had to go to work early the next morning, and to ask, 'Will you get up early?' Just then, a man came along in a great hurry and tried pushing open both the toilet doors. There he stood, squeezed close to Selvamani, waiting for one of them to open. Her eyes running quickly over the crowd standing in the passage, she was just thinking, 'So, this is the way it's going to be, all the way to Madras!' when a fat woman emerged from the toilet on the eastern side.

'Go in!' said Selvamani at once to Kokila, but before she could get in, the fellow standing next to him tried to shove his way forward. 'Wait, 'nga! Ladies first!' Selvamani told him, and sent Kokila in.

No sooner had she shut the door and locked herself in than the stench hit her. Shit lay around – dry as well as wet. The reek of urine grabbed at her very guts. Ten or twenty cigarette butts lay scattered around. Everywhere were gobs of spit and mucus. Nausea churned her stomach. Wanting to clear her throat and spit, she saw that the basin was glistening with saliva and smeared with phlegm, and strewn with the stubs of beedis and cigarettes.

Her lips and nostrils began to itch. Scrawled around on the walls were sketches of men's and women's private parts. Enduring it all, she tried to lower herself, and found the entire spot completely wet. Was it water, or was it urine? Even if she somehow managed to squat, there was no certainty that her saree would escape being smeared with shit and piss.

'It's even worse than back in the village!' she muttered to herself. What was worse than anything else, however, was the awareness of Selvamani standing there outside, and next to him, the other man, who was waiting to see when she would open the door and come out. And two feet away, there they would be, all of them – ten other men. She would have to get past all of them and enter the coach ...

where all the others would look at her. When she had left the coach, they all knew where she was going, and now they would know where she had come back from, and what she had been doing. Thinking about it, here inside the toilet, she felt an overwhelming disgust. She was just trying to decide what to do about it, when somebody tried to push open the door, and she rose and quickly opened it herself and came out … without emptying her bladder.

Shoving past Kokila, a man rushed inside the toilet. 'Move a little, 'nga, move, 'nga. Just move!' Selvamani kept repeating as he pushed and shoved their way back into the coach. Kokila followed him with downcast eyes, trying not to look at anybody else at all.

After they had got back to their seats, it took some time for Kokila to regain her breath. The itching sensation in her mouth and lips had not reduced at all. Drenched in sweat, her saree and blouse stuck to her body. It was amazing how much she had perspired in such a short time.

She turned her face to the window and breathed in the air. Even that did not help drive away the smell of urine that seemed to be clinging to her saree and blouse, and to every part of her body. She felt as though she had barely escaped from some kind of terrible calamity.

The train stopped. 'Tea!' 'Coffee!' 'Tender cucumbers!' came the calls of vendors striding on the platform alongside. 'Will you have tea?' asked Selvamani.

'Don't want.'

'Why?'

'In the middle of this crowd? How to drink in this place, with so many men around?'

'Can one worry about such things?'

'I don't want it!'

'Shall I buy cucumber?'

Selvamani bought some cucumbers and gave her one. She held it in her hand but did not eat it. Selvamani put four or five cucumbers in his bag, and proceeded to eat three more, biting into each with a 'Marak! Marak!'... Like a cow eating maize stalks. His mouth moved from side to side, like an elephant's. Watching it, Kokila felt like laughing.

'When will we reach home?'

'Another three-quarter hour it'll be. Train is late today. Why are you asking?'

'As soon as we go home, I have to go ... to the garden.'

'You went just now, no?'

'Didn't go.'

'Why, what happened?'

'So many men standing at the door, how could I go? On top of all that, that place...! It's even worse than the shit-jungle in our village – such a stink. Yei, Appa! If I had stayed a little bit longer there, I would have died. Couldn't bear the smell. Felt like it was tearing out my insides. Sweat was pouring. So horrible it was. And the train was moving, moving all the time...' Kokila tried to smile a little.

'Everybody who goes on the train goes only in that place.'

'I felt very ashamed, so I came out. Anyone who remains in that place for an hour is sure to drop dead.'

'Those who go there and come back – aren't they human beings?' Selvamani's tone and expression showed a marked change. 'Is this our own house? Our town? Can we choose any spot, when we have to go?' he remarked, and went on to talk about Madras ... To pass urine, even men had to walk three or four kilometres, he informed her.

Then, as though he had just thought of something, he said, 'Over there, near the Koovam, so many people are living ... What'll you say when you see them?' he asked with a smile.

'Koovam? What is that?'

All the way to Madras, until they had set down their bags, he talked on and on about that stream – the Koovam – upon whose banks stood shanties set up by tens of thousands of people. About how they lived in those hovels. He didn't stop talking until they entered a hut. With a rude jolt, she saw that the entire floor within would contain no more than three sleeping mats, spread out.

'To the ... garden. I have to go ... outside...' she muttered.

'Come,' he said, going back outside.

'Outside, there? Why?'

'Come! I'll tell you.'

He led her past three huts full of people to a room, and gestured towards it. 'Go!' he said.

'Here? Inside this?'

'Mmm! These are line-huts. So, each line has only one. For the nine houses in this line, this is the only one. For two thousand rupees rent, in Madras, this is a lot. Go!' So saying, he pushed her into the toilet and pulled the door shut.

'Not one leaf or bush for a girl to hide behind? Is there no spot in this whole world anywhere – not even a tiny place for a wretched female to stay safe, out of sight?' Tears blurred Kokila's eyes. Furious sobs fumed up from the pit of her stomach.

'How long are you taking? Come out! Look, the next fellow is waiting! If you take so long, there'll be a fight. Quick, come out!' Selvamani's yell threw Kokila into a panic.

Between her thighs, piss came trickling down.

Missing Persons

WALKING TOWARDS THE BUS TERMINUS, Kolanjinaathan spotted a bus. It seemed to be waiting just for him and ready to start. Reaching it quickly, he climbed in. There was not much of a crowd inside. 'One ticket to Kadalur,' he told the conductor, took out the money, paid it and got the ticket. He was just in time – the bus set off within a few minutes of his getting in. A lucky omen, he thought. 'This thing I'm going for – it'll all work out fine.'

'Come today at two o'clock to the wedding hall behind the Kadalur Police Superintendent's office.' That was the instruction he had received on the phone from the Karuveppilai-kurichi police station.

'Any news about my father?' he had asked straight off.

'Come to Kadalur, 'nga, let's talk then,' the constable had replied. He seemed to have no inkling of Kolanjinaathan's agitated state.

'Please tell me, saar?' he pleaded.

'You have to go to Kadalur first. Then you will know. Your ID proof, the ID proof of the missing person – you have to bring all that. And exactly at 2 p.m., you have to be present,' the constable warned, before he put the phone down.

It made Kolanjinaathan very angry. 'Why are they telling me to go to Kadalur instead of Karuveppilai-kurichi? Have they found out something about my father Kaliyamurthi, who's been missing? Is he alive? Where is he?' His mind throbbed with the questions he longed, and at the same time feared, to ask. What if they said, 'You have been told whatever there is to tell. Then why are you phoning?' All he wanted to know was if Kaliyamurthi was alive. That would calm him down ... Let them scold and curse him if they wished, he resolved.

No one picked up the phone. He dialled once more, and again no one answered. 'Can't they say just one word – that he's alive? What do they lose by it? Arrogance – because they're police!' he fumed.

Right after the constable's phone call, it became impossible any more for Kolanjinaathan to sit or stand in any one place. Over and over again he walked to the doorway and back into the house. Inside, he went round and round in circles. When Sumati said, 'Calm down, 'nga,' he vented his blazing rage upon her. 'Time ... time ... What's the time?' he kept muttering and peering at his watch. He wanted to leave for Kadalur at once ... What should he do? With whom was he to share this matter? In an agony of bewilderment, he finally rang up his elder sister

Parvathi and told her that the constable had instructed him to turn up at Kadalur.

'I'll come too,' Parvathi said.

'What this will turn out to be, one way or another, I don't know. Police haven't broken the news so far, whatever it is. I'll go find out and tell you. No need for you to run around,' he told her, and hastily put the phone down as though he had to get back to some urgent task.

It was more than three months since he had submitted a petition about the disappearance of Kaliyamurthi. He had made trip after trip to that police station, only to get no information at all. Now, on their own, they were summoning him. Would they be doing such a thing without cause? They must have some information, and that was why they were calling him now. With that thought, he strove to reassure himself as he hurried over his bath, and ate some food just to get that over with, paying no heed to what it was that he was eating … If he got into the bus at eleven, he would reach Kadalur by one o'clock. It had been eight that morning that the police constable had phoned him, and now at nine o'clock he was already climbing into the bus.

Once he had got in and sat down, some measure of calm came over him. What came with it was another worry. What were they going to tell him, there in Kadalur? A hope had taken shape after that constable's phone call – a hope that his father would be found. So had another thought –

that constable on the phone, was he hiding the fact that his father was dead? No, that must not be! To the deity after whom he had been named, he sent up a prayer: 'O Kolanji Apparey! He's got to be alive!' Would he be found alive, or as a corpse? Simmering with these two questions, his head was being drained dry, and his very brain seemed about to shrivel up.

It was on the morning after Deepavali that Kaliyamurthi had said, 'I'm going to the field.' Neither for the morning meal, nor for the midday meal did he return, but it was only when he didn't turn up at night that Kolanjinaathan and his wife Sumati began to worry. Immediately he called up his Akka, and his two younger sisters, and then his relations, one after the other. With one voice, they all said, 'He hasn't come here.' Then he questioned several in the village, going from house to house, in street after street, and got no information at all. Now fear seized him. 'Did you say anything to him?' he asked Sumati again and again. Could she really have said something bad to him, maybe? That possibility, too, lodged itself in his mind.

Not caring that night had fallen, he combed each patch of thorny wilderness around, but nowhere did he uncover any clue. The first two or three days after his father's disappearance, he had thought he might have gone to one of his kinsmen somewhere, and went to their houses, one after the other. That hope vanishing in two or three days, he went searching in village after village, and in temple after temple. He had posters printed and stuck on the wall, and ads put in the papers. He handed in a petition at the police station. From the time he got up in the morning to when it grew dark, he went searching in every village, every street. That was the only work he did.

Three months and twenty days had gone by since Kaliyamurthi had gone missing, and in all this time, not one word had his son heard that could raise his spirits … Until this morning, when the call came for him to present himself at the police station.

It was not often that Kaliyamurthi went anywhere outside the village. Even when he did attend a family gathering elsewhere, he would be back in almost the same time it took him to reach there. Though he had as many as three daughters, he never dropped in on them without cause. Where could such a person have gone? It was not just Kolanjinaathan and his family who did not know the answer, nobody in the village did, either. If Kaliyamurthi's disappearance was a riddle, a bigger riddle was the fact that there had so far been no news of him at all.

Had something provoked the old man to leave the house? A quarrel between daughter-in-law and father-in-law? You couldn't say that either. Kolanjinaathan's wife Sumati was Kaliyamurthi's own sister's daughter. When Sumati lost her temper or had a fight, it was only with Kolanjinaathan himself. She always treated her father-in-law with due respect, and not a single day had there ever been any tussle between them. The two children, too, were well behaved with him, he adored them both like his very life. And as for Kolanjinaathan himself, whenever he came back from work, or from out of town, the first thing he would ask Sumati was, 'Has my father had his food?'

In these thirteen years that had gone by since his marriage, not once had the old man had an altercation with his son or with his daughter-in-law and set off for one of his daughters' houses. Nor was he given to wandering around in the village, or going to a tea shop or an idli stall, or sitting on a bench in the temple premises. Because there was likely to be pushing and jostling in crowded places, he never attended any public events. All he did was go to the fields and come back home. He went nowhere else. It was such a man who had now gone missing.

'I will sacrifice a cock! Break a coconut into one hundred pieces! Just fetch the man and leave him in my house.' That was the vow that Kolanjinaathan had made at the temple of that family deity whose name he bore. Going all the way to Narasinghamangalam, he searched in the little towns around, and found an astrologer who arranged for a 'parrot prophesy', with birds nodding and pecking in answer to his queries. He journeyed to the great temple of Vaidheeswaran to get a kaanda rite[1] conducted, which would throw light on his father's whereabouts. He called

---

1 Kaanda rite: A rite involving astrological predictions said to be based on information inscribed on palm leaves. An ancient palm leaf, pertaining to any individual's birth star, is extracted from a cache inside the temple by the astrologer/ priest, who then makes cryptic utterances said to confirm the

upon the lord of Tirupati, vowing, 'I'll put money in your collection box! I'll tonsure my head!'

Every astrologer swore solemnly: 'Go home, 'nga! You don't have to roam around and search any more. Exactly ten days from now, he will come home all by himself!' All their oaths had come to nothing. It was when he was sunk in abject despair that the constable had called this morning. Was there at last some good news on the way?

Distracted by a sudden flurry of sound, Kolanjinaathan glanced about and noticed that the bus had reached Neyveli. Had it been going fast – this bus that he had got on at Karuveppilai-kurichi? Or was it running late? He had no idea of its speed at all. Usually, he would doze off soon after he had got into a bus, and how it was that sleep overtook him every time, he didn't know. Always he told himself not to fall asleep, and yet that was what always happened. Right until the bus stopped at his destination, he would be fast asleep. Today he just could not shut his eyes, to his own surprise, though he wanted to sleep off.

Upwards of ten people climbed into the bus, and eight or nine got off. He didn't feel up to taking note of who got in and who was leaving. There was no heart in him for all that. A man came and sat next to him. At first glance, he looked to Kolanjinaathan very much like his own father. But Kaliyamurthi was very dark and short, and his head

---

identity of the person, and to prophesy his/her future, along with warnings and good tidings.

was bald. This man sitting next to him was fair, with a full head of hair. To Kolanjinaathan these days, any old man he caught sight of looked just like his father. Such a thought would strike him, again and again, as he stared from afar at somebody, only to go up close and find that it was someone else entirely. He had actually believed, more than a hundred times in these past three months, that he had found his father, and each time what he found was that his eyes had deceived him.

The bus came to a stop, and did not move on, much to Kolanjinaathan's annoyance. Would he get good news or bad news, when he got there? His mind stuck in the mire between those two questions, he felt hot and cold all over. Fretting about what they were going to tell him, there in Kadalur, he stared out of the window.

'Ayya, saami … Do a good deed!'

An old woman outside raised her folded hands towards the man who sat in the seat ahead. That fellow not only did not give her any money, he said nothing – not even that he had no cash. Yet the woman did not move off. Kolanjinaathan decided that, if she came to him, he would give her some money at once. He looked for change in his wallet, and found a two-rupee coin, and another five-rupee one. Should he give her two rupees, or five rupees? At first, he thought the two-rupee coin would be enough. 'Let her come, I'll give her the five-rupee one … Or should I call her myself, and hand it over? No, let the woman come.'

He was still thinking over it when the bus began to move. Then, when he hastened to drop the five-rupee coin into the woman's outstretched palm, it slipped from his fingers and fell to the ground. Did the woman pick it up or didn't she? As he strained to see what was happening, the bus picked up speed.

Feeling a little sleepy, he had shut his eyes for just a minute or two when he thought he heard that same voice: 'Ayya, saami! Do a good deed, 'nga…' Opening his eyes, he saw that the bus had left Neyveli far behind. But there it was, that woman's voice beseeching him: 'Ayya, saami, do a good deed, 'nga!'

How could that be? He couldn't understand it at all. A pang went through him and seemed to set his guts on fire with the memory of that beggar woman's face … and then, his father's face … If Kaliyamurthi was begging somewhere, that was all right – just as long as he wasn't lying dead under some lorry or bus or train. And then he wondered – would that woman have picked up the five-rupee coin he had thrown? Kolanjinaathan tried to recall those he had seen begging on the street, and whenever he went to a temple. Not one face came to his mind … Had he ever, until now, and on his own, given alms to anybody?

'Got no change! Go away!'

'Is this a decent way to live?' And: 'Like bad luck you're showing up! Begging and blocking my way, just now when I'm stepping out. What kind of behaviour is this?' He now recalled that this was the way he spoke to any beggars who approached him. The realization that he had never of his own free will bestowed alms on anybody made him very uncomfortable. 'From now on, I must give alms to whoever comes to me,' he swore to himself, as if he were taking an oath in a temple.

The man on his right had plopped his head down upon Kolanjinaathan's shoulder and gone to sleep. He scowled down at him and gave his arm a sharp tap, upon which the man awoke and sat up straight – just for a few seconds, after which he nodded off, having deposited his head again on Kolanjinaathan's shoulder. Now really angry, Kolanjinaathan wanted very much to tell the man off. Trying to forget about the whole thing – both that man's temerity in using his shoulder as a pillow, and his own anger – Kolanjinaathan stared outside.

The bus had gone past Vadalur and was nearing Kurinjipaadi. 'So soon?' he thought, with surprise. Now, in half an hour, he would be in Kadalur … That unnerving thought made him feel hot all over. 'Must get good news, God! Just let him be found, wherever he is, and however much it costs, I must bring him back … And see that he never goes to the fields again. Never goes out of the house…' All sorts of plans to keep a watchful eye on his father went through his mind, as he talked to himself. That Kaliyamurthi should return home was his only prayer. But so far, he had heard not a word of it, nobody who told him, 'I saw him over there!' or 'He was right here, I just saw him!'

No sooner had the bus halted at Kurinjipaadi than it set off again. Kullanchaavadi was next, and then Thambipettai. Last of all, Kadalur. Was it a good thing that he was reaching early, or was it unlucky? He must be there, in time … For what? He flinched. Until his father went missing, he had never known such confusion.

… Should he take an auto to the office of the District Superintendent of Police, or take the city bus? Not even about that could he take a quick decision. 'It's a big headache!' he fretted, looking out of the bus, as it went past Kurinjipaadi … A beef shop at the further end of the village caught his eye. It brought to mind at once the curry that his father had cooked and fed the family.

Ordinarily, his father never touched meat. It was only on Deepavali, Pongal, and the eighteenth-day festival of Aadi[2] that he bought any. Then he would cook it himself, and when it was done, he would set down the curry pot and the rice pot and make his children – all four of them – Parvathi, then Kolanjinaathan himself, Kolanjiammaal and Deivanaayaki – sit around it in a circle. On each one's plate he would plop a ladleful of cooked rice, and two ladlefuls of curry. Both rice and curry would be too hot to eat, and 'chilli-hot' as well. You could manage the heat, but the 'kaaram' would bring tears to the eyes. If you said, 'It's

---

2 Aadi: The Aadi Perukku festival, on the eighteenth day of the month of Aadi (mid-July to mid-August), celebrating the onset of the monsoon and its promise of plenty.

burning, I'll eat it later!' he wouldn't let you off. 'Get your tongue used to kaaram!' he'd say, and wouldn't let you get up until you finished every morsel.

That meat curry he cooked up was terribly spicy – and so was his brinjal curry. Whenever he went to Vriddhaachalam to sell paddy, he would buy three or four kilos of brinjal and cook it all up on that very same day. Not chopped up for a kuzhambu, but putting in as much garlic as would go into a dry curry, all fried up and added to the gravy. And then he would feed it to them in the same way as he did the meat. If you cried out, 'It's hot! Don't want it!' he wouldn't listen. 'The body must become hard as rock. Eat it!' he'd insist.

Brinjal was the only vegetable he would ever buy in the village market. That was what he brought back with him, too, whenever he went out of town. It was available in plenty – and it was cheap. Apart from brinjal, the only vegetables he knew were ash pumpkin and red pumpkin. Greens for him were only the drumstick tree's bitter leaves, and the mouth-puckering sour leaves of the pulichcha keerai.

Sumati cooked a fine meat curry and prepared many kinds of vegetable fries. Yet it was Kaliyamurthi's meat and brinjal that would come to Kolanjinaathan's mind when he ate her meat curry or her brinjal fry. Whenever he ate meat or brinjal even in the best eating places, it was never quite like what Kaliyamurthi used to prepare.

Kaliyamurthi's cooking, and Parvathi's – those remained fixed in his memory, but what his mother had fed him had gone forever. When Nallammaal died, Kolanjinaathan had been seven years old. Somebody he didn't know turned up at his school and told him, 'Your mother died, come,' and led him away by the hand. That was all he remembered. 'She got bitten by a snake in the fields and died,' the village folk said, and that was all he knew about it, and now the memory of Nallammaal's face was a blur. His sisters Parvathi and Kolanjiammaal were fair-skinned and tall. All those who saw them remarked that they looked just like Nallammaal. Kolanjinaathan himself and Deivanaayaki were like Kaliyamurthi – short, and very dark. Just about twenty hairs were left on Kaliyamurthi's head, and now, on Kolanjinaathan's, only about a fourth of all the hair he ever had.

Parvathi was ten, Kolanjiammaal five, and Deivanaayaki was only three years old, when Nallammaal died. 'These are motherless children. And yet, just see how well he has brought them up!' people in the village would remark admiringly. The only one he got educated, however, was Kolanjinaathan. As soon as each girl came of age, he got her married. To Kolanjinaathan, when he came home after completing his studies, he said firmly, 'Until you get a job, no wedding for you.' For three whole years, his father cooked and served him his meals, and it was only when he had a proper job that he arranged for his marriage.

Had his father ever taken him anywhere? He thought about it. No … he had never gone out of town with him … Except to Vriddhaachalam. Year after year, that was where his father took him, at the time of the annual Maham festival. It wasn't to attend the festival, but to make an offering in memory of Nallammaal.

Once he started to work, whenever he asked his father, 'Do you need any money for expenses?' the answer was always, 'What expenses do I have?' If he offered him money, he never took it. If Kolanjinaathan insisted, he would say, 'Give it to your Akka. That sister of yours – never let go of her. That child has brought you up just like a mother cares for her own son.' When he bought him a new vaitti and shirt, his father would protest, saying, 'Why are you burning away your cash?' If Kolanjinaathan went to work in the fields, he would send him back, saying, 'That hand of yours is meant to hold a pen, not a spade. Go home!'

When Kolanjinaathan began his studies for the plus-two exam, his father stopped addressing him familiarly by his name. Nor did he, after Kolanjinaathan left for college, call his son thambi[3] any more, for to Kaliyamurthi this was no longer a little boy but a grown-up, educated person distinctly above his own station. Not given to talking much, now Kaliyamurthi would only answer when spoken to, and when he did have something to say, he would add a polite

3 Thambi: Younger brother. Also a term of endearment for a child – rather like 'little boy'.

'appa' to every word. 'Come, 'ppa' or 'Go, 'ppa' was the way he spoke…

'If I, his son, were to tell him to stay put in one place, my father would have stayed right there, unmoving as a rock, in that very spot…' thought Kolanjinaathan. 'Not even one day has he ever behaved like a man who's lost his sense of right and wrong. How could such a person have gone off?' he kept asking himself. This was not even as if he'd left home because of some quarrel … There had to be something that had made him go off. Some cause … 'Without an axle, a temple chariot won't run even as far as three arm-lengths.' This was a proverb his father often repeated, he remembered now.

'Our mother gave birth to us, but even she wouldn't have looked after us like he did. No fighting, no scolding … never any hard words from him. How can it be that he has gone off somewhere?' he asked himself, and suddenly his eyes filled. To hide his tears, he turned his face to the window. The bus was entering the terminus at Kadalur when his cell phone rang. It was his elder sister, Parvathi.

'I've come to Kadalur, I'm going to the SP's office to talk to him. You please stay calm. I'll call you as soon as I find out what's the matter. There'll only be good news, that's what I think,' he told her rapidly, and hung up.

As soon as he got off the bus, he looked at his watch. It was not even twelve o'clock. 'Let me have some tea to drink,' he thought, and was only about ten steps from a tea stall when something occurred to him. Abruptly, he turned around and walked to an auto stand.

'I have to go to the SP's office. Will you take me there?' he said to the first auto in the line.

'That is where I am going,' the auto driver told him. 'One person is already inside. If you want, you can also come.'

'I don't mind sharing. I have to get to the SP's office, that's all.'

'Get in, saar,' the auto driver said and started the auto as soon as Kolanjinaathan sat down. Glancing at the man sitting next to him, he saw that he was clearly a person of some culture and breeding. Could be a government official, he thought.

'Are you going to the SP's office, saar?' he asked. To which the gentleman replied with a mere nod. 'It seems there is a wedding hall behind the SP's office, 'nga. Do you know it?' Kolanjinaathan enquired and received another nod in reply. When he followed it with, 'Are you also going there, 'nga?' the gentleman turned to gaze outside. Not put off at all by his silence, Kolanjinaathan continued to speak: 'My name is Kolanjinaathan. Government schoolteacher,' he volunteered. The other did not even say, 'Is that so?'

'Saar…' began Kolanjinaathan, once again. Before he could again ask, 'Do you know the wedding hall behind the District Superintendent of Police's office?' the man seemed to have understood why he was being thus addressed. 'My name is Ramalingam. LIC employee,' came his brief reply.

Seizing on those few words as sufficient reason to continue the conversation, Kolanjinaathan went on, 'Saar must not mistake me, please! My father has gone off somewhere, we don't know where. I gave a complaint at the station. Today, after three months they have called me to come. I'm just going for that now. Is saar also going to the mandapam?'

To that question, the gentleman gave no reply. Maybe it was just that he was a quiet sort, thought Kolanjinaathan … Of all places, they were on their way to a wedding hall. Maybe the police had taken it over for what was going to happen there, today … And what was that? He was just turning it over in his mind, when the auto came to a stop right in front of that mandapam.

Kolanjinaathan got down first, and then Ramalingam. 'Which way, saar?' asked Kolanjinaathan, and the other replied, 'Come, 'nga,' and began walking on. Falling in step with him, Kolanjinaathan saw the office of the Superintendent of Police, and behind it, a large open ground. That expanse of exceptionally clean ground looked as though it might be thirty or forty acres in size.

'Have you been here before, saar?' he asked wonderingly.

'For four years, I have been coming and going,' said Ramalingam. Four years! What could have brought him here, Kolanjinaathan wanted to ask, when his phone rang.

It was the same constable who had called him that morning. 'Have you reached Kadalur? At one thirty sharp, you must be in the mandapam.'

'I have come, saar. I'm just on the way there now.'

'Don't go anywhere else, stay right there. I'll call you when I reach,' the constable said, and hung up. This was the second time the constable had called him. He was panic-stricken … Maybe it was because he hadn't wanted to convey some bad news over the phone. Was something being hidden from him. 'No bad news, God … let me get only good news, da!' he prayed.

'Is this the first time you are coming?' Ramalingam asked him.

'Yes, saar,' he answered, looking around. People were walking towards a building in the distance, towards the east. That must be the mandapam, he surmised, looking around him. Behind him were others headed in the same direction.

'Police must be having some news, saar?'

'Don't know.'

'Just the day after Deepavali he said he was going to the fields and left, and now for three–four months he's been missing, saar…' Quite unasked for, the story was spilling from Kolanjinaathan.

They walked about ten or twenty steps more. 'A quarrel in the house?' Ramalingam finally asked.

'Nothing like that, saar. On Deepavali night, he ate quite well and went to bed.'

'Was there any kind of problem? Was he given any treatment?' enquired Ramalingam. It was clear what he was getting at. 'No, no mental problem or anything, saar!' Kolanjinaathan replied, 'He wasn't able to hear very well – that's all. And sometimes he would sit down in one place, and just stay there – just sit. That's all. Otherwise, he was quite all right.'

'Age?'

'Seventy, saar.'

'Did he often go off like that? May have been some problem which you didn't know about.'

'First time this is, saar…' began Kolanjinaathan, and before he could finish even those words, tears gushed out of him. 'Saar! If today I have a job, and I sleep in a house with two floors, and eat all three times a day, the reason for all that is my father, saar. From the day he went away, out of sight, whenever I sit down to eat, I feel like vomiting! Can't pick up even one handful of rice and put it in my mouth. Without my father in the house, I can't sleep, can't even lie down, saar. Feel like I'm lying down in a house which doesn't have any door. I have been through a lot, saar – with no money, not even enough for food, I couldn't study … Had no mother, but not one day did my father ever let us go hungry. We were never sent to anybody else's house to stand around and wait for them to feed us. He worked very, very hard, saar. Now he has gone away and left the house burning. Three months have gone by, with me standing guard and waiting, thinking, "He will come back! He will come back…" Lightning has struck our house, saar. Finished.'

He looked down in an effort to conceal his tears, then looked up again at people passing by. Then, without walking on, he stood gaping after the one or two cars that went past, and at the two-wheelers. Ramalingam, too, had come to a standstill.

'Better if he had just died, not just disappeared. That would have been good for him … Good for me, also. But he's just nowhere to be seen! Just missing! That is the big problem. It's enough if we knew if he was hit by a lorry and died, or if he was run over by a bus or train. Even if he fell into a lake or a pond or in the river and died, that's all we want to know. Without knowing anything about it, how can I decide on my own that he's dead?' he implored, with bowed head. That he was now crying openly in front of a man he had never known no longer mattered to him, he was sobbing like a child being beaten.

'Don't worry, your father will be found soon.' Instead of telling him this, what Ramalingam said was: 'After some days, you will get used to it.' But Kolanjinaathan was not listening, he was blowing his nose vigorously. After two or three loud sniffs, he took out his kerchief from his pant pocket and wiped his eyes and face. Then, as though he knew the way forward, he strode ahead.

Falling in step with him, Ramalingam asked softly: 'Are you your father's only child?'

'Four children we are, saar,' Kolanjinaathan began, and then went on at his own pace, not waiting to see if Ramalingam was actually listening. 'Six kaanis[4] of land my father used to have, saar. And one house with a tiled roof. That was all the wealth he had. Even when my elder sister said, 'Appa, come and spend a couple of days with me,' he would not go there. My younger sister Deivanaayaki's husband drinks a little. So he would never go to that house at all, just because of that. If he ever went to Akka's house, or to my first younger sister's place, he wouldn't spend the night … From the day my father has been missing, all that my Akka has been suffering cannot be put into any words. She must have gone around searching four times as much as I myself have roamed…

'My Akka is like a mother to us. From the age of ten, just like a grown-up woman she has been cooking rice, making kuzhambu … doing everything. Even if my mother were there, she wouldn't have taken care of us like my Akka, saar!' Kolanjinaathan burst into tears once again. Then he stood stock-still, his eyes scanning the whole ground as though he were looking for something he had lost.

Ramalingam also came to a stop. 'Some people are like us. They search for whoever has gone missing. And some others think, "Whoever has grown old, let them get out …

4 Kaani: A land measure equal to nearly 1.32 acres. Six kaanis would be almost eight acres. In this rainfed terrain, it cannot provide for much more than a bare existence.

let them leave the house."' This time, it was Ramalingam who spoke without being asked. As though he were talking to himself: 'Your father went away on his own. But with my mother it was different.'

It took Kolanjinaathan some time to grasp what he was saying. Wiping his eyes, he leaned forward as though about to hear something secret: 'What, saar, what happened?' Ramalingam stood there as though he could not make up his mind whether to speak or not, with Kolanjinaathan gazing intently at his face.

Finally, he spoke: 'My brother said to my mother, "Come, let's go to Tirupati," and took her away with him. On the way, he got down at some station or other. Said he was going to fill his water bottle … He didn't come back. Train left, mother went with it. Was it a train going up north, or was it going to Tamil Nadu? He never told me.' Ramalingam spoke in his usual tone, and his face was impassive.

Speechless with shock, Kolanjinaathan forgot that he had himself just been weeping over his own predicament. With difficulty he finally managed to ask, 'Saar! What are you saying?'

'He could have given her poison and killed her, and we could have thought he did it in anger and forgotten about it. Such things do happen in this world. When I questioned him, "Why did you do it, da?" he turned around and asked me, "Don't I have to take care of my wife and children?" What could I say to that? Seventy-four years old, she was.

Had high blood sugar and BP. Maybe if she had been young, she could have got some work to do somewhere … To somehow stay alive. No chance of that … For the past four years, I have been roaming around searching for her.'

Hurriedly, before Ramalingam had finished speaking, Kolanjinaathan exclaimed, 'Do people really do such things, saar?'

'All kinds of people are there in the world,' answered Ramalingam, as he started to walk on, slowly. Kolanjinaathan walked with him. 'Why did your mother go to him?' he asked.

'She was with me for fifteen years. When my younger brother lost his job, I thought let her be with him, that will give me a reason to send some money to my thambi. And then he did this.'

'How awful, saar.'

'His own mother who gave birth to him – how he could even eat again, after leaving her like that in a running train, I don't know. He could have just brought her back and left her with me. My mother loved him more than she loved me. "He is suffering," she kept on saying.'

Just then, three cars went past, one of them a police car.

'So cruel, saar!' declared Kolanjinaathan. Ramalingam did not respond at once. They walked on ahead for about twenty or thirty feet. Then, as though he had just remembered something he had forgotten to mention, 'There was a person who worked for me, named Selvaraj,' he said. 'His mother left the house after a fight. No one knew where she went. For three–four years he searched, and then he felt she must be lying somewhere – as a corpse. Abandoned … So he had the last rites performed. They even began to observe a fast in her memory, every new moon. After that, how could they go on searching for her? So they gave up, and left it at that. Then they stopped sending money every month for the search to go on … Suppose it worked and she turned up again? What was to be done after that?'

A shudder went through Kolanjinaathan at what he had just heard. 'Just can't believe it, saar.'

'It's the first time, for you. That's why you don't know. You will hear thousands of stories like this when we reach the mandapam.'

On either side of the mandapam reserved for the use of police personnel stood at least two to three hundred cars. There were more than a hundred two-wheelers as well. Thrown into a state of bewilderment, Kolanjinaathan stared at those vehicles. With fear and trembling, he began climbing up the steps. At the entrance to the hall was a table, with four policemen standing next to it.

'Come here, saar,' said one who looked the oldest among them. 'Which police jurisdiction are you coming from?' he asked, and when he received the reply, held out a printed form. 'Write down the name of the missing person, age and address, 'nga. Then write your name, address and mobile number and put your signature,' he instructed. First Ramalingam and then Kolanjinaathan filled out the information required, and signed the papers. 'You may go in now, saar,' said the policeman. They both went into the mandapam.

Two policemen immediately offered them tea and biscuits, as though they had been waiting for them to show up. 'No,' said Kolanjinaathan, disposing of the offer in that single word. 'This condition that we are in – does it call for tea and biscuits?' he thought to himself. But Ramalingam took both the tea and the biscuits. As if that were not bad enough, 'Take it, saar,' he said.

'Don't want it, saar.' Kolanjinaathan turned away. The mandapam was large enough to hold two thousand people. Some two or three hundred people were seated there already. On the stage, five policemen were intently attending to some kind of work. Ten or twenty more going around, serving tea and biscuits to those in their seats. Taking in all that was going on there, he asked Ramalingam, 'What is all this crowd, saar?'

'More will be coming, just see, 'nga,' Ramalingam told him.

'So many people? Are they all looking for somebody who's missing?' he asked, sounding like a small boy. To that, Ramalingam's answer was a mere nod.

They set up a portable screen on the dais and arranged six chairs around it. A policeman carried in a loudspeaker, and two others walked back and forth, talking on their cell phones. From all that was going on up there on the dais, it was evident that a Very Important Person was expected.

A woman came up to Ramalingam and said, 'How are you, saar?'

'Not bad,' he replied in a neutral tone.

'Did you get any news, 'nga?'

'No…' came the polite answer.

'We have also not heard anything till now. It'll be good if we get some news today at least. Coming here again and again, hoping and hoping every time – it's like dying,' the woman said, tears blurring her eyes. Such a beautiful woman, weeping like this! Kolanjinaathan wondered at it. Neither skinny nor fat, she had a strikingly attractive face. Must have been under forty years old. The saree she wore, the blouse, the chains on her neck, the bangles on her arms – all of them proclaimed that this was a woman in good circumstances. He kept gazing at her, he couldn't look away, she was so beautiful.

'It would be enough just to know that it's all over. We could perform the last rites. Now there's no way to get even that done!' the woman said.

'No need to hurry,' Ramalingam answered quietly.

'My saar is sitting there, in the back. We can meet when it's time to leave.' The woman moved to the back of the hall. He turned, but couldn't see where she was seated. The hall was more crowded than it had been a little earlier.

'Who are they, 'nga?' Kolanjinaathan asked.

'Met them just like I met you. Got to know them. For four years, I have seen them here,' Ramalingam said.

'In four years, they still haven't found that person?'

'Mm.'

'Who was it who got lost?'

'His older sister.'

'How old was she? When did she disappear?'

'Don't know,' Ramalingam was just telling him, when two women and a man came and sat on his right. Turning around, he saw people streaming in as though it was a wedding they had come to attend. 'What a crowd … All these people – does each one of them have a family member who went missing?' he wondered. Silently, he beseeched his namesake and family deity: 'Kolanji Appa! Never mind all that, you just bring me some news about my own father, da!'

Someone came and sat next to him. The mandapam was fast filling up, but sounds were greatly muted. Those who spoke seemed to be whispering secretively to one another. The police presence on the dais had swelled, and among them were two policewomen. All of them were darting around busily. He sat there, his mind in a welter of uncertainty about what they were going to say … 'What are they going to do? Shall I ask Ramalingam?'

He decided against it. The man was sitting there with his eyes closed as if in meditation … When were they going to come out with some information? So hard it was to just keep sitting like this … He looked at his watch. It showed two o'clock. How had time gone by, he thought, bemused.

Up there, all of a sudden, the police rushed about, making way for five officers who had just arrived. Almost as soon as he got there, one of the officers began to speak into the mike, beginning with a greeting: 'Vanakkam, to all of you … Many of you may have already come here before. Some may be newcomers. I would like to clarify the matter to the newcomers–' he announced, and stopped. Immediately, a policeman who stood behind him came forward and handed him a file. Taking it from him, he began to speak once again.

'Who is that, saar?' Kolanjinaathan enquired.

'District SP,' Ramalingam informed him.

'And those standing there?'

'Four deputies. One assistant district superintendent of police,' Ramalingam said in a low voice. 'We'll talk later.'

'On the screen that has been set up here, first you will see people who are staying in destitutes' homes. Next, you will be shown those people lying around in bus stands and railway stations. Third will be people at the gates of temples, and those begging on roadsides. Fourth, those who are wandering around in a bad mental state. After that, you will see the unclaimed bodies of those who were hit and killed by lorries and buses and trains … Corpses found in rivers and lakes, and at sea. You will then be shown bodies of those who have been stabbed to death. You will see photos of dead bodies, and if you have a connection with any of them, immediately you must get up and tell it.' Having spoken, the District Superintendent of Police went and sat down in his chair. It was only after he had seated himself that his deputies took their seats.

The screen on the dais lit up. Kolanjinaathan prayed fervently for his father's photo to be the first one to appear on it. Filled with a nameless dread, he quivered slightly. But it was the face of a woman they showed first, with her name and age, her physical details, as well as the name and address of the ashram where she was lodged and how long she had been there. Next came another photo – also of an old woman – and then, one after the other, a succession of others in ashrams and asylums. After that, they began on those who were found wandering the streets … His hope that his father would be found in an ashram had proved false. It wrung his heart.

'Zoom, please,' a man in the audience stood up and called, as photos of those sitting and begging outside temples were being shown. At once, the scenes on the screen were alternately magnified and miniaturized. As both detail and perspective took form in picture after picture, Kolanjinaathan's heart beat faster and faster. Kaliyamurthi was not there, in the lines of beggars.

Next came those who were not all right in their heads. Let him at least be among them, hoped Kolanjinaathan, and broke into sobs when his father was not to be found among even those. Feeling that he would piss, right then and there, out of sheer terror, he mumbled: 'God!'

At that moment, a woman rose and said something to the policemen on stage. 'Come to the dais when the meeting is over,' a policeman told her.

Now they began on the unidentified corpses. Kolanjinaathan thought, let my father at least be among them … They showed pictures of twenty to thirty dead bodies. His father was not there, and yet Kolanjinaathan's desperation only worsened … Bodies of those flung on the seashore were shown. Would he be among those? He looked closely at the photos. No, his father was not one of them…

Kolanjinaathan could not sit still, he felt he was going mad … If his father was not among any of these people, then where was he? What had happened to him? He fell into a sweat of anxiety. Such was his trepidation that he could not follow all that they were saying about each of those dead bodies that appeared on the screen. His morale began to sink – that faith in himself that, a few moments ago, he had believed to be indestructible.

When they had finished projecting all the pictures, the District Superintendent of Police rose and spoke into the mike: 'Until now, out of all the photos we have shown so far, only six persons have been identified. The family members of those six persons may please come backstage, bringing all their credentials with them.'

From among the audience, quiet all this while, arose the buzz of voices, and about ten or twenty people hurried to the back of the stage. Once again, the Superintendent began to speak into the mike. The hall fell silent.

'In our district of Kadalur, between 2014 and 2020, the total number of missing persons is eight hundred and seventy-six. Eighty-three per cent of them are women, and twenty-seven per cent are men. Of the total number of missing women, sixty-four per cent are under fifty years of age, and thirty-six per cent are older women. Of the total number of missing persons, twenty-one per cent are from villages, and seventy-nine per cent are from towns.'

Kolanjinaathan was in no state of mind to hear what the DSP was saying. If he had been by himself and not in a crowd, he would have wailed out loud – and that he could not do. All he could do was sit there helplessly. It was unendurable ... 'My father is not anywhere!' he gasped, gulping the air down, open-mouthed. What his nostrils took in just wasn't enough.

From the time he had left home, right until he had entered the mandapam, he had been lamenting that it was his father who had gone missing. To know, now, that that father of his was just one of eight hundred and seventy-six missing persons staggered him.

'In all the district capitals today, at this same time, are being shown all the details and photographs of these missing persons whom you have seen here. As and when information is received by us about those missing persons who are originally from our district but have been residing in some other district, it will be passed on to the police authorities in that district.'

He heard it – what the Superintendent was saying. His brain, however, was in no condition to grasp it. He was sobbing, his head buried in his chest, when Ramalingam gave him a gentle tap and said, 'Please sit up straight.' Wiping his nose with his kerchief, he blew his nose half a dozen times before he straightened up.

'Leaving the house because of a love affair or some family problem is one thing,' the DSP continued. 'Driving someone out of the house because we can't care for them is something different. This person whom we are driving out – it's nobody else but our own appa or amma, or their parents – our thatha or paati. Some close relation – uncle or aunt, father's brother or sister, mother's sister … Family members only. Will a tree or a creeper grow if there is no earth under it? It's just like that: without old people, we would not be here. Everyone in the world has their old people, and they themselves get old.

'Those people we see begging on the roads, or lying as unclaimed bodies – who are they? Majority are only old people! From birth itself, did they start begging? No! Each one must have had a house, some money, some belongings … And a family. Will any person go begging if something like that is there for them? No, they go only when their children, their belongings and house, and property don't feed them – isn't that so? Money and jewels, property deeds – such things we lock up safely in our almirahs. Car and bike we lock up in the shed. None of these have any life in them. But living people … we drive out of the house. And that, too, those who have given birth to us. It's in the towns and cities, where people are more educated and well-off, that so many go missing…

'Those who die and end up in the burning ghat are not a problem. It's only the ones who go missing and aren't found who are the problem. Whether it is the missing person, or the one who is searching for him, or me, here, talking like this – one day, everyone has to go to the burning ghat, that's the only place where it will all be over, for every one of us. Today it is them, tomorrow it is me. Only the date is different. There is a date for each person, and that date will never change…

'So! Everybody, see if you can live happily! See about keeping those near you also happy. As long as they are in the house, you keep driving them to the door, and then you go roaming around searching for them! What kind of good deed is that? The hardest thing to do in the world is to beg, and to die as a destitute…'

What Kolanjinaathan thought would happen – that this speech that the SP had just made would be followed with a great round of applause – did not happen. Not a single person clapped. A hush had descended on the hall. Not the tiniest ripple of sound arose from among the more than two thousand people gathered there. The SP must have been not more than thirty years old. Tall and strapping, he was a typical police strongman from the looks of him. But his words had pushed not only Kolanjinaathan but everyone in that mandapam into a gigantic well of silence.

The SP resumed: 'Don't quarrel over petty matters, please! Let go of small things, just give them up. Life is like that only! Giving charity to the beggar is nothing to be proud of. It's seeing that nobody has to beg at all that should make us proud. Those people who have in some way or the other made our birth possible, helped us to grow and to live – we are making paupers out of such people. We are the ones who give them alms, and we are also the same ones who turn those beggars into homeless destitutes. How do they go on and on appearing, how do they show up, age after age – all these beggars and paupers? That is what I don't understand … Now, let nobody feel anxious that their person has not been found this time. Go back with the confidence that there will be news, next time.'

The SP finished speaking. The policemen standing here and there on the edges of the crowd now came forward to say, 'Please come for a meal, 'nga.' It astonished Kolanjinaathan that police constables could conduct themselves thus, as though inviting guests to partake of a feast.

'Looks like I'm going to be wandering around searching till the day I die,' he muttered, rising from his chair. 'What now, saar?' he enquired. 'They won't let you go without eating,' Ramalingam informed him, and began to walk towards the dining hall. Kolanjinaathan fell in step behind him.

They couldn't find seats next to one another. When Ramalingam found an empty spot, he said, 'You please have food, we'll meet afterwards.' Kolanjinaathan sat down reluctantly, two rows ahead. To sit and eat there, as though he were attending a celebration of some sort among a batch of guests, felt utterly repulsive to him. But here he was, all because the constables were plainly insisting on it.

'What brings you here, saar?' The person seated on his right began a conversation all on his own. In one breath, it all came spilling out like a pot of water being overturned – Kolanjinaathan's entire family history. Having listened patiently to all of it, the man said, 'I am also a teacher. Name's Ezhumalai.'

Dragging out the words, Kolanjinaathan asked, 'So, the reason you have come here…?'

'Two years ago, my wife said she was going to her mother's house. She didn't come back. I am still searching.' Even as he spoke, he burst into tears. As though the only treatment for the fit of grief into which he had fallen was water, he reached for his bottle and gulped some down.

The policemen set about serving the meal, and Ezhumalai began to eat.

'From which town are you, saar?'

'Panrutti.'

'How many times have you come here?'

'Three times, so far.'

'This meeting – do they have it every month?'

'Once in six months, or once in a year.'

'You haven't heard anything for two years?'

'If I had, why would I come here now? Money, jewels, property – if all of that is lost, it doesn't matter, saar. But it's the wife who's gone! I've got two children, saar … it's very, very hard.' Ezhumalai got up, having barely eaten half the food in front of him. Kolanjinaathan rose with him. He, too, had eaten only for form's sake. They both went and washed their hands.

Kolanjinaathan looked around for Ramalingam. He was not in the dining hall, nor in the main mandapam. He went to the entrance and looked around. No sign of him … Where could he have gone? He felt distressed that he hadn't got his cell number from him. Thinking about how to get to the bus terminus, he noticed people leaving in cars and on two-wheelers.

His cell phone rang – it was his Akka, Parvathi, trying to call him. 'No result at all,' he told her tersely. 'Only thing that got done was all this running around. Rest of it, I'll tell after reaching home.' He hurriedly put away his phone.

People were climbing into the autos parked in a row outside the SP's office and leaving. 'Bus stand,' he said as he got into one, and within a quarter of an hour, it arrived at the terminus. Looking all around for some bus that might take him to his village, he saw one standing there, quickly got in and sat down. 'When will it start, 'nga?' he called out to the conductor. Then he shut his eyes, muttering in desperation: 'Not one god has come to help me!'

'Ticket?' said the conductor, coming up to him.

'To Pennaadam, one ticket.'

'Pennaadam? This bus is going to Chidambaram. Why did you get in?' The conductor's question threw Kolanjinaathan into a frenzy of confusion. Feeling as if he was burning from head to foot, he stammered, 'I saw … I even asked you!'

'You only asked when will the bus start, you didn't ask where it is going!' the conductor snapped, glaring at him. Humiliated, he sat silent ... Suddenly, he was furious with Kaliyamurthi. 'What kind of man is he? What-all sorts of shame he's left me in and gone off!' If that father of his were right there, he would even have cursed him in filthy words, such was his wrath. 'A mental case ... That is what he is. Let him die and get lost!' he hissed from between his teeth.

'Ten or fifteen kilometres have gone past. Next stop is Vandipaalayam. Get down there, 'nga, and take the Kadalur bus. If you don't do that, ten kilometres after that Bhuvanagiri will come. You can get down there and change to the next bus,' the conductor told him, before he moved on towards the next passenger, calling out, 'Ticket!'

Kolanjinaathan felt his head would burst, he felt so angry. To whom could he exhibit this anger? That was what he couldn't decide ... 'How did I get into the wrong bus? Should I go to Kadalur and change buses, or should I get off at Bhuvanagiri? Which was closer to home? Whom should I ask about it?' He just didn't know.

'Buy a ticket to some place, whatever it is, 'nga! This is a government bus. If a checking inspector gets in, I'll lose my job,' the conductor yelled. Without a word, Kolanjinaathan took out a hundred rupees and handed it to him. Taking the money, the conductor demanded, 'Vandipaalayam or Bhuvanagiri?' Sitting there as though seized by a fit of madness, Kolanjinaathan went rigid.

The bus picked up speed.

Payback Time

Crossing the road with the child straddling her hip, Seeniamma headed towards the illuppai[1] tree, east of the women's police station. Beneath its shade sat her mother, brother and sister-in-law.

'What did you buy for the boy?' enquired Megavarnam.

'Tea, bun…' Seeniamma answered in a lifeless tone, her eyes on the police station. She turned, tears welling up at the sight of her brother Sundaram squatting there. She tried glancing this way and that, to hide them, and finally burst out, 'Don't think badly of me because I have made you come and sit here! What I've gone through for one whole year – you know all that, don't you?' All three of them broke into tears along with her – Sundaram and Thavamani, and her mother.

---

1 Illuppai: Mahua (*Madhuca longifolia*), a tree valued for its medicinal properties, with sweet-tasting flowers used to brew a mildly alcoholic drink.

'This girl of mine – how I gave birth, how I brought her up! And after all that, I've gone and married her off to Yama himself, ayyo!' sobbed Megavarnam.

'Why are you crying?' Thavamani demanded of Seeniamma. 'As if I'll have to light up another fire just to cook for you and your son! For your brother, your life is also his life – that's how he always feels about you, don't you know?' She nodded mutely.

Still standing there, Seeniamma was staring down the road at some eight or nine schoolchildren who were riding home on bicycles. 'Sit down,' Sundaram told her. But she did not sit down with them under the tree. Instead, in a resolute tone, as though she were under oath, she declared, 'Never will we become a burden on your head – not me, and not my child! Till my dying day, I won't do anything to make you hang your head in shame. I'll show I'm not some fatherless nobody!'

'Why are you talking like that? Stop crying,' scolded Thavamani. 'So long as you have your brother, what more do you need?' Taking the baby from Seeniamma's arms, she settled it on her hip.

'Ayyo, what a terrible thing has got written on my girl's forehead!' wailed Megavarnam at the sight of Seeniamma standing there looking forlorn.

'Why are you also sitting all hunched up and crying? Like a female!' Thavamani berated Sundaram. 'Go on, go drink some tea. If you three go on sitting here together, you'll all be talking only of the same thing over and over again. Mind will get all confused … Get up, I'll also come.' She all but dragged her husband to the tea shop near the police station.

As she lowered herself next to Megavarnam, Seeniamma's eyes went towards the police station. Paandi had arrived, and a great many men stood there with him. 'I'll put an end to his whole story, today. Finished!' she vowed angrily.

'Who knows where that woman was born, which village she grew up in, who gave her a child! As if it wasn't enough that she gobbled up her own husband, she's tearing off my girl's taali!'[2] Megavarnam cried, and began to curse Prema under her breath.

It was more than five years since Paandi and Seeniamma had got married. Both were from the same village, from the same street in that village. He had no bad habits – didn't smoke beedis or cigarettes, didn't drink saaraayam. And he had a regular job – he was supervisor at the village noon-meal centre. That's why they got Seeniamma married to him.

Then, the cook there retired. A woman by the name of Prema was given the post. She must have been of the same age as Seeniamma, about twenty-five or twenty-six. Her being a widow had got her the job – her husband had got killed by a stack of ripe sugarcane stalks which fell on him

---

2 Taali: A thread strung with certain symbols knotted by the groom around the bride's neck, at the time of marriage.

as he was loading them. She had three children. Within two or three months of joining duty, certain changes became apparent in Paandi's behaviour. At first, when Seeniamma asked him anything about it, he would retort, 'Don't you go around imagining things!'

But within one or two months, even the schoolchildren knew that he and Prema were having an affair. Then the teachers came to know of it, and the whole town. Seeniamma was the last to hear about it. Each time she questioned him, he would shut her up by snapping, 'Did you yourself see anything?' No, she had not, she would have to agree, and leave it at that.

Until somebody or the other said, 'Your man and that girl – I saw them there myself!' Or, 'Right here, I saw them!' Blood rushing to her head, she would confront Paandi again, and he would silence her again with a mocking remark: 'If I really wanted to hatch an egg somewhere else, would I go to a female who cooks in a block development office?'

Or he would swear to her, 'On my own son, I swear it is the truth! Nothing is there at all like what you are thinking.' When he swore like that, she would believe him totally – all that day. And all day long she'd be a little happier, but that was it. That happiness didn't last, because the very next day someone would turn up and say, 'I just saw them both – your man and that woman. Laughing and talking together, right now in the school!' She would be stung by a poisonous rage that rose right up to her head.

Not one stroke more of work would she do in the house. She would sit down in one spot, and there she would wait, without budging, for Paandi to return.

'Why so late? It took so long, is it? To finish having fun with that … that "baby"?'

'Both of us are working in the same place! Sometimes we have to talk, right?' Mollified for the moment, she would tell herself that what he said was reasonable enough. And then it would happen again. She'd be on her way to the provision store, or to the well, or it would happen in the vegetable orchard where she worked: somebody would tell her something.

'So! Where did the two of you go together, yesterday?' And if he denied it in a normal tone of voice, she would not believe him, until he swore to it. Any day that Paandi returned late from the school noon-meal centre, she would assail him with, 'So! School won't let you go home, is it? School is hugging you tight? Sticking to your body, isn't it?' If he left punctually for work, she would ask, 'So! Your baby ordered you to show up right on time, did she?' Paandi would reply, 'That new headmaster – he's troublesome, keeps poking into everything.'

Everything he said sounded quite believable, and Seeniamma did believe it, at the moment when he came out with it. And then she would start all over again. 'What word did she say, what magic spell did she cast on you?' she'd ask sarcastically. Upon which he would strike himself on the forehead in a hopeless sort of way, as if to bemoan his fate that he had such a shrew of a wife … Every day someone or the other would drop in, churn up the contents of her mind, and then go off.

Having tried her best to cope with it, one day when Paandi had gone out of town, she went straight to the school and spoke her mind to Prema.

'Who are you speaking to? And what are you saying? Don't you dare talk to me like that! One more time you talk like this, you'll be in a bad mess!' Prema made a huge fight of it. The whole school stood by and laughed. Having come to know of the fracas when he got back home that evening, Paandi demanded, 'Why did you go to the school?'

And then he hit her. It was the first time after their marriage that he actually struck her…

'No need to go to school today, just last night we have fought and I have hit her,' Paandi must have thought the next morning. It was Seeniamma now who started it all again. 'Why are you sitting here in the house? Someone or the other may just carry away your dear baby, don't you know? Go take a look and come back!' she jeered.

'Baby, or old woman – she may be anything – so what? What is it to you?'

'Could have caught a nice new one for yourself, but you went and caught an old cow! Three calves she's got! Why her?'

'Calf, or cow with many calves – whatever she is, why are you bothered?'

'You've slipped your foot into a filthy slipper. New or old, a seruppu like her is only fit to touch the road. Nothing else.'

'So, let her be a seruppu, what has it got to do with you? Don't dare talk about her…'

'I *will* talk about her! Only her, nothing else!'

'You are not fit to speak about her.'

'"Which fellow shall I catch? When can I trap him?" That's what *she* is thinking, and *you* are saying, oh, *she* is the one who's as good as gold, and *I* am not fit even to talk about her. Okay, if she's pure gold, why not just go and stay with her? Why come here? Even "Goldie" has the same piss place, no? The town cow – that's what she is! A common stray.'

'So what? Let her be that – the town cow. You just keep being the house cow. Don't listen to people giving you bad advice and dance to their tune!'

'Never mind me dancing … you stop dancing with that stray donkey.'

'Will you shut your mouth? Or take a beating with my seruppu! … You donkey, you're calling me "nee! nee!" No respect!'

'Those who do bad things get beaten with a seruppu! Why should *I* take that kind of beating?' Hardly had she come out with this rejoinder than he slapped her hard across the cheek and went on to thrash her up until his paroxysm of anger was sated.

A week later, when he came close and tried to touch her, Seeniamma snarled, 'Chhee! Take your hand off! You go and touch any old dirty bitch and then touch me? Take all your man-stuff and go show it off to that Goldie of yours!'

That night, she was beaten and kicked so hard that for three or four days she lay in bed, unable to get up and walk.

School closed for the summer holidays, and the noon-meal centre shut down. Seeniamma thought that the affair might peter out. But every day at nine o'clock, as he had before, Paandi left the house. It was only at three in the afternoon that he came back from wherever it was he had gone. She waited for a day, another day … A week and then ten days went by, and she could no longer hold herself back from asking him about it.

'Who are you to ask me all this?' he retorted. 'A man goes out! He doesn't just sit in the house!'

She bore it for four whole days. Half an hour after he left home on the fifth day, she set off and went straight to Prema's village. It was well within walking distance. There, outside Prema's house, stood Paandi's bike. This should be enough to prove it, she thought, and began to walk back. What would he have to say to that, she asked herself … Just the usual 'Have you seen it?' That was Paandi's usual rejoinder when she accosted him with any of her suspicions. Now she had proof.

… But he wouldn't believe her if she told him! And so, halfway home, she turned and went back to Prema's house, and knocked on the door. It was Prema who opened it.

'Go call your new lover boy!' Seeniamma shouted angrily. Coming out of a room inside and seeing her, Paandi stood there stunned, bereft of speech. Without a word more, she turned and left.

Back home, she gathered up her clothes and was about to leave for her mother's house when he arrived. Not stopping even to take a breath, he demanded, 'Why did you come there? You didn't believe me, did you? Do you know why I went there?' and began to hit her. Hearing her screams, the entire population of that street turned up. Some tried to stop Paandi, and so did Thavamani and Megavarnam, but he rained blow after blow upon her, yelling, 'Why did you come there?' Unable to withstand the blows, she ran out of the house and into the street.

That didn't stop him. Snatching up a cattle whip, he gave her a flogging so violent that she urinated and defecated right there, in the middle of the street. Because he did not, even then, stop beating her, she scrambled up and hurled herself down the street. Into the temple she ran, and it was only there that Paandi was stopped from chasing her further by some seven or eight men, who were lounging in the courtyard playing cards.

… She, who had been hiding in her house, had been driven out and mauled so badly that piss and shit had burst out of her in full public view. The whole village had seen that ugly spectacle. She wanted to die. She must die …

Tormented as she was by that thought, she shook it off. Resisting her mother's and her sister-in-law's attempts to restrain her, she went to the women's police station and handed in her complaint.

Three days later, because nobody there took any action, she went there again. This time, she paid five thousand rupees. Only after that was done did two policewomen show up just yesterday evening, asking for Paandi. This morning, a third policewoman turned up to order Seeniamma and Megavarnam to present themselves at the station in the evening for an investigation. It was for that process to begin that they waited now, outside the building.

Sundaram and Thavamani came back from the tea stall. The baby on Thavamani's hip leaped at once to Seeniamma's arms and settled in her lap.

'When are they ever going to call us?' Thavamani was remarking, just as a crowd of ten to twenty people arrived, with a woman whose head was battered and bloody. They hurriedly entered the police station. 'Looks like every day there'll be at least one or two cases like this,' Thavamani observed.

'Five cases here, on the day I came,' Seeniamma said. 'All husband–wife fights. Men's police station is all empty, no crowd at all like this. By mistake, I went there first … Nothing going on there. It's all empty, there's only wind there. Blowing in and blowing out.'

Talking loudly among themselves, the group which had just entered the station was shooed out by a policewoman.

'Go and shout out there, far away! No noise allowed here in front of the station. Only Seeniamma-case people can come in. Come, 'nga! Police Amma is calling you,' she announced, before going back inside. It was only after Paandi and the men standing with him near the door had entered that Seeniamma, Megavarnam, Sundaram and Thavamani could get in.

Seated in a well-lit space, with her chair facing east, was the assistant superintendent, Ms Aarthi. Less than thirty years of age, by the looks of her, she surveyed the two groups who stood opposite. 'Ei!' she called out, with a glance towards the inner room. Answering her summons with 'Yes, 'mma?' Pushpa emerged and presented herself.

'Have you examined this case?'

'No, 'mma.'

'Do you know the case details?'

'Husband–wife fight. Case for separation, 'mma – petition has been given.'

'Okay, you go.'

Pushpa went back inside. She must have been ten or fifteen years older than Aarthi. Yet, when Aarthi summoned her with an imperious 'Ei!' Pushpa had responded with a submissive 'Amma' … Aarthi ran her eyes over the two groups facing her. With one of them was Seeniamma … Face swollen. Bandaged head…

'You're the one who gave the petition?'

'Yes, 'nga,'

'What is the problem?'

Seeniamma told her the whole story – how she and Paandi had got married five years earlier and now had a two-year-old male child, that Paandi got a job as noon-meal supervisor at the childcare centre, that the cook there had retired and had been replaced by Prema with whom he developed a relationship, which had led to a lot of fights in the house … How she, Seeniamma, had gone to Prema's house five days ago and seen them both, and how when she came home, Paandi had beaten her up … How she had run to the police station and given in her complaint.

'Which one is her husband?'

Paandi stepped out a little from among the crowd, saying, 'It's me, 'nga.'

'You, is it?' Aarthi remarked indifferently. Then, raising her voice, she queried, 'Is it true – everything she is saying?'

'It's only words, Amma. Just a quarrel, nothing else,' he said meekly.

'"Only words?" Would a woman write and say she does not want her husband because of "only words"?'

'It was nothing 'nga!' protested Paandi. He sounded even more servile than before.

'See here, Amma!' cried Seeniamma. Handing over her child to Megavarnam, she raised her saree up to her thighs, laying bare the open wounds, the bruises, the still-swollen flesh. Then she showed her mangled right ear, turned to expose the welts on her back, revealed the cuts on the back of her head, and on her brow. By the time she had seen them all, one after the other, Aarthi's expression had changed.

Glaring fiercely at Paandi, she demanded, challenging him to contradict her, 'So! This is how you do it? You beat up a woman with "only words", do you?' Not daring a reply, he stood there with bowed head.

'Why just ask for separation? Say he demanded dowry and I'll send him straight to jail!' Aarthi told Seeniamma, and proceeded to rain abuses on Paandi. Angrier than ever, she roared, 'Fold your arms! Show respect, you rascal! Standing there as if you're a hero or something.' At once, Paandi crossed his arms abjectly over his chest, looking stricken to death. The sight of him standing there, quelled and spiritless, gave Sundaram and Seeniamma some satisfaction. 'Serves him right!' they thought. 'Let him just stand there with his arms crossed!'

'See, 'mma! He hit me and beat me enough to kill me! As if that's not all, he's now saying I am the one who did the wrong thing. And he has gone and got the whole village to come here!' Seeniamma cried.

'Why are you getting our village into this? It's all because you have no respect for our village that you have come here, isn't that it?' growled the panchayat president Sadayaandi.

'Is it the village that is giving me the food I eat?'

'Woman, only when you grow old will you know the value of the village!'

'Any village that won't feed a young woman – why will it feed her when she's grown old?'

'Too big mouth you've got – whole village knows that!'

'Yes, yes, it's all because of my very, very big mouth – and what about that mouth of yours? All the time wanting brandy!'

Outraged by the cut and thrust of her retorts, and this dig at his drinking habits, Sadayaandi bellowed, 'Talk with respect! If you had said this inside the village, something very, very different would have happened to you.'

Aarthi flared up. 'Is this your own house or what, for you to shout and make a noise and curse like this? Do all that on the road! Understand?'

Upon which Sadayaandi was joined by village councillor Murugan, ward member Lingam, and village headman Periasaami in protesting, 'How can that woman talk like that – insulting the whole village!'

'This is 2018! A woman being beaten like this, even now? Is this your village custom?' Aarthi demanded.

The villagers fell silent for a while. Then they began to talk amongst themselves in low voices – about how disgraceful it was for Seeniamma to have taken a family quarrel to the police station. There were more than twenty of them there with this opinion, and finally Aarthi had to hear them out.

Seeniamma knew exactly why the whole village had united against her. It was because she had not gone at once to the house of the village headman, or of the councillor.

She had not appealed to either of them to summon the village council, saying, 'My husband beat me. Ask them why he did it.' Nor, when she went to the women's police station to hand in her complaint, had she sought out the company and got the support of any of the important personages in the village. When she had set off this very evening, she hadn't called anyone, she hadn't cried out, 'Somebody please come with me!'

As soon as they found out that she had gone to the women's police station and handed in a complaint, people not only from the same street but from all over the village had descended on her, upbraiding her: 'A man will be a man! Little bit like this, little bit like that. It's just a quarrel between husband and wife – why take it to the station? Tomorrow you will have to live together, won't you?' One or two of the men declared, 'This kind of thing can't be allowed. This habit will spread to all the females in this town!'

No one said, 'What he did was wrong.' Not a single person confronted Paandi with the question, 'Why did you throw her down on the street and thrash her?' Or, 'Why did you take up with Prema?' This very thing had infuriated Seeniamma so much that she had stopped speaking to any of them, let alone ask them to come to the station with her. And she had forbidden Megavarnam and Sundaram to speak about it to anyone. Which was why they had also not approached anyone for support, or invited anyone to accompany them.

'How can you go off to the station without saying a word about it to any of us here in the village!' remonstrated the village councillor Sekhar. Seeniamma took no notice of him, she didn't even glance in his direction. And Aarthi snapped, 'If you people are going to ask whatever questions you want, why should I be present at all?'

'No, no, madam, you please ask, 'mma!' Sekhar pleaded, duly admonished.

Aarthi's interrogation began, surprisingly, with Megavarnam, who was holding Seeniamma's child. 'Who are you, 'nga?' she demanded, firing the first question.

'The girl's mother.'

'Your daughter has given a petition. Do you know that? What should be done?'

'Daily she is being beaten, day by day she is dying … We can't stand to see it!' Megavarnam said, between sobs. The child on her hip began to howl.

'And who are you, 'nga?' Aarthi's next query was to Sundaram.

'Her elder brother, 'mma.'

'Her own brother? Born to the same parents?'

'Yes, 'mma.'

'What do you think about all this?'

'She is a wife, she is the woman who has the right to live with him. But if she herself says she does not want him, what can I say, Amma? Only if she is the one who has done wrong can I ask her why.'

Aarthi addressed the crowd standing with Paandi: 'What about the people of the village? What do they think about this?' Some three or four began to speak all at once.

'Talk one at a time!' she exclaimed, driven to exasperation. Spotting an elderly man among them, she called out, 'You, 'nga! Please speak.'

It was the village headman. 'That girl has tried to hang herself two or three times, 'nga.'

'So?'

'She is a hot-tempered girl, 'nga. If he gets angry and gives her a tap or two, she might drink poison or something. Life will be in danger.'

'So, what's to be done about that?'

'Even if each of them lives alone, at least there will be no danger to life. So let us separate them, 'nga. Later, if they feel the need, they can come together,' said the headman. He brought his hands together in a pleading kumbidu, which clearly meant: 'Madam, you simply must help us to settle this matter!'

Just then, Aarthi's cell phone rang. Glancing at it, she called out to Pushpa, 'It's our Thamizharasi. Find out why she's calling,' she ordered, and turned to Seeniamma. 'So, what do you say?'

'You yourself saw how he has beaten me. At the back of my head they put seven stitches. Five days ago if you had seen me, you yourself would know what big cuts I got.' Tears came in a gush, even as she spoke. Seeing her crying, the child on Megavarnam's hip wailed and sprang towards her. Seeniamma took him in her arms.

'Never mind all that! Do you understand?' Aarthi demanded. But Seeniamma did not answer, all she did was weep even more.

'"Somehow or other I got angry and came to the station, from now on I won't do such a thing, please unite me with my husband!" – isn't that what you should be asking? Instead, here you are, standing and talking like the opposition party in the legislature! Don't you need a man who can be called a husband – at least in name?' It was Chellamuthu, a member of the local ward. Though hearing him offer his view of the matter drove her to fury, Seeniamma managed to speak in a level tone:

'I was not born with a husband.'

'Your mouth is really too, too big,' pronounced Chellamuthu.

'But *my* mouth is with *me* only, isn't it? Is it with *you*, for *you* to control?'

'It's no good talking to you! A good family woman would never have come to the police station, no?' Chellamuthu said accusingly.

'I'm a bad woman. No morals! That's why I am standing here, in the police station. Your wife is an oh-so-great chaste lady! That's why she is at home!' Seeniamma was saying, when Paandi broke in. 'Look, 'mma! Even before you she is showing no respect! See how she is talking, 'nga!'

'Chhee! Shut up! How you've beaten her!' exclaimed Aarthi, outraged. 'Just for that you should be put in jail! It's only because of your work at the noon-meal centre that I'm thinking what to do. Otherwise, I would have booked a case against you right now! On a charge of dowry demand and assault, you rascal! You marry a woman and make her have a child, and then you join up with another woman? Beat your own wife enough to kill her, will you?' she said threateningly, and went on to taunt: 'That fancy woman of yours – where is she? Hasn't she come?'

Paandi and his entire cohort of supporters stood there, heads bent.

'That woman!' Aarthi gnashed her teeth. 'Should book a case against her, first of all…' She turned to Seeniamma. 'Do you want to live with him? Or do you want to separate?'

'Ask *him*, 'nga,' came Seeniamma's answer.

She was using the respectful second-person plural…

'What! After getting such a beating from him, you are still saying "avar"! Such respect you give him, even now?' Aarthi gave a bitter laugh. Guffaws broke out among Paandi's men.

'Have you ever come to the station before today? Or complained in public to the village panchayat?' she queried sternly, continuing her interrogation.

'No, I never do that sort of thing, 'nga! It's not a habit or anything. This is the first time … my *pust*!' Seeniamma avowed, using the English word for added emphasis.

That made Aarthi look fixedly at her, though it was hard to tell what she had in mind.

'What is your final decision? Say it,' she said finally.

'Ask *him*,' repeated Seeniamma. Again, that respectful pronoun…

'Go to him, then. Try one more time. If it's still not okay, come straight to me. I'll put him in jail.'

'First tell him to leave that woman.'

'Ei!' Aarthi called out contemptuously to Paandi. 'What do you say to that?'

He stood there like one who has no mouth, no tongue to speak with.

'Are you going to drop her or not?'

'There is nothing between me and her, 'nga! Just sometimes talking, that's all. Both are working in the same place,' declared Paandi. 'How can I leave a good job like this one, and go off somewhere else?'

Immediately Seeniamma lowered the child perched on her hip, and laid him on the floor at Paandi's feet.

'This is your child, isn't it? Step over him now and say, "There is nothing between her and me!" Swear to it, if it's the truth. Let's see!'

Paandi did not swear to it. Instead, he scowled fiercely at her, as though he would burn her up, if he only could. He bent down and was just about to pick up the baby, who was screaming shrilly at being deposited there on the floor, when Seeniamma slapped away his hand. 'Chhee! Don't touch my baby!' she spat out.

'Why don't you swear to it? It's all you have to do, no?' Aarthi prodded him, as he kept standing there, head hanging. Between clenched teeth, Seeniamma hissed, 'This bull's a brute – he won't change.'

'Get to the point! No time to waste,' Aarthi looked at her wristwatch, her eyes narrowing at what it showed.

'See if he'll say he wants me and doesn't want her, 'nga!' Seeniamma dared. Paandi said nothing at all. Nor did he so much as glance towards her.

'If I had gone to some man and come back, the way *he's* gone to another woman and thinks *he* can come back, would *he* or would *he* not have set me on fire and burnt me up? Ask *him* that!' she shrieked. Again, that pronoun – used, now, with unmistakable contempt.

'Isn't she asking you? Answer her!' Aarthi commanded. But there Paandi still stood, with his head slung low on his neck and his mouth shut. He didn't look at Aarthi.

'Here you are, 'nga, asking him questions, but is he opening his mouth? See, 'mma, how that woman has got him hooked with her medicine…' Seeniamma exclaimed.

And then she came out with a cry: '… Set me free, 'mma! I will say he died! I will cook rice for his death feast and feed it to the crows tomorrow. A sacrificial offering, for this heavy curse on my head that I have just got to pay back. I'll push it off and go dunk myself in the river, head first! Then I'll be clean at last.'

'How she talks, right in front of you, Amma! How can I live with such a woman and join up with her?'

Paandi's plea did not produce a reply from Aarthi – it was Seeniamma who snarled: 'What! Join with me? That brand-new one you've caught, that Goldie ... Go join with her.'

The respectful pronoun was gone at last.

Again, Paandi was silent. All he could do was gnash his teeth and fling another burning look at her.

'Does your wife have a bad character?' Aarthi continued with her investigation.

'No...'

'Before marriage, or after marriage – did she do any bad thing?'

'Nothing like that.'

'Would she do something like that in the future?'

'No, she won't.'

'Then why do you want to separate from her?'

'She shamed me in front of the whole town. Now here in the police station also she is throwing dirt on me. She is an arrogant woman!'

'You are going around with that cook-woman – isn't that shameful and dirty?'

His mouth stayed shut.

'Is your wife a mean and nasty person? Does she waste your money?'

'... I can't say she does all that.'

'She listens to the talk in the town and does this drama. And as for you, you round up the whole town and bring it here.'

'Let her cut loose and go! But she has to give me my so–' Hardly had he finished than Seeniamma cut in: '*That* is not going to happen.' There was no mistaking her firm tone.

'I will give back the four gold sovereigns, and all the dowry items…'

'You don't want me – right? So then I don't want any of those things.' With those few words, Seeniamma cut the talk short.

Megavarnam turned on Seeniamma. 'You don't want him, you are leaving him, no? Then why leave our valuables to him – what for? For him to eat?'

'Just keep quiet, Amma!' Seeniamma shut her up.

Exasperated by the exchange of words, Aarthi cut it short. 'Just talk about the main issue. Are you going to take her back or let her go?'

'When she has made me come to the police station and stand here, arms crossed like this, how can I take her back? Will anybody in town have any respect for me?' Paandi demanded, his voice gathering force.

'So you can't take me back – isn't that so?' Seeniamma repeated, her wrath boiling over.

'Right!' said Paandi determinedly. It drove Seeniamma to a level of vehemence that seemed to come from some unseen source.

'Since I am not there, how can the child be there for you?'

'The child is mine, no?'

'Did you give birth to him? Did you give him milk? Did you wash off the shit and piss from his clothes?' Seeniamma yelled out, forgetting entirely that she was in a police station. Immediately Aarthi turned on her. 'Could you, all by yourself, produce a child?'

'No!' Seeniamma shook her head.

'The child must be given to me,' declared Paandi.

'That will never happen!' Seeniamma announced boldly, without the least hesitation.

'Why not?'

'If I say it won't happen, it won't happen. You can do what you like!' Her answer came like a knife-slash that had found its mark.

'Stay together, or separate – that's another matter. But doesn't he have a right over the child?' asked Aarthi.

'When he has said he does not want me, then why does he want the child? Only the child? What for?' Seeniamma was not about to give up.

Back and forth between Seeni and Aarthi and Paandi, Seeni and Aarthi and Paandi, went the same questions, the same answers-as-questions … Once again, Paandi reiterated his position:

'She has given a petition in the police station and dirtied my name in the whole town. From now on, even if it means I won't live, I will not live with her. I don't want her, I want only my child.'

'After saying you don't want me, how will the child go to you?'

'So you won't give me the child? Is that it?'

'I won't.'

'Why?' he asked again. And this time, her answer rang out like a stunning slap across the faces of all those present – from Paandi to Sundaram to Thavamani to all the rest.

'The child is not yours.'

All of them stared at Seeniamma in a state of shock.

'What a terrible thing you have done now, di!' shrieked Megavarnam. Right across the cheek she smacked Seeniamma, who turned her face not away, but towards her striking arm … Defiantly, as though to say, 'Go on, hit me hard!'

Not one tear fell from her eyes. It was as though she had gone numb all over, as she stood there like a solid block of wood, without even wincing as Megavarnam slapped her again and yet again, and finally struck herself, on her own face and screamed, 'She said she was going to shame him! But it's my whole family that she has shamed!'

An angry squeal came from the child she carried on her hip. Grimacing in utter disgust and hating to remain there any longer, Sundaram turned and walked out.

Tearfully, Thavamani quavered, 'What have you gone and done, dear?'

'Do you really mean what you're saying?' Aarthi enquired.

Unperturbed, and without any trace of the fury she had exhibited earlier, Seeniamma calmly responded: 'Would anybody lie about a thing like this?'

Everyone present, including Paandi, looked devastated. What he and those with him wanted terribly was to beat Seeniamma to death right then and there, and they had to control themselves because, after all, it was a police station. Paandi felt as though he were standing on smouldering embers. Bawling, 'You have brought dishonour on our entire lineage, di!' Megavarnam hit Seeniamma once again on the cheek.

Distraught and quivering from head to foot, perspiring profusely, Paandi strove to quell his fury as he asked Seeniamma straight out, 'Didn't you have this child because of sleeping with me?' It came out as a stammer.

Not hesitating in the least, and utterly unafraid, she came out with her reply, and it was clear: 'No.'

'Are you saying I'm not a man? That I can't…' Paandi stuttered.

'*That* I don't know!'

'Then, if the child wasn't mine, whom did you sleep with, to have it?'

'No need for you to know all that.'

'Then that means you roamed around the town and got this child somehow, isn't that it?'

'Yes.'

'If that is true, then you keep the child yourself.'

'Why would I hand over a child who isn't born to you, anyway?' Seeniamma's tart reply was followed by a blow across her lips, delivered by her sister-in-law, who hissed, 'Just because you have a mouth, will you dare to say whatever you feel like?'

'Give her two more slaps, di!' Megavarnam urged Thavamani. And then she went up to Paandi and tried to thrust the baby into his arms, saying, 'This is your child! Take him!'

He turned away. Catching hold of his arm, Megavarnam tried to make him take the wailing child, who was straining to reach Paandi's reluctant arms. Drained of all spirit, and trying his best not to look at the baby, he muttered roughly to Seeniamma, 'Give me the taali I tied on you.'

'I will not!' Seeniamma said with finality.

'When you have already said you didn't get pregnant with this baby by sleeping with me, that taali I tied should not remain on your neck.'

'...'

There was a pause. A silence...

And then he continued, 'You said I'm not even a man? You said I can't...? After what you said, that taali doesn't belong on your neck.'

'She's a dirty-filthy rag full of dung! And you are very, very close to her, no? So then, go! Be with her! From now on, you will never see me or my child, I swear it! On God, I swear it.'

'You have to give me that taali I tied!' Paandi said again and again, but his angry remonstrances only stiffened her resolve.

'It was tied in a temple. I will untie it in a temple and give it back to you. The whole town will know if I am a pure woman or a prostitute when my corpse is taken to the burning ground. For five years you were a god I carried in my heart. But when you wanted another woman and went to her, that very moment you turned into a stone – a chip of stone that's used to wipe off shit from the arse. Who cares about you now?'

There was nothing uncertain in her manner, and no confusion in her speech. She was very clear. And she was calm. She was not perspiring, her limbs did not quiver, her eyes were not blurred with tears. It looked like she had finished what she had to say. A great feeling of relief had come over her, now that she had lifted from her head the heavy load that had been thrust upon her. She had set it down, at last. She could stand up straight.

It was Paandi who could hardly stand, who could not speak, who couldn't look anyone in the eye. His expression was that of one who had lost his all in a gamble. 'Why are you talking to that wretched woman?' Sekhar urged him. 'She calls you a useless fellow, she says you're not a man at all, so why do you want her taali? Get along, tear yourself loose! Come on!' But two or three men moved menacingly towards Seeniamma, demanding her taali. They looked ready to strike her dead, but she stood her ground like a carven statue. She said nothing to them, she didn't even look at them.

'She's made weak females of us all, da, your wife!' bewailed Paandi's kinsman Jayabaal. He turned abruptly and hurried out.

Having heard Seeniamma and Paandi out, Aarthi sat there, ready to close the matter. 'So! You have both finished everything right here, isn't it? Or do you want to go to court?' Paandi himself had nothing to say, but all those with him affirmed, as though in one voice, 'We will finish it right here! Right now!'

'Shall we wait for one more week?'

'No, 'mma!' they chorused again in unison.

'Then both of you get it written down that you want to separate, and bring it here,' instructed Aarthi, sending out Paandi and his group.

She was quiet for a while. Then she looked at Seeniamma and said, 'You also go and write it and bring it here.' As though something had just occurred to her, she suddenly asked Seeniamma, 'Why did you say that?'

'"Whore" – that is my title now. I have given it to myself, I know. It won't go away till I die. My boy will be known hereafter as the child of a whore … Not only did he go to another woman, but didn't he get the whole town to come and watch the fun while he beat me on the open street till he had squeezed the shit and piss out of me? That very day I lost my dignity, didn't I? So let him lose *his* dignity now! That deadweight on my head is gone. From now on, who cares? He can marry whoever he wants, as many women as he wants. Even if he has children, will the town ever believe that they are his children? Let him walk with bowed head till the day he dies! Now let me see how he dares to wear a vaitti and tries to walk on the street like a man…' She paused.

Then she said, quietly. 'Let him die. That's why I said it.' And she walked quickly out of the police station.

One of Ours

THAT HE WOULD LAND UP on a motorbike at the house in a wilderness of cashew trees, far from the town, was something nobody expected of RKS.

Not since 1989, when he first became a minister, had he ever ridden on a motorbike – nor in any car which wasn't air-conditioned. Not only while he was a minister for two terms, but even during that time when he was just a member of the state legislative assembly, he always saw to it that there were at least four or five cars in his cavalcade as he arrived – whether it was a party function, or a wedding he was attending. Nowhere did he ever travel without getting local and city officials to send three or four cars for him.

Whether he belonged to the ruling party or to the opposition, he always made it clear that he was the one who counted in his district. He saw to it that his prestige and his reach remained undiminished. Whenever a party member came to see him, he never asked him to sit down. That was not only when he was actually a minister or an MLA, but even when he held no office at all. A full five minutes would go by before he addressed the person with the question: 'Why are you standing?' Even then, he would never actually say, 'Sit down.' He would also have seen to it that there was no chair next to his. An ordinary party worker would have to keep standing for a half hour, or even a whole hour, in order to speak with him. It was only VIPs and officials to whom a seat was offered. Nobody else sat down in front of him – Big Brother. He was the Party's king in Koodalur.

'Annei![1] You're the raja in our district!'

That's what they all told him, to his face, and every time they said it, he would just smile. From the very day that RKS became the district chief, the Party had been whatever he decided to make of it. Only the men whom he approved of got any party posts. For twenty-eight years, as the party chief of the district, it was he who selected the municipal and panchayat union secretaries.

At every party event, his arrival was greeted by posters: 'Welcome, District Party Chief!' and even 'District Party, Welcome!' equating his person with the Party itself. R.K. Selvam – that was his real name. But you never saw it in print, or on any party poster. 'Minister' – that's what everyone had called him – partymen and others alike – from that very day in 1989 when he had first become one. And that was how he was known even afterwards, when

1 Annei: Anna – elder brother.

he stopped being a minister. When he was no longer even an MLA.

For such a personage to turn up on a motorbike – who would have believed it?

Shocked at the sight of RKS alighting from a motorbike, some people who stood chatting on the terrace hurried downstairs. RKS's assistant Murugan also came running. Like a wallop across their faces came RKS's roar, as he glowered at those who had come to see him: 'Why are you all coming here? Go back up!' Which sent them all scurrying back up. Only Murugan stayed back.

RKS looked at the line of motorbikes parked in front of the house. There was not a single car among them. He looked up at the three tube lights in the veranda, then at the multitude watching him from the terrace. Some folded their hands in greeting. Incensed at the sight, RKS turned to Murugan, saying, 'Tell those standing up there to sit down. And why so many lights?'

'Please sit down. Nobody should stand!' Murugan called out to those who stood on the terrace gazing down at RKS. 'One light is enough. Switch off two.' Those on their feet sat down, and two of the tube lights were turned off – instantly. Because when Murugan told them to do anything, it was as though it were RKS himself giving the order.

RKS's glance swept over the surroundings. Everywhere he looked, there was darkness. Behind the house and on either side was a thick growth of cashew trees. That anyone would build such a big house in this jungle a whole two kilometres away from the town seemed strange to him.

'Has everyone arrived?' he said finally.

'Already at eight o'clock they have all come.'

'How many are there?'

'Only the people on the list you gave,' Murugan replied, lowering his voice. Dhanapal, who had driven RKS there on his motorbike, said, 'Let's go inside, Annei – it's better. You should not be standing outside.' As though okaying the suggestion, RKS stepped inside the house. Murugan and Dhanapal hurried ahead and held open a door into a small room. There was just one chair inside. Having seated himself, RKS told Dhanapal, 'Switch off the light outside.' Dhanapal immediately went out, and as soon as his back was turned, Murugan shut the door. He also turned up the speed of the ceiling fan.

'Who are all the important ones among those who have come?'

'Must be around ten from our party. Could be ten or twenty from the Central People's Party, and about thirty from the other parties. Then there are the others – the ones from the government staff union, teachers' union, construction workers' union. And the fan clubs have sent their people, too, Annei.'

'How many from the women's self-help group?'

'Twelve.'

'How much are we giving each?'

'If it's an ordinary person, five thousand. If they're in charge of the district branch or the block, it must be twenty, as you told us, 'nga.[2] All put into covers.'

'How many have come from the fan club?'

'Seven groups have come, 'nga. Looks like they will ask for fifty thousand.'

'Any suspicious-looking fellow?'

'All of them are ours. Whoever has come is one of ours. Each and every one of them is loyal to you.'

'This matter … it must not be known outside.'

'Right, Annei.'

'The fellows who are going to stand for election – I asked them to pay for expenses. Have any of them shown up?'

'Six out of those eight have come and given something, 'nga. Two of them said they will come – that's all.'

'The fellows who came – how much did they bring?'

'Ten L,[3] Annei.'

'The two who didn't come – who are they?'

'Sivabalan and Dhandapani.'

'Liars! Get those dogs on the phone and tell them to come. They're our own-caste dogs only, but both are district bosses. So they will do such a big drama.'

---

2 'nga: A short form of the second person plural pronoun, expressive of respect.

3 L: Colloquial short form for 'lakh' (one hundred thousand).

To these remarks of RKS, Murugan offered no answer. He just stood there, looking meek.

'When this gets over, come straight back to the House. Tomorrow night you have to go from door to door in our constituency, delivering a thousand for each vote,' instructed RKS. 'Now let's go upstairs.' At once, Murugan opened the door and hastened ahead up the stairs, before RKS began to heave his massive body up behind him.

As he reached the top of the stairs, all those seated on a jamukaalam[4] spread on the floor sprang up at once and brought their palms reverently together. In a marked departure from his usual practice, RKS said, 'Sit down, please!' when he saw them all standing and saluting him.

'Annei, you sit down first, 'nga!' cried the crowd, upon which he sat on the chair kept ready for him. It was only then, and with hesitation, that those assembled seated themselves. Kumar, who was the only one among them who had not sat down, raised a shout: 'Long live our District Party Chief!'

'Long live!' came the seated multitude's instant response. It enraged RKS. Glaring at Kumar, he demanded, 'You're Kumaran from Nandimangalam, no? What are you doing here? Sit down, you dog!'

---

4 Jamukaalam: Large handwoven cotton mat, usually brightly coloured, often used to seat the general audience at public events.

The slogan-raiser sank down shamed, hanging his head. Quelled by this display of RKS's anger, the crowd fell silent. RKS ran his eyes over every face in the crowd that sat before him, doing a spot check to separate the ones he could fully trust among all those present, from others who could only be trusted to some extent, and from those who could not be trusted at all.

Eager to be included in RKS's gaze, the entire crowd kept thrusting their faces forward to register their presence. In all those seated there, there was not one who deserved to be doubted. All of them were his loyalists, all had come to their present posts only because of him, and each one had gained something from him. It was only after he had scanned all those faces that there was a visible slackening of the tension that had gripped his own face.

Before RKS sat nine rows of people. To the left, along the wall, were the women's self-help group members. Those in the last row were in dimmer light. They were not at all sure that RKS could see their faces. Old Ganapati, who was third in the row, suddenly got up. 'Vanakkam,[5] 'nga!' he cried out, raising both his arms straight above his head and bringing his palms together, like a worshipper at the feet of the Supreme.

'Oh, it's you, huh?' remarked RKS contemptuously, nodding a haughty okay to him to sit down. When the old

---

5 Vanakkam: A term of respectful greeting, meaning a bow, the same as the namaste or the namaskaar of North India.

man had seated himself, Muthusaami, the man who sat next to him, sprang up and threw himself down at RKS's feet, prostrating with folded hands as though before an image of God. RKS smiled faintly, without actually telling him to rise. That he had looked at him and smiled at him was enough to make Muthusaami feel very happy indeed. He sprang up and went back to his place.

After Muthusaami, three or four people rose and did exactly the same thing. As a result, every one of those who had stayed seated so far now got up to fall at the big man's feet. When some were paying obeisance and others did not, for anyone to be counted among the defaulters clearly meant trouble.

But then, RKS shouted, 'Why are you all standing up? All this can be for later.' Afraid that he was going to get angry again, they stood there uncertainly, not knowing if they should brave it and offer a kumbidu[6] at his feet or sit down obediently. 'Sit down!' he ordered in a growl, and it was only then that they went back and sat down in their places, crestfallen that they had not been able to deposit their prayerful gestures at RKS's feet.

All except for Mathiazhagan. Defying the big man's orders, he pushed forward and flung himself at his feet. 'I know you, da!' remarked RKS with a chuckle. 'Don't put

---

6 Kumbidu: Hands folded in respectful greeting – a namaskaar often accompanied by a partial or a whole prostration.

on a drama!' Taking it as a great honour to be scolded thus, Mathiazhagan strode proudly back to his seat.

RKS narrowly observed the people seated before him. Then he eyed the two men standing behind him, like two policemen on security duty, with their hands folded across their chests – Murugan and Dhanapal. Since they said nothing, he decided to come out with it himself.

'Do you know why you have been called here?' he asked the people seated before him.

'Don't know, 'nga,' came the answer from the ones in the first row.

'Didn't Murugan tell you anything?'

'No, 'nga!' shouted the entire assemblage.

Gazing solemnly at the multitude and speaking very slowly, he asked: 'This time, should I become Minister, or should I not?'

Electrified, the crowd shrieked, 'What are you saying, 'nga? Why are you asking like this?'

From the first seat of the second row, Suresh, the chief of the Youth Wing in the Nadunaattu Makkal Katchi,[7] bounced up and announced, 'You are going to become

---

7 Nadunaattu Makkal Katchi (Midland People's Party): The author's take on a well-known but not overtly designated political configuration of middle-level castes in Tamil Nadu. Some have a martial background, others have a sizeable base in agriculture, industry and trade. In political life, these middle castes have replaced the first high-caste, non-Brahmin leaders in the Dravida movement.

Minister! That is certain! We will give our lives for you to become Minister, Annei.'

'Don't need your life, don't need your ****! Just do what you're told, that's enough.'

That he had used that particular epithet did not worry Suresh. Everyone in the district knew that of any ten words spoken by RKS, at least two of them would be that one. Everyone in the district knew it, and nobody ever got upset with him about it. Suresh, too, was not offended by it. Because all you had to say to RKS was, 'I'm one of yours, saar!' or, 'He is one of ours, 'nga,' as you introduced a would-be loyalist to him, and the task that the man wanted done would be accomplished. When he swore at anyone, it meant that he had done that person many favours. As a consequence, the district party workers and others never took his curses amiss. This matter was known to the Party High Command. Since he belonged to the majority caste in the district, the leadership did not take action against him.

'For so many years, ever since you first became Minister, we have been listening only to whatever you say. Even when ours is another party, have we ever gone against your orders?' Suresh declared in a resounding voice. Which made RKS flare up:

'Why are you shouting? Is this a wedding celebration going on here or something? Don't you have any sense?'

Not only Suresh, but the whole crowd calmed down after that. Invariably, during RKS's years as Minister, no one – neither his own partymen nor anybody else – dared to stand close to him and speak to him. One stood at a distance of two to three yards from him and kept one's mouth all but shut, even one who was actually speaking to him. And one could not raise one's voice. If one dared to do that, some very bad words would emerge from his lips, and it was out of fear that this might happen that many stood six or eight feet away during a conversation with him. It was a small gathering, convened by him alone, and Suresh was a caste fellow, although he belonged to another party.

Which emboldened him to speak as he had. If that were not the case, he would not have spoken at all.

Drawn by the bright tube light, a small beetle fluttered down and sat on RKS. Slapping it away, he addressed the crowd. 'What is the situation in the constituency?'

'What problem will be there for you, Annei? You'll get a margin of victory of thirty to forty thousand votes and become Minister, Annei!' declared Gopi, from the third row. He was the head of the Tamil Hero Fan Club.

'I was not asking about my constituency. I'm asking about your constituency!' came RKS's retort, like a smack on the face. For a moment, Gopi looked crushed, and then he rallied, declaring, 'Your party is going to win in our constituency also, 'nga. We will all work hard and make you win, Annei!' RKS gave him an even closer stare than he had done before. What could be the reason for such a look, thought Gopi confusedly. Maybe RKS was displeased because he had not crossed his arms over his chest in the dutiful attitude proper to one such as himself, he decided, and at once crossed his arms.

With the intention of pleasing RKS and gaining his approval, the union secretary Dravida-Mani rose to make an announcement: 'We'll win in our constituency and show you, Annei!'

A strange change came over RKS's face, as he challenged, 'So! You're going to work very, very hard, is it? All for *me* to win?'

'I didn't say anything bad! So why is he so angry?' thought Dravida-Mani, bewildered. There he stood, without uttering a word – he, whose very name meant 'Jewel among Dravidians'. Not daring to move – until RKS brusquely gestured to him to sit.

Having glanced contemptuously at Gopi and Dravida-Mani, RKS addressed the assemblage once more: 'Do you know why I told you all to come?' he demanded. To say 'Yes!' would be to invite a further question: 'How do you know?' To say 'No!' might make him shout an even trickier question at them: 'When you don't even know why I told you to come, why did you come? What for are you sitting here?'

They all sat there with their mouths shut ... In everyone's mind were the same questions. First of all, with elections around the corner, why had he called only those who belonged to the Kadambur constituency instead of summoning people from his own constituency? And that, too, only some of them, as though he had carefully handpicked them?

And why had he got them to come all the way to this house in the middle of the jungle, secretly, at ten o'clock in the night? But when that question had been put to Murugan earlier, he had given just one answer: 'Minister says you must come. I don't know what it's about.' Not one of them knew why RKS might have instructed him to make an appearance. What was certain was that he would fly into a temper and abuse them if asked for a reason. And so, there they all sat – every man present, and every woman in the self-help group as well. It was as though none of them possessed such a thing as a mouth.

There were Gopi and Dravida-Mani, still on their feet. Pointedly ignoring them, he spoke to the crowd: 'The two terms that I was Minister – did I or did I not do whatever you all wanted?'

'Yes, Annei! You asked us what we wanted, and you did what we asked. And even when we didn't ask, you did what we wanted, Annei.'

'If you hadn't come to power as Minister, our people wouldn't have been able to show their faces in this district. Even though we were in our own caste party, not one day did you ever set us aside or let us down. Never have you refused to do what we wanted done for us. We're more beholden to you than we are to our own party!' declared Suresh. RKS's response was a dismissive nod – as if to say, 'I know all that!'

Anxious that Suresh alone would make a name for himself by praising Minister to his face, Dravida-Mani said, as humbly as he could: 'Minister only has to say what we must do. No need for Minister to say what he is thinking! No need to even point his finger. One look is enough – we will do it, Annei! With an abrupt motion of the hand, RKS made Dravida-Mani sink to the floor without uttering another word. 'We're your loyal followers, Annei!' Suresh declared.

'This loyalty of yours – show it in your work. Not with that mouth of yours,' admonished RKS, waving him down, and continuing: 'Should I become Minister? Or should I not?'

Shouts erupted from the emotionally charged crowd: 'Annei! What is this! Same thing you are going on asking, ever since we came here! If you don't become Minister, which dog will dare to take your place?'

'So, all of you feel that I should become Minister?'

'Yes, Annei!' they screamed.

Manjula, of the women's self-help group, got up, folded her hands with utmost respect, and declared, 'As long as you live, for us in this district, you will be Minister, 'nga!' At that, he gave her a look and a smile, from which Manjula understood that she was permitted to sit down again.

The crowd sat quiet, as he eyed them sternly. Then, his voice taking on a harsh rasp, he warned: 'If any fellow doesn't do just as I say, he can never again come and look me in the face!' Unnerved and perplexed, they wondered why he spoke thus, as though holding some kind of dire penalty over their heads. What was he going to demand of them, what sort of mess was he getting them into? They couldn't ask him directly, it would only infuriate him, everyone knew that. And so, not one single person rose to ask, 'What do you mean?'

For a long while, RKS kept staring at the crowd without speaking a word. It seemed as though he was about to say something but was as yet undecided about how to put it to them. At last, apparently having come to a decision, he gave a command: 'For me to become Minister, our Party must not win in Kadambur. Your constituency.'

What was he saying? And why was he saying it? Those in the crowd did not at once grasp his meaning, and many were utterly dumbfounded. Did he really mean what he was saying? Or was he testing them in some way? One or two thought that maybe they should get up and ask, 'Would you please repeat what you just said?' But he would get furious and yell if they were so presumptuous as to make such a request. So they just sat there speechless, not asking him anything.

For a while, RKS watchfully took in the crowd's silence. Then he spoke in a deliberate and measured tone: 'That one is a senior in the Party. Three times he has been defeated. This time if he wins, he might get a ministerial berth. If he wins and becomes a minister, there'll be two Ministers from this district.' And he fell silent. Those sitting there finally understood what RKS had just told them.

Now he spoke again, 'For me to be Minister in this district – and also for *him* to be Minister? He'll dare go around in a car with a wailing siren, will he? How can *he* be a Minister! He should not be, he just can't do it! That I am sure of. That is why he lost three times. But by caste he's not one of ours, he's one of *them*. Because he's low caste, he may win the election this time. And just because the fellow tried three times before and got defeated, if he wins this time, the Chief might reward him with some ministerial post or other. Out of pity! Then what's to be done about it?' He gave them all a look, as though to say, 'You make up your minds now about what's to be done.'

'You are Minister forever in this district! Only you! No other fellow can come. You don't worry, 'nga. We will take care of it right at the booths!' The speaker was Kumaresan – the chief of the district's construction workers' union.

Up rose Dravida-Mani, at once. 'For fifty years in this district, only our men have become Ministers. Whichever party comes to power, it is only our men who can become Ministers in this district. Nobody else can be made a minister. Because you are one of *ours*, that's why *you* are Minister! You only! That's the truth, we swear it!' He swore to it by placing the palm of his hand on the crown of his head. At that, Suresh stood up and added, 'Your name is not just any name, Annei. You are *one of ours*! A treasure for the whole community – our Selvam!' Everybody sitting there clapped loudly. It was only when the clapping ceased that Suresh sat down.

'This matter that I have just told you, have you understood it?' RKS's question was to all of them. In one voice came the crowd's response: 'We understand, Annei! No need now for you to say any more! We'll take care of everything.'

Rajendran in the fifth row stood up. He spoke with intense feeling: 'If you had just told us to do this on the phone, it would have been enough! We would have done it. Just for this, should you leave your important election work and come all the way like this?' Then, raising his voice, he boomed, 'If anyone in this whole district dares to disobey our Minister, that fellow won't be able to show his face any more – because he will not have a head any more!' When they began to clap again, RKS's upraised arm signalled: 'Enough! Sit down!'

They stopped, Rajendran sat down, and now Ananthan, the Nadunaattu Makkal Katchi's district head, ventured to rise. 'So! You are going to give a speech?' RKS asked, smiling broadly. Forgetting whatever he wanted to say, Ananthan timidly stayed on his feet.

'I got your wife a teacher's job – in the noon-meal scheme[8] – remember?'

---

8 Noon-meal scheme: The well-known welfare measure to address malnutrition in growing children, the Saththunavu Thittam, a free midday meal programme for children in government run and aided schools, was begun in the 1980s under the chief ministership of M.G. Ramachandran. Those employed under it, though not teachers, enjoyed a certain prestige thanks to the fact that they worked in schools, in addition to being government employees. Noon-meal staff

Thrown into a tizzy by RKS's query, Ananthan quavered, 'What, Annei! What is this you are asking, 'nga? It was you only who changed the government order that had given the job to your own party union secretary's wife, and you gave that job to my wife. And you didn't even take one paisa for it! We will never, never forget it!' he cried out, close to tears.

'Don't do anything just because I did something for you while I was Minister. I'm one of yours, who's speaking here. Your own caste man. Do it just for that, all of you.' A thrill went through the crowd at these words of RKS.

The first man in the fifth row, Ezhumalai, now rose. Respectfully he said, 'Minister does not have to speak so much. You have told us the matter. We will finish the job. If you don't believe us, we will swear to it!' Three or four women stood up and started to call out their oaths. The mass spectacle of oath-taking commenced, and came to a halt only when he finally thundered, 'All of you sit down. Would I have asked you to come if I didn't believe in you?'

Peering at Ezhumalai, RKS demanded, 'Have you been drinking?'

'No, 'nga!'

'Then why is your mouth so wide open?' Grinning abashedly, Ezhumalai sat down.

---

jobs provided an avenue of patronage and influence for local politicians. Many states have subsequently adopted the scheme.

'If I become Minister, it is like all of you have become Minister!' RKS announced. Immediately, several in the crowd shouted, 'We'll go now, tonight! … Yes, just now we'll go and talk to all our own people in the constituency … Let's finish the job now, tonight!' And Manjula shrilled: 'I'll talk to all the women in the self-help group in the constituency and get it done.'

'Doing what I am telling you doesn't mean you have done me a service. Not talking about it outside is the real service,' RKS told them solemnly.

'Please don't say such big-big things, like service and all, 'nga!' protested some in the crowd.

'In this 2016 election if he wins, he will be a big enemy for our people. After that, it will not be easy to get rid of him,' he warned.

'He must not become Minister, 'nga!' they shouted.

'What you have done for our people the whole world knows, Annei. Same caste-blood that's flowing in your body is running in our bodies also! From nine parties we have come here, all of us. What for? Because Minister said, "Come!" That one word was enough. Whatever Minister wants will happen. We will make that very thing happen!' A burst of applause greeted these words of Kannadhaasan, who spoke up in the fourth row. Well satisfied that he had said what he wanted to say, Kannadhaasan sat down again.

'If the Party leadership gets to know of this, I'll be barred. They'll shame me, put me out of circulation. Finished! So watch how you do it,' RKS said calmly, measuring every word, even as he rose from his chair. 'I am leaving now. People from my constituency are waiting for me at my house. Only four days are left for the polling. Then, six days for counting the votes. So, that's ten days in all. Then I'll become Minister. Whoever wants anything, just come and I will do it. If I say it, I will do it – all of you know that,' he finished, faced the assemblage and brought his palms together in a kumbidu.

At once, the entire crowd rose and did the same to him.

'Whatever the other constituencies do, as far as your constituency goes, whatever party our people may belong to, they will vote only for you, Annei – the whole lot of them,' Suresh said loudly. Then, moving closer to RKS and lowering his voice, he made a humble suggestion: 'About all this – if you also drop a word to our Leader, it will be good, Annei.'

'Already last week itself I have spoken to him, and he told me, "You will win and become Minister. My first blessing is only for you!" That's how he has blessed me,' RKS informed him, and then he went on, 'As far as the Leader is concerned, he is always with me. If you are also with me, well and good…' His tone was grim.

Turning once again to the crowd, he announced: 'The other seven people standing for election in the district are all newcomers. They won't create any problems. It's only *that* one who'll bring trouble. So, be careful what you do.' Once again, he saluted them with a kumbidu. He took a few steps forward, and then halted, saying,

'I am leaving now. Murugan will tell you the details. After I leave, he'll take care of you all.' He began to descend the stairs. Along with him went Murugan, Dhanapal, and a group of about twenty more. Soon, Dhanapal turned back to inform Manjula that RKS had summoned her. Those upstairs began to slink down the stairs, one by one, instead of waiting for Murugan's return as RKS had directed them to do.

In the last row stood Murugesan and Aasaithambi, uncertain if they should wait for Murugan to come up, or just go down like the others. Having made sure that RKS had left, Murugesan lit himself a cigarette. 'Give me one!' said Aasaithambi. Lighting it up, he said, 'Come this way,' and walked towards a corner of the terrace, with Murugesan next to him.

'What's all this, 'ppa – what is in Minister's mind?' asked Aasaithambi. Glancing around to make sure that no one was nearby, he whispered, 'Talk softly…'

'One partyman is trying to pull down a fellow partyman – it's an amazing thing. Happens only in our Party.'

'Shh … Who knows whose ears it'll get to!' hissed Murugesan. 'As far as I know, *that* one has been in the Party for twenty-eight years. Loyal as a shadow, he has been. To defeat such a man for the fourth time – isn't that a sin?' he said and peered around to see if anybody was approaching them. Throwing his cigarette butt on the floor, he rubbed it out with his foot. Watching one person after the other going down the steps, he finally said, 'Shall we go down?'

Without responding to that question, Aasaithambi remarked, 'Twenty-eight years he's been district secretary, twice he has been Minister, once an MLA. A third time he'll become Minister. Do you see the way his mind works?'

'Pushing the man in front of you out of the way to stand in his place – that is politics. If you were in his place, that's what you would do. And if *I* were in his place, that's what *I* would do,' in a barely audible voice, Murugesan shared this secret with Aasaithambi.

'If the district secretary himself does this kind of thing, how will the Party ever come to power?'

'It will come to power! You just keep your mouth shut. You're standing here, in this place, and talking like this? All over Tamil Nadu, every fellow who's been district secretary, every fellow who's been a minister, every one of them sees to it that nobody else can raise his head. They all act only like this.'

'In every party, this is what goes on! You just better not spill it from that mouth of yours!' warned Murugesan. 'He is the district secretary, he has been Minister, he is going to be Minister again. He has done good things and bad things. Above all, he's a fellow caste-man. When it's something to do with one of ours, how can we let him down?' he finished.

He began to descend the stairs.

A Man of the Party

HAVING TAKEN OUT A FRESHLY laundered dhoti and wrapped it around himself, Ponnusaami pulled out a shirt and put it on. He oiled his hair and combed it. Then he looked around among his clothes for an upper cloth.

There was none. He searched in all the usual spots, one after the other, but no … No upper cloth. The thundus that were among Meenaatchi's clothes were dirty. Seizing them and flinging them away, he rummaged in the place where his own things were kept. Not one towel fit to be draped over the shoulder was to be seen there.

'What is it you're looking for, 'nga?'

'Thundu.'

'Vaitti and shirt you have put on, no? What else d'you need?'

'If no Party thundu is here, on my shoulder, it's not right.'

'Going on a trip out of town?'

Noting the taunt, he silently continued his search for an upper cloth.

'So, it's election time! Now you'll be rushing off to seize the fort … Even some invader in olden times wouldn't have rushed about like this!' remarked Meenaatchi. Ponnusaami glowered at her. She paid no attention and continued to needle him.

'A fine wedding boy, going in a procession! To which town are you going today?'

Let alone look at her or reply, Ponnusaami didn't even turn in her direction. On any day that he dressed himself up in a freshly laundered vaitti–chattai plus shawl, this was the question she always asked, and he never answered it. Nor did he answer it now.

Ponnusaami's vaitti–chattai–thundu – his Party shawl – were all kept separately in a wooden almirah. Never would he keep his clothes all mixed up with those of others. If he ever found them lying around with others' garments, he'd get into a temper. 'What is this! A washerman's house or what?' he would shout. Whatever else he had or did not have in the house, he certainly had his crisply laundered vaittis and shirts. Whatever else he may have spent on, when it came to getting his clothes laundered, he spent lavishly. He might leave the house without a paisa in his pocket, but he would never leave wearing anything but impeccable chattais, and vaittis edged with the Party colours. Quarrels often broke out between Meenaatchi and himself on this account. But no matter how much she fought with him over it, he would clinch the issue with one answer: 'A Partyman is known by his vaitti–chattai – what else?'

Kathiravan, who had just entered the house, saw Ponnusaami busy searching for something and asked, 'What are you looking for?'

'Thundu.'

'Shawl?'

'Yes.'

'It's out there, in the back of the house. Drying on a line.'

'How did it go there?' demanded Ponnusaami, and strode off to the back of the house when Kathiravan said nothing. There it was, his thundu, hung out to dry. It made him very angry. Pulling it off the line, he pleated it neatly several times and put it over his shoulder, thinking, 'Who took it out of my almirah? Who's used it? Must be Kathiravan only.' He went back inside and told Meenaatchi, 'I have to go out somewhere.' As he was slipping his feet into his chappals, Kathiravan went up to him.

'It's today, isn't it – the Party interview?'

'Yes.'

'Cash paid, no?'

'Mm.'

'I'll come too.'

Ponnusaami threw a questioning look at him – as if to ask 'What is this? A new practice?' But before he could say anything, Kathiravan told him, 'Wait, I'm coming,' and went inside. Having dressed himself in the Party vaitti, he wheeled out his motorbike from behind the house and stopped in front.

'Climb on, let's go.'

'I'll go see for myself and come back,' said Ponnusaami.

'You are going to ask for a seat in the election! If a man goes all alone to the Party, just one man all by himself, who will give any respect?'

'Don't even know if I'll get it or not…'

'Each fellow who's going there to ask for a councillor's seat takes one hundred or two hundred people with him. In cars! To show his power and prestige! More than a lakh he'll spend, even before he knows if he's getting a seat or not. Only when he can show he has a big crowd behind him, he can give the block and district chiefs a good scare, no?' demanded Kathiravan.

The question made sense all right, like whatever else Kathiravan was saying. Yet Ponnusaami only said, 'I'll just go there and come back.'

Bringing his motorbike to a stop, Kathiravan got down and went up to Ponnusaami. 'If you don't get the Party ticket this time,' he warned, 'you better not wear the Party vaitti ever again!'

Ponnusaami stood silent.

'Last assembly elections, the two other parties told me, "Come to us, we'll give you our party ticket." Right then I should have done it. I would have become councillor by now if you hadn't stopped me!' Kathiravan glared at Ponnusaami.

'They wanted to start a fight between father and son, that's why they told you that. Not just to give *you* a ticket.'

'Father in one party, son in another party – both living in the same house. It happens like that sometimes, no? One of them may even be in power.'

'Isn't that shameful?'

'If you are so fussy about shame and all, can you be in politics? Can you remain in power? This time, you just have to get a ticket! It can be for block councillor seat, or for district councillor. If you don't get it, I will go to another party tomorrow itself.' Kathiravan spoke with finality.

... Never had he imagined that such words would come from a son of his. Now over seventy, Ponnusaami had joined the Party at the age of twenty-one. In all of Mangaloor taluk, he had been the first to hoist the Party flag. He had spoken to his neighbours in the village and got them all to do it along with him. It was he who had collected members for the Party, not only in his own village but in the neighbouring ones as well, he who took them to rallies. He would ride around on a bicycle distributing notices and posters, and attended every single rally held in the district capital. Not a day passed without his having read the Party newspaper.

Not only going to rallies, but going to prison, too, was a festive occasion for him. Protests, demonstrations and blockades, bandhs, fasts and jail bharo agitations – when any of these were announced by the Party central committee, he was never one of those who fled to a relative's house or to the jungle, fearing that the police would nab them. Even when the police didn't turn up at his house to arrest him, he would present himself at the station. Whenever he set off to participate in any agitation, he'd take along a couple of sets of extra clothes, just in case. Eighteen times – that's how often he had been to jail, and not once had he paid bail and come out. Whenever anyone advised him to just hand over the bail amount and walk out of jail, he would say, 'Why take part in the struggle at all, if I'm just going to come out on bail?' One time, he spent a full six months in jail, and that time, too, he didn't pay bail to get released.

When any Party conference was to be held, he would set off as though to a grand wedding. If any member sent him an invitation to a wedding, he would never miss attending it. No matter if the man did or did not honour him with the customary gift. And when he heard news of the death of any Party member, he would immediately get himself to the house of mourning.

'Why do you have to go for this sort of thing? All the time you are running around like this!' Meenaatchi would protest.

'When a Partyman passes away, shouldn't there be at least four partymen to pay their respects?'

All the party members in the district knew Ponnusaami. Whenever a meeting or a rally was held, until the district Party chief and the chief speaker arrived on the scene, it was Ponnusaami to whom the mike was entrusted. He would hold the crowd together with his oratory about the Party's entire history – about the struggles that it had conducted, and about each of its achievements whenever it was in power. He would speak in detail about speeches that the leader had made, and quote, 'Brothers! You who are my very life!' from his missives addressed to the people. He could cite the exact date and year of each peroration. Because he backed it all up with impeccable statistics, people in the party referred to him as 'Law Point' Ponnusaami.

… For two or three days after the Party lost any election, he would not eat at all. And when he spoke again in public, he would turn each defeat into a victory. 'We have not been defeated. It is the people who have been defeated. Welfare schemes have been defeated. Our principles have not been defeated, it is those who stood against our principles who've been defeated,' he would declare. 'Our leader's Tamil has not been defeated – it is Tamil's enemies who have been defeated.'

When embittered by the allotment of the constituency's MLA and MP seats to candidates of other parties in the coalition, Ponnusaami could complain, in informal conversation: 'Why has our "Sottai" done this? Breaking the arms of our own men? That's what Baldie wants – just four words of praise on the mike from any fellow!' Yet, when he himself spoke into the mike, he would proudly declare, 'What our leader speaks, what he writes – that's not the only Tamil in him, da – Tamil is his very walk! Tamil is in his actions! Mother Tamil herself is alive only because of our leader!'

… How was it that Ponnusaami came out with dirty words only when he held forth about those belonging to the opposition party? Those were the persons he freely grilled and tossed up. Over the mike, it was Ponnusaami who would promote their Party line and speak about all issues in a way that the block and district chiefs never did. It earned him great respect within the party. As for Ponnusaami himself, making a speech through the mike was something to relish, like rice and mutton curry.

He had held many positions – that of the district representative, the secretary at the block level, and the chief of the Party in the village assembly. Even now, he was the chief of the block unit. Three times he had been appointed member of the Party unit in the rural development bank, and in the agricultural cooperative bank. He had never held any higher post than those, but when the Party came to power, it was he who brought electricity to the village. And roads and schools, primary health centres and irrigation tanks. He was respected in the village. But not in his household, despite the regard he enjoyed locally, as well as among the party rank and file. From the family, all he ever heard was: 'How much did you make?'

Noticing her father-in-law and her husband standing and talking there in the doorway, Thilakavathi went to Meenaatchi to inform her of it:

'Your son and your husband are having a fight.'

It sent an instant shudder through Meenaatchi. Rising with difficulty, she dragged herself up to Ponnusaami.

'What is it?' she quavered.

When he didn't answer her, she turned to Kathiravan, 'What happened, 'ppa?'

But he didn't answer her either. Her panic grew. Had they both had such a bad quarrel? It must be because Kathiravan had confronted his father, he must have said, 'Why are you going around after "Party! Party!" all the time?' That would have incensed Ponnusaami and made him fight back, she guessed.

'At this age, why are you rushing around for "Party! Party!" Is the party good for even ten paisa worth of property?'

'I am not in the Party for money!' Ponnusaami turned the outrage he felt at his son's behaviour on her.

Hoping that Kathiravan would simmer down if she gave his father a good scolding, Meenaatchi accused, 'You don't care at all about how to run your life! How many more years are you going to run after "Party! Party!" For all your running about for Party, what has Party done for you?'

'So, what didn't Party do?' countered Ponnusaami.

'You get to wear a white shirt, a white vaitti. Daily you get into a car, daily you shout into a mike. What else?' Meenaatchi berated him.

'One minister, two MPs, four MLAs – I got them all to attend, when I got the first girl married. For the second girl, I got two ministers, one MP, and two MLAs when

I married her off. And three ministers, two MPs and six MLAs – for your son, I got all those to be present at his marriage. Who else in this whole area conducted such grand Party weddings? As for the Party, the Party will do just what it has to do.'

'"Minister is coming! MLA is coming!" That's what you kept saying. Flag hoisting, setting up a platform for some rally or other – that's what you spent all my money on. Made us all into debtors! Only you can talk big about your Party. Every time, for each girl of ours, you said, "I will perform her marriage only after the Party comes to power!" And isn't it only after each girl grew old and all dried up that you at last got her married off?' demanded Meenaatchi. Ponnusaami gave her a black look.

'You know the way his mind works, no? When he puts on a white shirt and a white vaitti and gets into a car, it's like some madness has got hold of him. Don't you know that?' she said to Kathiravan. He averted his face, saying nothing.

Meenaatchi persisted. 'He's an old man. Why are you getting in a wrestling match with him?'

'You don't understand the matter at all, Amma, so just don't keep on talking!' Kathiravan growled. 'You go and lie down.' Turning to Ponnusaami he demanded: 'Shall I take out the bike or not?' His tone was relentless, although he had no idea what his father was going to say.

Seeing Ponnusaami standing there, unable to assert himself, Meenaatchi felt miserable. 'Let him be, boy, if he's not coming! You go ahead,' she pleaded. But Kathiravan stood there stiffly, as though what she had just said hadn't entered his ears.

'He's calling you, isn't he? So why don't you just go with him? What can happen?' she begged Ponnusaami. That he was standing there, speechless, was a pitiful thing for her to see.

This Ponnusaami, this husband of hers – in the village, and in the Party, too, everybody listened to what he said. And it had never been his habit to do as others told him. It was only what seemed right to his mind that he would come out with, straight away, no matter who it was that he was addressing. That he had never been promoted to any high position had not happened just because he lacked material resources, it was also because of that mouth of his. That such a man now stood there looking crushed brought tears to Meenaatchi's eyes.

'I was thinking there is no other father and son like you two in this town. That is also gone, is it?' she cried.

'You don't understand all this, just keep quiet, Amma!' Kathiravan glowered at her.

'Bring out the bike,' Ponnusaami said at last. When Kathiravan wheeled it out, he seated himself on the pillion. 'Go inside and lie down,' he told Meenaatchi, as Kathiravan started it up.

Whether it was a family function, or a party event, he always went by himself and returned alone. Kathiravan did that too – going out alone and coming back alone, whenever he went out. They were never in the same place together. Usually, Kathiravan never showed up where Ponnusaami was present. Nor did he ever speak more than he needed to. Why was such a reticent fellow being so stubborn? Supposing he told him this time, too, as he did after every election, 'We'll see next time.' What would Kathiravan think of him? Perched there on the bike, behind his son, Ponnusaami thought about it.

Supposing this time, too, Ponnusaami came out of the interview hall, saying, 'Maybe next time … We'll see,' as he always did after every bid to get a ticket? How would Kathiravan react? Sitting on the bike behind his son, Ponnusaami felt as if they were two lifelong enemies, riding together. Here he sat, perched behind his son, saying nothing at all – he, Ponnusaami, who didn't come to a halt very easily whenever he started speaking. Almost always, he wouldn't allow anyone else to speak, or even give an ear to what that person was saying. When the other person was an opposition party member, he wouldn't even let him open his mouth … Not a word out of him, now.

He saw a van coming along with a flag stuck in its back. In the blink of an eye, it overtook them.

'Isn't that our Party van? Could it be the district chief?' asked Kathiravan.

'Interviews will start at ten o'clock, they said. But when did it ever take place at the time they said?' remarked Ponnusaami in a disinterested tone. He tightened his hold on his vaitti and thundu, as they fluttered in the wind.

'Don't depend on the block fellow. Go straight to "District". It's only then that the job will get done.' When Ponnusaami made no answer to that, and doubting that he had been heard at all against the roar of the racing motorbike, Kathiravan yelled, 'Do you understand what I said?' as if he were speaking to an ignorant child.

'As if District can meet me in private! A hundred people are surrounding him whenever you see him. They're all over him – as if they're filming a dancing girl.'

'If we can't see him here, I'll get hold of a car and go to District's house. We will see him there,' Kathiravan declared firmly, as though he were issuing a command.

'Let's see what happens. You just hurry a bit. Could be our bad-luck time – he may be coming right now.' Ponnusaami's words of caution spurred Kathiravan on to increase the speed of his bike. Two vehicles whizzed by just then, fast as the wind. As that van and tempo overtook him, Kathiravan steadily increased his speed. It was only when they reached Pennaadam town that he slowed down.

'Interview is at the mandapam, isn't it?' he queried.

'Parvathaambaal Mandapam,' Ponnusaami pronounced each syllable distinctly, as though he were conveying directions to a wayfarer. Twenty to thirty large vehicles stood in front of the mandapam, and parked around were two or three hundred motorbikes.

The bike came to a halt and Ponnusaami alighted. Kathiravan secured his bike and ordered, 'Come, let's go.' The way he pushed on ahead of him towards the hall made

Ponnusaami fume. It was difficult for him even to put one step forward and get inside the hall, and to find a place to stand was impossible.

'If the Party leader of the district council himself comes late, how will it look?' remarked a man.

To which Ponnusaami retorted, 'Is everything happening only because of a Party chief?'

'What is this, Annei!'[1] scolded the other, laughingly. 'If a Party VIP himself talks like this, what will happen?'

'Today, does any true Partyman have any value?'

To that, the other made no reply. Instead, he asked another question: 'Have you paid the cash?'

'I have paid it,' Ponnusaami said, and asked, 'But you will get the seat this time also, isn't that right?'

'Three times already I have contested the election. So this time, District has told me not to contest. Let the damn thing go, I also thought. Why give my own money, from my own house, and fall at the feet of every fellow I see, and do kumbidu? I thought – what for should I do it? What a way to live! What can I achieve as a councillor of a party that's not even in power!' finished the man, with a laugh.

'Then whom have you come here to support?'

'My sister's son has paid to try for the seat. I've come for his sake, Annei,' answered the man.

'Okay … I'll just go and meet the block chief,' Ponnusaami said, moving off to look for Dhandapani.

---

1 Annei: Anna – elder brother.

He was stopped on the way by three or four Partymen who wanted to chat with him. 'Go and find out where the block chief is,' he told Kathiravan, who took off at once, slipping into the crowd.

Coming up to him, one of those in the women's wing enquired, 'Annei, how are you? Doing well?' She added, 'When is District arriving?'

'Don't know, 'mma,' Ponnusaami replied.

'Annan himself does not know?' she smiled. Then she asked, 'You have paid the cash, 'nga?'

When Ponnusaami nodded in assent, she declared, 'Then Annan's seat is confirmed!' and gave a laugh. 'I've come with my village people, Annei, I have to go and meet them … I've already paid for the twentieth ward seat, Annei. Put in a word for me to District, 'nga!' She hurried out of the hall.

'Vanakkam, Annei!' Ramu, the assistant secretary of the party's block unit, called out on his way forward. Ponnusaami asked him, 'When is District going to arrive?'

'Should have come by now. Already one hour is over after he said he left the house,' Ramu called back and disappeared into the crowd.

Ponnusaami was chatting with some others, when Kathiravan turned up to tell him, 'In the groom's room…'

'I'll just go and meet District and come back,' Ponnusaami announced and began to walk towards the interior of that hall normally used for wedding ceremonies, heading towards the room meant for the bridegroom's party.

'Long live District Secretary!' 'Long live our Man-of-Gold!' Slogans fit to split the whole building broke from half a dozen throats the moment Thangam entered the hall. Two other persons pushed ahead, parting the crowd with shouts of 'Way! Make way, 'nga!'

Raising his hands in a kumbidu to one and all, Thangam moved on towards the groom's room. Taking along only the party's district assistant secretary, treasurer and the Youth Wing organizers, Dhandapani ushered Thangam inside and closed the door, leaving Ponnusaami and Kathiravan standing outside with some twenty or thirty others.

'Why only them? Such big shots they are, hanh?' fumed Kathiravan, furious that his father had not been admitted.

'Only Party organizers will be let inside,' Ponnusaami told him. 'You just keep quiet.'

'Just go inside and meet District yourself!' urged Kathiravan, refusing to listen.

'Don't be in such a hurry,' Ponnusaami said, and just then Dhandapani opened the door and called out, 'Those who have paid for contesting as councillors in the first ward – come inside. Only those!' More than ten persons pushed and shoved their way in, with Dhandapani shutting the door behind them. A continuous stream of complaints, muttered under his breath, came from Kathiravan, anguished and enraged as he was by the sight of his father standing outside … as though he were just some ordinary Party member.

The contestants for the second ward were already right behind them. Most of them greeted Ponnusaami with a respectful 'vanakkam'. Many were talking about the Party's chances of victory in this ward or that ward … Many were complaining about Dhandapani. They said he was taking bribes from would-be contestants. To their complaints, Kathiravan added his own grievance.

After the first lot of contestants had been sent out, Dhandapani sent in the ones for the second ward. It took only ten minutes for these to be similarly sent away and a third lot to be let in. Batch after batch was being moved in and out, one after the other.

'Eleventh ward persons may come, 'nga!' came the call, and at once several went in. Ponnusaami went with them, along with Kathiravan. There were fourteen aspirants contesting to be the candidate for that councillor's seat.

Thangam greeted Ponnusaami at once: 'Come, Annei, come and sit down!' A boy in the Youth Wing vacated his chair for Ponnusaami.

'How much will you spend?' Thangam asked the man who sat ahead of Ponnusaami.

'Three to five lakh, 'nga,' announced the man humbly.

'And you?' Thangam asked the next person.

'Just give me the seat, 'nga! I will win and show you!' came the smiling rejoinder.

Thangam now asked the third in line, 'Tell me, 'nga – what is the amount you will spend? And by how much will you win?'

'I will give ten lakh,' declared the man. 'Tomorrow I will bring the money to you, District, if you tell me! And I'll give it to the party.'

Ponnusaami gave him a scathing look. Just seven months had passed since this man had switched parties. He was in the real estate business, and he possessed no fewer than four Poclain excavators,[2] two trucks for transporting sand loads, and two paddy harvesters. Once given the ticket, he would use every crafty stratagem the world has seen to win the election somehow or the other. His goal was to become chairman, and it was for that alone that he had joined the party. Knowing quite well that he was a money-minded businessman, Dhandapani had become a buddy of his.

Right now, this man had brought with him some five hundred people from three villages around – and a quarter-bottle of country liquor and a packet of biriyani to distribute per head. Plus, a sum of five hundred rupees. It was common talk in the party that he was ready to spend as much as a crore of rupees to become chairman of the district council. Ponnusaami knew all about it. 'Only a man

---

2 Poclain excavators: A brand of heavy-duty bulldozers used in construction sites.

with cash belongs in the Party … Even in the world…' he thought.

'Tell me, 'nga…?' Thangam asked the fourth in the queue. A woman.

'If I am given the ticket for the eleventh ward council seat, it's a sure victory for the party, Annei,' the woman declared. She quickly whipped out a shawl, presented it to Thangam, and dropped down at his feet with a kumbidu. Immediately, her husband prostrated himself too at Thangam's feet, doing *his* kumbidu.

'What is all this? What sort of habit is this? Get up, 'nga. Don't make our Party like all the other parties, with this falling-at-the-feet business.'

Ponnusaami looked them over, both husband and wife. 'He wants a seat, so he shows off his woman…' he surmised. When it was the turn of the sixth in the queue for Thangam to ask his question: 'Tell me, 'nga…?' the man came out with, 'We people have a majority in three villages, 'nga. If Annan puts his heart into it and gives me the ticket, I will win!' With that, he flung himself at Thangam's feet.

Thangam broke into a laugh. 'Everyone is saying, "I will win! I will win!" If all of you are going to win, which one is going to lose? However many people stand for election, only one will win. Isn't that so?' A few of them laughed.

At last, having finished asking them all the same question, and listening to their avowals of sure success if only they were allotted tickets to contest for the seats,

Thangam declared: 'What I really want to do is to allot each and every one of you a ticket. But I can give a ticket to only one person per ward, right? Much more than in elections to the state assembly or parliament, it's in local body elections that there can be back-stabbing going on, all because of which village a candidate comes from, what caste he is, who he's related to. We can't let all that happen in the Party! For us, what is important is the Party. So whoever we give the ticket to – we have to make that person win! No member should make trouble within the Party and set off Partymen against fellow Partymen, with complaints like "They didn't give the ticket to me!" or "They didn't give it to you!" And unless we win more seats in our district than others in other districts, I won't be respected by the Leader!' said Thangam solemnly.

'How many seats for the coalition partners, 'nga?' It was Gunasekharan, standing in the line for the sixth-ward ticket.

Thangam chuckled as though he had just heard a priceless joke. Since District himself was laughing, all those in the room guffawed loudly. 'None of the coalition fellows comes out in the open, even in daylight, when we look for their support! Why does Leader need to go to them at all? For coalition? What for? Only at election time will they show up – that's when they'll jump at our throats. Wearing our Party shawls, they'll demand money for standing at voting booths! And for cars to go about here and there … And if you ask them why they're there, they'll say, "We are a national party!" A real nuisance, these coalition fellows. It's because too many MLA seats have been given to them that we're not able to come to power. A curse! Don't know how to get rid of it.'

'Annei! Shall I call the persons for the next council seat?' Dhandapani hastily cut in.

Answering him with a brief nod, Thangam addressed the crowd once again, 'All of you have to see that the party wins, do you understand? Go ahead – I'll come when it's time to ask for votes.' He raised his hands in a kumbidu. All of them saluted him likewise, and went out of the hall.

Ponnusaami now said, 'I have also paid the cash, saar.'

'You, of all people – how can I ask *you* questions, 'nga?'

'It is the Party procedure, isn't it?'

'Just for that to question a senior Partyman, 'nga? How can I do that?'

'Both for the district council and the block council seats, I have paid the money, 'nga.'

'I'll take care of it. You can go now, Annei…'

'For every election, I have paid the ticket money. Not even once has the party seat been allotted to me.'

'If you get it, will you win?' What was going on in Thangam's mind as he came out with this sudden challenge? It was hard to say.

'In all these years, I have never stood in an election. So, I don't have a bad name either. If I stand now, I will win.'

'For block councillor it will cost at least ten lakh, Annei,' Thangam told him.

Ponnusaami did not seem to have heard him, as he spoke in a broken voice, 'Everyone in my house is asking me, "For years you have been in the Party, what have you got to show for it?"'

Not taking the least note of it, Thangam persisted: 'How much will you spend?'

'Will anyone be allotted a ticket for a Party seat only if they have money? Is that the way it is, Annei?'

Ponnusaami's query annoyed Thangam intensely. It was only because of the others present that he held in his wrath. If it had come from anybody else and not Ponnusaami, he would have roared, 'Get out!'

Now he remained silent. It was hard to tell what was going on in his mind, until he finally spoke:

'Only a man who has the money can stand for election these days. It doesn't matter whether he is a good man or a bad man, or what his party is. People have changed. They will only vote for the man who spends money. Lots of money. You know that yourself ... Tomorrow you bring ten lakh, and I will give you a ticket. And if you win the election, I will make you chairman!' Knowing that Ponnusaami didn't have any – which was exactly why he kept on talking about money – he went on: 'The ruling party will spend a lot of money to get the chairman's seat, Annei.'

At this point, Dhandapani put in a word: 'Just go out and have some tea, Annei,' he advised Ponnusaami. 'After the interviews are finished, please come. Then we can talk alone.'

That infuriated Ponnusaami. 'So! Must all those who have been working and toiling for the party be let down like this? Is it like that, District?' he demanded.

Impatiently, Thangam now informed him of certain facts: 'For the past five–six years, nobody knows who hoisted flags, put up banners, built platforms, set up mikes and loudspeakers! They are all working on contract basis. Party itself works just like a corporate now!' He sounded bitter.

It provoked Ponnusaami to question him further: 'So, Party will give a ticket only to a fellow who has defected from another party? Or somebody who has a real estate business?' Guessing to whom he was referring, Thangam countered with a laugh, 'It's only they who have the money, no?'

'It's only in our Party that you are asking, "How much cash will you spend?" Other parties are not like that!'

Ponnusaami's complaint made Thangam laugh more loudly than before. 'That's a cinema party! Our Party is a party of principles! Just for nothing people will vote for cinema actors. But to vote for *our* Party, they demand money. And even if we give it, they don't vote for us! Then what do you want us to do?' he demanded.

'It's fifty years since I joined the Party.'

'Being a Partyman is important. But more important than just being a Partyman is winning,' Thangam said with unmistakable firmness.

'An old Partyman is unwanted. Isn't that it?' said Ponnusaami.

Thangam winced. 'Already every fellow is making fun of our Party, saying it's an old men's Party,' he said gloomily. 'Party High Command says, "Give importance to the youth!"'

'So then, no more need for the old ones, Annei?'

'Only a horse that will run has any value at all, right?'

'... Twenty years old I was when I rented a cycle and rode twenty kilometres to the block secretary…' murmured Ponnusaami. 'At that time, it was Raasu. I didn't go to his house – I went to his brick kiln on the riverbank. Told him I wanted to join the Party. "Is that so?" Raasu laughed happily, told me to fill out a form and send it to the leadership. Took me along and gave me four idlis ... And poori–potato. First day I ever tasted poori–potato. He gave a rupee and a quarter for the hire-cycle and sent me back ... From that day to this, I have been shouting until my throat goes dry, for the Party – don't know how many, many times! If I am a real, true Partyman, give me the ticket – if not, then let it be,' Ponnusaami said, at last.

As though reminding Thangam, Dhandapani said, 'Annei, you have to go to the next block.' Meaning that there was no need for District to be chit-chatting with Ponnusaami, and that he should be sent out…

Standing nearby, the district party secretary now scolded Ponnusaami: 'Is this interview being conducted to find out who are the "real, true Partymen"? It's election time, Annei!' Like a blow across his face came Ponnusaami's retort:

'I am talking to District! Not to anyone else!'

Realizing that now he was really very angry, and fearing that he would scandalize the proceedings and openly declare, "I paid for the ticket, but I didn't get it! District is playing favourites!" Thangam now tried to reason with him. 'I am only doing what you would do if you were district secretary. I didn't say there is no ticket for you. I only asked if you would win the seat. Tell me that you will spend, and that you will win the seat! Who will say there is no seat for you, 'nga? Question is, when the election is there, will you spend, and will you win? That's all! That is what happens to the Party High Command also, don't you know?'

'All right, Annei. Give the seat to the man who has money,' Ponnusaami told him.

'So many years you've been in the Party, what is there that you don't know about all this? You know, don't you, how much even a fellow who is standing for ordinary village president spends? Block councillor has three villages under him. District councillor has forty-five villages. You tell me if you can handle it … One lakh, two lakh even, is not enough to stand for election now.' Thangam was decisive.

'Am I a Partyman or not?'

'If you go on and on saying the same thing again and again, I'll have to just push you towards the coalition party

… What for am I telling you this? If you don't understand that, no need to talk!' Thangam took off his glasses and began to wipe them. Everybody in the district, whatever their party, knew that when Thangam was at the end of his tether, he would take off his glasses and wipe them.

'You allot tickets to whoever has crossed over from another party. But you pack off a Partyman to the coalition partner, 'nga?'

'Floor crossers! What party have those men not belonged to, at one time or another? Whether someone is a man from the Party is not the point – will he win, or will he lose? That is the point!' said Thangam, grimly.

That he had now lost all patience was very clear. Any more talk and he would just say, 'Can't give it. Go see the Party High Command.' That would be the last word from him, Ponnusaami felt.

Humbly lowering his voice, he said, 'From the time your father was district Party secretary, then minister, and after that when you became district secretary, and then minister, I have been in our Party only, till today. Never have I gone and changed party. Never have I changed the way I wear my vaitti. "Father in one party! Son in another party!" – that kind of thing never happens in my family. Just one time, let me stand for election on the party symbol. Doesn't matter if I lose.'

'If every councillor loses, how can we get the chairman's seat? Who'll answer for it?' demanded Thangam.

'Who will stand with folded arms to be scolded by the High Command?' he challenged imperiously.

'Till now, I never said to District that you must do this or that. Whatever District said, I have obeyed, and done only that.'

'I did not say you didn't! And when I was minister, did I or didn't I do whatever you wanted for your village?'

Ponnusaami did not reply.

'Am I thinking you shouldn't get a seat? Is that what I mean, 'nga? Standing for election means spending money! You have to go to all sorts of fellows and fall at their feet! And after doing all that, you have to win! Or you'll be in debt for several crore. Even if you win and become a councillor, you can't do anything if the opposition party comes to power. Then not a single fellow will come to you even to get you a cup of tea. The debt won't go away. Those partymen who have stood for election and got defeated – you know what condition their families are in. When a Partyman wins, everybody will shout '*Vaazhga!*' and wish him a long life. But if he loses, they won't even turn to look at him. Should a person like you cheapen yourself like that? A person of your worth, in front of ordinary fellows? So, please, you just be a respected senior Partyman, like always.'

'District! In my house, my family won't let me be just that…They don't understand politics, that's why. They don't know that even a Partyman can be betrayed within the Party itself–'

Even as he spoke, the assistant district party secretary cut in. 'Already it is two hours late, Annei. They're phoning again and again – the people from the next block.'

'Let it be,' Thangam said.

'He is getting old, 'nga,' Kathiravan spoke at last. 'At least once if he stands for election, there will be some respect for us in the village, Annei.'

'Do people cast their votes these days after considering a candidate's party and his character? You saw how one thousand rupees have been given per vote, to win an election! If that is what goes on in an MLA election, how will it be in a local body election? If the party were in power, and I were a minister, I would myself make your father a councillor. Even the chairman! But I am not a minister now. If I say anything, nobody will listen to me, they'll act like they are listening, that's all. You know that! But if, in spite of all this, you still want the ticket, I will give it! Go stand for election, then!' Thangam finished.

And at that, Ponnusaami's heart melted. 'I know you, I know your character!' he burst out. 'I know what it means to be a Partyman, Annei. Our leader is not some lightweight person, he will never lose control of his emotions and waste one single word. He is super! A hero! He was the one who gave you this name of 'Thangam'! That itself is a wonder in this world!'

The other smiled faintly.

'Give the ticket to somebody who will win, 'nga. In my council, the Party should not lose! But there is one thing I want from the Party.'

'Please tell me.'

'When I die, you should come from wherever you are and put a garland on my body. And cover it with the Party flag. That is all I want.'

'What are you saying, Annei! If someone like you dies, how can we save the Party?'

'Your father was district secretary for two terms, and minister for one term. For three or four terms, now, you have been MLA, for two terms district secretary. One term you were minister. I'm only an ordinary man, but you have spent all this time talking to me. Because you felt that otherwise I might get angry! This is what our Party is, Annei. This is what our leader has taught us.' Ponnusaami broke into tears as he spoke.

'After my father died, when I stood for district secretary in the election, all the fellows who voted for me were the ones who had taken money from me. You were the district Party representative, and you were the only one who voted for me without taking money. I haven't forgotten that. It's not that I don't know who is like *this* and who is like *that* in the party!'

'How well your father managed everything! But you have gone one hundred steps above him! Whether you give me the ticket or not, I am not one to switch parties and cast my vote!' Ponnusaami said. Gazing at his tear-blurred eyes,

Thangam declared, 'As long as there are persons like you, our Party will never get destroyed, Annei.'

Ponnusaami had never put down any cash to buy an entry ticket to contest for a seat in the election to the state assembly. Or to the parliament. Aware that trying for an MLA or MP seat would require much more money than he could afford, he had left those elections alone. All he had been trying for was the chance to win a seat in the local body elections, as a block or district councillor, and it was for that chance that he paid the usual fee. And every time, he would appeal to the district secretary to give him the seat. The response, each time, would be, 'This time please let it go, 'nga. Let's see, next time.'

That would calm him at once. 'Never mind if I don't get it. Please give it to some partyman who will win. What I want is for the party to win,' he would say, and leave. Even if he was annoyed by the rejection of his bid, it would not deter him from performing his election duties. Night and day, he would go around tirelessly canvassing for votes, more than the candidate himself.

What Dhandapani and Thangam both expected was that he would leave at this point, as he always did. Why was he so stubborn this time? Didn't make sense…

'Annei, just wait outside for a little time,' Thangam suddenly said, as though he had something on his mind, 'I'll finish the meeting and call you.' Ponnusaami immediately raised both hands in a kumbidu and left the room with Kathiravan.

The moment they left, the assistant secretary complained, 'You are spending so much time on one man – half an hour has been lost! By this time, we could have finished one whole block.'

Thangam smiled gently at him, 'Forty-fifty years ago, before we were all born, when it was not known if the Party would grow, if the Party would ever come to power or not, this man was the first to raise the party flag in this block. It was he who planted the flagpole and rode on a bicycle from village to village to distribute the Party notice. Men like him have planted the tree, and from that tree we get the fruit we're eating. Do you understand that?'

Ponnusaami and Kathiravan emerged from the mandapam. 'Let's get some tea to drink,' Kathiravan said, and went straight on ahead towards the tea stall. Undecided whether to go with him or not, Ponnusaami finally followed, fearing that his son would get into a temper and begin to shout. Handing him his tea, Kathiravan began to sip his. 'Can't we manage to collect ten lakh?' he demanded exasperatedly. 'They will give a seat only to a man who has money!'

The remark did not seem to have entered his father's ears, as he quietly drank his tea.

'So then why stand here for nothing? Come, let's go home.'

'Wait. We'll go soon,' Ponnusaami said.

Kathiravan gave him an accusing glare. 'You should have fought it out with the district secretary!'

'To get this much respect from a district secretary is itself a big thing. He could have easily said one or two words – "Won't do it! Get out!" And what could we have done then? … The district secretary is the raja of the district, in our Party. And the Party is what he wants to make of it, in that district. What he says is what the Party High Command listens to. Did he say he won't give us the seat? What he asked was just, "Can you spend money to win it?" … All these years, if I had only had money in my hand, what-all positions I could have held! What I didn't have was money! At least caste could have been on my side. That also I didn't have … But on top of all this, you have to have it written on your forehead! You can want something as much as you like, but without that, you don't have a chance of winning it.'

His son flung him a look of utter disgust. Trying to placate him, Ponnusaami reasoned, 'We have done a lot of running around for the party, roaming from place to place. But that's all – we didn't invest any capital. Only if we are putting something in, we can expect some gain, no? If not, in our party, at least we can get some respect. That's because of this man. That is the kind of man he is. And that is only because he is in *our* Party.'

'*Everyone is all the same! All are equal!*' Kathiravan mockingly intoned the often-quoted Party line.

'Don't talk like that. He is the only man who doesn't even look at a man's caste! Doesn't choose to take along just his own caste fellows in his car, doesn't work just for his own caste people. Compare him with the party secretaries in other districts! This man fits his name – he *is* gold.'

'So, what did he do for us when he was minister?'

'What favour did I ever ask, for him to refuse anything? I never put pressure on him for anyone's sake! Not a single fellow approached me, hoping that I would put in a word with the minister to get his job done. Anyone who wants his help goes to him on his own … In the old days, only if you went with a Partyman could you get them to do anything. Nowadays it's not like that, you just need to have money … When he was minister, only the fellows with BA degrees earned his respect. Those who knew he was crazy about books just took him books and got some benefit. But all he earned then was a very fine reputation!'

'Whose fault is it if he doesn't know how to get on in the world? He may not need to. *His* father would have left him enough money!'

Kathiravan's insolence goaded Ponnusaami to retort, 'His father Pandiyan also didn't earn much. And he wasn't a loudmouth show-off like the other district party secretaries. That's why father and son have been able to win continuously, in seven or eight constituencies. They're not the types who spend their nights with caste-party fellows, and spend their days with our Partymen!'

'Yes, yes, *they* will win! But to you they'll say, "No ticket!" Now come on, let's go! When has the party ever done anything worthwhile, for them to do anything now?' demanded Kathiravan irately.

Having completed the interviews, Thangam emerged from the hall. 'Are they finished so soon?' exclaimed Ponnusaami, as he hastened towards him. 'It's all just for name's sake, this interview business,' griped Kathiravan, as he fell in step with his father. 'The block secretaries have already put down the names of those who've been selected. They're the only ones who are going to hear from him.'

As Thangam climbed into his car, the crowd swarmed towards him. 'Whoever gets the seat must win!' he exhorted them. 'We must not let the Party get defeated. Don't shame me before the Party High Command!'

'We will never go against your wishes, Annei!' they all shouted in one voice.

Ponnusaami went up close to the car, hands lifted in a kumbidu. 'Next time I will do it for you, Annei!' promised Thangam with folded hands. He turned to salute the crowd.

The car started and drove off, with four more cars whizzing behind.

The Petition

HAVING REACHED THE TEMPLE OF Kolanji Appar, Thangamani looked around to see where to tie her prayer-chit. Approaching a worshipper on his way back from the god, she followed his directions and reached the spot.

It was a vanni[1] tree. Pierced into its thorny branches as high as a person could reach were twenty or thirty small tridents. Each of them not only had five hundred or more bits of paper tied to it, but for want of space on the trident itself, whole bunches of these prayer-chits had been suspended from the threads of those already fastened to it. Perplexed, she searched for a gap to squeeze in her chit. But nowhere on those tridents was there even a needlepoint of space. Taking out the chit she had tucked into her waist, she rolled it up tightly and then realized that she didn't have thread to tie it with. She looked all around. Nothing that could pass for even a scrap of thread lay on the ground.

---

1 Vanni: The Indian mesquite (*Prosopis cinerariaa*), a native thorny dryland tree valued for its timber and its bark, unlike the invasive Mexican *Prosopis juliflora*.

Should she just poke it in between the others tied to one of the tridents? She thought about it, and decided not to do it. Her prayer-chit might fall off the very next moment with a gust of wind, and the task she wanted done would not be carried out. She was just about to turn, with the idea of walking up to the main road and asking someone at the shop that stood there, when she saw a man walking towards a room nearby. Hurrying after him, she asked, 'Do you have a bit of thread?'

'What for?'

'To tie this chit, 'nga.' She showed him the rolled-up piece of paper in her hand.

'Did you write it down at home and bring it here?'

'Yes, 'nga.'

'Then your chit is useless. Can't be tied.'

'Please! What's this you are saying?' she pleaded pathetically.

'If you turn up here and tie your chits on your own and go off, why are we sitting here and running this office?' he asked contemptuously.

'Will you give a chit, then?'

'Yes, yes, 'mma! "Petition" – that's what it's called. We issue a thing that's called a petition! You have to fill out the form and show it here. Only if you give a chit like that will we send the Saami to answer your prayer. All the chits here have been tied only after that.' As he spoke, he entered the room and seated himself on a chair.

Thangamani was baffled. 'Go tie a chit!' was what Saroja and others in the village had told her. Why hadn't they told her about all this? When she set off, she had gone straight to the headmistress of the village school and had her write down her prayer to the god on a piece of paper. That woman hadn't said a word about this matter either. It made her so angry that she wanted to fling away the rolled-up piece of paper in her hand.

At the same time, it occurred to her that it was just a piece of paper after all. She could get another one written, and give it in. Going up to the man seated on the chair, she asked, 'Please give me a chit.'

'For what?'

'Just a chit, 'nga. I want to tie a chit.'

'Not a chit, 'mma. Petition, it's called! If you want to submit a petition, it will cost two hundred.' Having said this, he looked her up and down. Then he began to arrange the papers on the desk, placing them one on top of the other. Opening the desk drawer, he took out a pen and set it down, and then a key. Opening the cabinet nearby, he brought out a notebook that resembled a letter pad, and another that looked like a bill book. Setting them all down on the desk, he locked up the cabinet and asked Thangamani:

'From which village?'

'Kazhuthoor, 'nga.'

'How far from here?'

With the hope that he might be more sympathetic if she mentioned a far-off place, she added five miles to the distance she mentioned.

'So! Then you please add one hundred to the petition amount.'

'But just now you said it was two hundred!' Adding those miles had turned out to be such a mistake, she thought, dismayed.

'Two hundred for Saami. One hundred for Saami's horse,' he said with a slight smile.

'Money for the horse?' Thangamani exclaimed, astonished. Not noticing the smile.

'Will the god come on foot to your house to check out what you have written down in your chit and see if it is all right? He will come on horseback, right? And will the horse come for nothing? It has to eat millet and hay, right? It has to carry Saami all that way! Both man and god need cash. Do you understand?' the chit-dispenser asked her. He grinned.

Thangamani stood bewildered, at an utter loss for words.

'What, 'mma? Why are you looking like that? How does the bus man let you into the bus and take you to your village? This is also just like that,' he told her.

'A brand-new jewel it was, saar!' she burst out. 'A gift I had to make, for my brother's daughter's wedding. Just day before yesterday evening, I mortgaged half a kaani[2] land to buy it. I put it carefully in my box and locked it and went to work yesterday morning. Came back in the evening and looked for it … The box lay open, and the jewel was gone. Gone! Two pavuns![3] "Why didn't you keep it safe? You didn't listen to me and went and mortgaged the land!" On and on my husband kept saying this and beating me – all night long. Blows of all kinds he gave me! And all sorts of kicks … He left nothing out, saar! "If you don't get back that jewel by the end of this day, I won't leave you alive!" he told me and went off. Only three days are left for the wedding, saar. If I tell my brother the jewel is lost, his wife won't believe it. I can't see any way out, saami! These hands of mine are empty, saar!'

Having said all this, Thangamani broke into sobs.

'Don't cry, 'mma. From now on it is not your job to look for the jewel. It's Kolanji Appar's job. Just submit your petition. He'll take care of the rest. However big the thief is, he can't escape from Kolanji Appar's eyes.'

Despite the faint tremor of hope set off by the chit-dispenser's words, Thangamani asked doubtfully, 'Will it really happen like that, saar?'

'The thing you want done will be a success. Where have you come to submit your petition? Here, at Kolanji Appar! Understand? In this whole district, there is no one

---

2 Kaani: A measure of land, about 1.32 acres.

3 Pavun: Pound – a measure of gold.

who can defeat him in the hunt, do you know that? Why don't people go to the police, why do they come here? Do you see how many prayer-chits are tied here? Why do we take money for them? So that the Saami won't forget any details of any case!'

'Will Saami forget, saar?' asked Thangamani, amazed.

The chit-dispenser looked about to lose his temper. He snapped, 'Do you think Saami is like you, sitting at home doing nothing? Just like you, so many people have come! They have already submitted their petitions! Don't their jobs have to be completed? One by one, as each job is finished, one or two might be missed. God is just like a man, no? Whatever a man can forget, a Saami can also forget! So, it's better to put some cash down. To remind him.'

'Chit-money, and on top of that more cash?'

'Yes, 'mma. If you want your job done by the date you have specified, there's an extra fee. You have to come here and pay it. Only then it will be done.'

'Will the job be finished, then? With that extra fee? Only three days are left for the wedding, 'nga!' Even as she spoke, Thangamani broke into tears.

'After you submit your petition, within eighteen days your work will be done. If not, then the very next day you must come and pay the first instalment of the extra fee. If it still isn't done, you have to make a second instalment. Now you go and buy your petition chit, and get it filled up and submit it. Fast!' he urged. He seemed to be in a great hurry from the way he talked and behaved.

'Eighteen days? Will it take so long?' she asked hopelessly, in a wan voice.

'It's a rough guess, but it will take that much time, at the very least. Hasn't the Saami got to have some rest? Does he have only one job to do, like the rest of us? And if it isn't finished in eighteen days, another instalment has to be paid. Or nothing will happen.' A shock went through Thangamani at the chit-dispenser's words. 'Ayyo, he's saying it won't happen!' she thought, her mind in a whirl.

'Won't the job be done with one payment?' she begged.

'Yes, yes, it'll be done! No need even for a second payment. It won't take that long. But we people have to speak like this, just to make the terms clear. Don't worry, it'll get done by then.'

As he spoke, his eyes went towards a couple at the door. They came straight in and asked in one voice: 'Please, we want to tie a chit.'

'Is this the first time you are coming?'

'Yes, 'nga,' said the man and the woman together, once again.

'Give two hundred. Also, the charge for the horse.'

Taking the money, he wrote out a receipt in the bill book, signed it and handed it over. Then he tore off a printed sheet from the notebook that resembled a letter pad. Addressing the woman, he said, 'Write down your application on this. Then go straight to the priest and give it to him. That Aiyar will put it at Saami's feet for the blessing. After that, you come here. I will tie thread around it and give it to you. Then, you take it and tie it to the trident on the tree. And the job'll be done.'

'You will be here then, won't you, 'nga?' the woman asked anxiously.

'I'll be right here. You go and come back!' he said in a booming voice.

Saying, 'We'll come, 'nga,' the couple went out. The chit-dispenser turned to Thangamani.

'Why are you just standing here, 'mma?' he demanded. 'Quick, go and get the petition filled up and bring it here. The later it gets the longer it'll take, and your number will fall behind the others. This god does these according to seniority.' Opening the desk drawer, he took out a box and began to count the money in it.

'Will it be too late, 'nga?' Thangamani asked, tears blurring her eyes.

'When a chit comes to me, I give it a serial number and send it on to Saami. Saami will go and do each and every job only according to its serial number.' His entire attention seemed to be on the counting of the money.

'Can't my chit be sent earlier?'

The chit-dispenser laughed gently. 'This is a government department. Everything is done according to the rules. Saami also goes only by the rules. Who is Saami? Is he a relative of yours? Is he the same caste? Rules and regulations are for Saami also. Whatever rules and regulations have to do with him, those rules and regulations Saami will never go against. Never! But we'll talk about all that later. First you get the petition written out and bring it here,' he told her. 'The rest of it can be seen to only after all that.' He gave her a hard stare.

Thangamani hastily took out the cash and handed it over. Taking it from her, he took out the notebook that resembled a letter pad and tore off a page. 'Get your application written down on this. Put the whole thing down in one or two words, Saami won't have the time to read a lot of blabber. As soon as it's written down, go straight to the Aiyar and give it to him. He will place it at Saami's feet and get the blessing. Then bring it right back here. I'll take care of the rest,' he said, as he gave her the receipt for the money.

'I don't know how to write, 'nga. Please write it for me!' To Thangamani's appeal, his response was a stern refusal: 'This is a confidential matter between you and Saami. On top of that, I am a government employee! There is no question of my interfering. You can go outside, if you want, and get it written by some unknown person.'

There was just nothing she could do about it. A young girl and an old woman came in with their petition. Disconsolately, Thangamani went out and began to search for somebody who might write down hers. Hesitant about whom to ask, she looked at some who were coming out of the shrine after offering worship, and at others who were on their way in. Approaching a lone man coming out of the shrine, she broached the matter.

That man's terse response was, 'No pen, 'mma,' as he walked on. Next, she looked around for anyone with a pen visibly clipped to a shirt pocket. Although there were many men going in and out of the temple, not one had a pen in his pocket. All she heard from anyone was, 'No pen.' Even those wearing trousers and shirts, watches and rings, chains around the neck and on the wrists possessed no pens. Where even men didn't have pens, how could women be expected to have any? Reasoning thus, Thangamani refrained from asking any woman there to fill in her petition.

Going up to a somewhat stout person, she asked, 'Please could you write out this chit for me, 'nga?' The man took her chit and read it through. 'This should not be written by anyone else, 'mma,' he told her. When he handed it back and walked off in a great hurry, Thangamani had a terrible urge to open her mouth and bawl out loud, then and there. Yet her eyes kept searching for someone to ask. She saw a man perched on the outer wall of the temple. He had a pen. She went towards him, showed him her petition, and entreated, 'Please could you just write this out for me?'

The man said nothing.

'I can't write, 'nga. If I had known it would be like this, I would have brought somebody from my village along with me. If I go back to get it written, my number will be pushed back, it seems.'

It was clear from her tone that Thangamani really believed the jewel would be returned to her if only she could somehow get the petition written and handed in. But it didn't look as though the man had heard a word she said. 'Go that way!' he told her, pointing in a westerly direction.

She felt consumed, at that moment, by a burning frustration so immense that it seemed to have no end to it. Bemoaning her fate, she began to walk on, towards the west.

Her anger turned on Saroja. Maybe she should not have listened to her at all, and come all this distance! When the theft of the jewel had been discovered, the whole town had collected to watch Thangamani screaming and striking herself. People, known and unknown, had tried to pacify her and to offer consolation. Nobody's words penetrated her hearing. Go to an astrologer, they advised. Blow on an egg and bury it, they said. But she heard none of it. Nor did she stop wailing. Her husband returned from work and asked a thousand questions: 'What happened? How did the jewel disappear? Did you lock the house or not?' But even when he thrashed her as if she were a mere cow, demanding, 'A man tells you something, and still you won't listen?' the pain of it was far less than the agony caused by the sheer loss of the jewel itself. Having wept all night long, she rose at dawn, bathed, and went to the Mariamman temple to light a piece of camphor. When she got back, she met Saroja.

'Why are you sitting here crying? If you hit yourself and howl, will the jewel come back home all by itself? Until you do what has to be done, and do it in the proper way, only then it'll come back, no? Just listen to what I'm saying. Go at once to the Kolanji Appar temple and tie a prayer-chit. That jewel will come back all by itself,' declared Saroja.

'What are you saying, Saroja?' countered Thangamani, refusing to believe her. 'In the village where I was born, if anything went missing, they'd go and fetch a fortune teller, get him to rattle his drum and point it out!' Immediately, Saroja came out with the story of the disappearance of a jewel from her brother's house which had been found lying in the backyard just three days later.

'The very day that jewel disappeared, my brother went to the Kolanji Appar temple and tied a prayer-chit. Came back and told the whole town about it. And on the third day, early in the morning, the jewel was found lying right there behind the house. Whoever stole it returned it on their own, just terrified of Kolanji Appar Saami. If they hadn't brought the jewel back, a leg or an arm would have got broken … Our father Kolanji would have crippled the fellow. Or had him crash against a car, or a bus, or a lorry. Finished! They knew that'd happen, and that's why they brought it back. Was it some thief from out of town who stole it and went off? No! It had to be a thief from right here in the village. So you better go see about tying a chit there, and getting back here.'

As she couldn't quite believe Saroja, she asked, 'What you're saying – is it really true?'

'What will I gain by lying? Four months ago, my brother lost a jewel worth eight pavuns, and that's a fact. Three days after the chit was tied, the jewel came back and was found behind the house – that's also a fact. I'm not just saying this for nothing. On my three children's names, I swear I'm speaking the truth!' Saroja was not a person given to telling fibs. She was known in that whole street to be a kind person. Why would she come and lie to her, Thangamani thought.

'Why couldn't my husband have been here right now?' she burst out.

'Now why are you looking around for your husband at this time?' Saroja retorted, frowning.

'"Not only have you let the jewel get stolen, you'll go off on a jaunt, will you?" That's what he'll say. And he'll beat me!' Thangamani sobbed.

'You can go there and get back before he comes. Go, run quick!'

'Only three days left for the wedding. And they're all killing me! Even if I work till I drop dead, I'll never make enough to buy even two pavuns! Will those who stole from me ever do well? Or will they end up as wretched beggars?' she wailed out loud.

'Don't keep on saying the same thing over and over again! Go right now, tie the chit, and come back. Will that jewel come back, or won't it come back, in just two days? Just see!' Her words set off a cool gush in Thangamani's breast. The exhaustion of having wept continuously ever since yesterday, the fatigue of not having eaten anything that night, the jitters she had suffered when she found the jewel had been stolen – all of it together had all but laid her low. Never mind all that now, she thought, as she listened to Saroja. What she wanted was just to get the jewel back.

'If the jewel is found, I'll cook meat curry and rice for you!' she promised Saroja.

'We'll see about all that later. You go now!' insisted Saroja. The more Thangamani listened to her, the more she was convinced that tying a prayer-chit was all that was needed for her to get the jewel back. And so, borrowing five hundred rupees from Saroja, she had caught the bus, and gone to the temple. It seemed to her now that she could have got here yesterday evening, if only she had known then that she would have to wander around like this, hunting for some way to get her prayer-chit written down and tied to the tree…

Going to a coconut seller nearby, she showed him her petition and asked him to fill it out for her. The fellow called out to another sitting some distance away. 'Yauv! Write out this chit and hand it over!' To Thangamani he said, 'Go to him, 'mma.'

'Sit,' that man told her, taking the petition. He read it through, placed it on his lap and brought out a pen from his shirt pocket.

'What's your village?' was his only question. And the whole story came out of Thangamani in one breath:

How, when her daughter came of age and had to be given the ritual turmeric bath, her brother had made a gift of a two-pavun chain. How, in order to pay off the loan taken to meet the expenses of that very ceremony, she had had to mortgage that chain. How the interest on the loan built up, and she could not redeem the chain. How her brother's daughter was to be married now, in three days, and how she had gone against her husband's wishes and been compelled to mortgage half a kaani of land to buy another chain for her brother's daughter. How that chain was found to be stolen, and how she had wailed and rolled on the floor … How her husband had beaten her … And how she had turned up here to tie a prayer-chit … All of it gushed out of her in a single breath.

Having listened patiently, the man calmly announced, 'Can't write down your whole story, 'mma. One or two words is all that can be written. They've printed this petition just like the exam papers that they give schoolkids, with gaps to fill in the blanks.' Sternly he told her, 'So, just answer only what I ask you.' Thangamani's face took on a stricken look, as he went on in a businesslike tone:

'Which village?'

'Kazhuthoor, 'nga.'

'Husband's name?'

'Annamalai.'

'Street name?'

'East Street.'

'Circle, district – all that I will fill up myself,' he announced, and proceeded to write it all down. Then he turned to her to ask, 'What is your request?'

'The stolen jewel must come back to the house, 'nga.'

'Arm or leg to be bent or broken?'

'No need for all that, saami! I just want to get back what belongs to me!' cried Thangamani tearfully. Having filled out the petition, the man pointed to a blank space in it, and held it out to her along with a pen, saying, 'Put your signature here.'

Even on a good day, Thangamani had difficulty writing down her name properly. How could she write when she was in such a state of anxiety over the theft of the jewel? When she took the pen, her hand began to tremble and tears filled her eyes. She couldn't even write her own name. Instead of writing 'Thangamani', she scribbled down some egg-shaped squiggles.

Taking the petition from her, the man announced, 'I am reading out what's written on this chit, so listen carefully. Afterwards, you must not say I have not written anything that you have told me.' After this warning, he proceeded to read out:

'Kolanji Appar Sri Murugan Sannidhi Manavaalanalloor, Vriddhaachalam, date 18-07-2016, Monday. To the holy congregation of the blessed Kolanji Appar Saami: I, Thangamani, from Kadalur district, Thittakudi circle, Kazhuthoor village, East Street, wife of Annamalai, and member of his household, am bowing down at the feet of Saami and writing this prayer-petition on this day of 18-07-2016. A two-pavun chain has been stolen from my house. I humbly request that the said article be returned to me. When my request is fulfilled, I shall pay the above charge for the petition and take possession of the article. O Divine Being! Requesting you to have my article returned to me, and to bestow every good fortune upon me and my family, I humbly prostrate myself at your feet. Signed, Thangamani.'

Thangamani was wholly satisfied. She received the petition from him. Then she remembered the yellow receipt she had tucked at her waist, and handed it over. The man glanced at it and said, 'This is nothing, 'mma. Just the receipt for the money paid by you, the charges for the petition, the charge for the summons, the fee for having the big thamukku drum beaten, the down payment fee, and the per-kilometre cost. That's all.' So saying, he gave her back the receipt. 'The Aiyar will go home now, for the noon meal. It's already time. Run!'

'I'll go and come back, 'nga,' she said and went off, carrying the petition in her hand as if it were a big block of solid gold. The Aiyar took it, performed a rite of blessing, and gave it back at once. She ran with it to the chit-dispenser's room. Instantly he received it from her, rolled it up and tied it neatly, left a length of thread which he anointed with turmeric and vermillion, and handed it back to her without a second's delay. Neither the Aiyar priest nor he had wasted a moment. Nor had either of them told her to go and come back later. Everything had got done as soon as she went to them, and this auspicious omen firmed up her belief that the jewel would be recovered. Prayer-chit in hand, she searched for a spot to stick it on the branch of the vanni, where it would not be shaken down by the wind or the rain. Having tied it securely to a trident, she prostrated herself upon the ground, with folded hands devoutly stretched above her head. 'So far in my life, never have I ever desired anything belonging to someone else. Never have I touched another person's property. Yet someone has taken a thing that is mine. Just fetch it back and give it to me! I look upon you as the protector of my family, I pray to you as our Saami! Only three days are left for the wedding! If I don't make a present of a chain, my brother and his wife will never let me hear the end of it! And if the chain doesn't come back, my husband won't let me live any more. You alone must save me, Kolanji Appa!' she beseeched. Her heart felt as though it were melting within her. Reverently, she touched the trident to which her chit was tied, and raised her hands in worship…

At that moment, a lizard made a clicking sound near her left arm. The sound reinforced her conviction that the jewel would now surely be found. Her heart brimming over with faith, she rose and started to walk towards the bus stand.

There he stood, waiting for his bus – the man who had written out her chit. He gave her a look and asked, 'Finished the job?'

'I have tied the prayer-chit, 'nga.'

'Who sent you here?'

'Why are you asking like that, 'nga?'

'Just like that!' Something in the way he spoke kindled a doubt in Thangamani. 'Why are you asking like that, 'nga?' she probed.

'Kolanji Appar and such deities are peaceful saamis. They are for keeping in the house only. For jobs like this that you're talking about, there's Neivaasa Vedapparu, Aavatti Aagaaya Karuppu, Poyyanpaadi Aandavaru, Melmalayanuru Sudalai, Thiruvakra Kaali, Konjikuppam Ayyanaaru. It's to such saamis that you have to go. Because those are angry saamis.'

'Is that so? I didn't know!' The enthusiasm she had felt earlier ebbed from Thangamani's voice.

'White pumpkin and sweet pumpkin, lime – all such offerings can be cut up and given only to peaceful saamis. That kind don't have any fury in them. You have to slaughter a cock or a goat or a pig and get blood flowing.

Then you add a quarter bottle[4] and go to a saami who accepts such things. Do you know one of those? Go to him and get your job done quick. When such offerings are made, that sort of god will get into a terrific fury! Rattle a hand drum, clash cymbals, and his power goes up and up.' The man smiled a mild smile. He looked away – towards the east, to see if the bus to his village was on the way.

'I didn't know all this before, 'nga! Couldn't you have told me earlier? The people in my village told me to come here. Won't my work be done at all?' she asked, on the verge of tears. Anxiety seized her. Not only would her husband beat her up when he found out she had gone to tie a prayer-chit in a temple, he would beat her up even more if she told him what the chit-dispenser now said about it.

But first she had to get home, and it was that worry that loomed largest just now. As she looked out for an approaching bus, the man remarked, 'Gods like Kolanji Appar are all mild Saiva saamis.[5] Not much heroism in them. Around here, it's the hunter god. Our Vedappar is

---

4 Quarter bottle: English term commonly used to refer to a measure of country liquor (arrack or saaraayam).

5 Saiva saamis: Deities who are manifestations of Siva, worshipped in grand temples with a Sanskrit liturgy conducted by Brahmin priests. The speaker here says that these represent a 'high' tradition which is far removed from the tastes and needs of ordinary folk. Folk gods and goddesses are worshipped in village shrines with the deities often identified with legendary ancestral heroes and heroines.

famous as far away as Madras. Among the saamis, he is the best! If you say to him, "I've come to you because I believe in you! You only must save me!" and sacrifice a cock and pour a quarter bottle, that will be enough to wake him up. That very same night, he will make a complete job of whatever work it is that has to be done. It's only to him that you have to go, when a goat or a cow goes missing, or any jewellery.'

The more the man talked, the more worried Thangamani grew that she would never get back her lost jewel. But neither Saroja nor anybody else in the village had told her to go to Vedappar. Was this man lying? He sounded so earnest, as though he really believed what he was saying ... The more she thought about that, the more befuddled she felt.

'If that's so, then what way is there for me to get back what belongs to me?'

'Wait for a week or ten days. If it doesn't happen, go straight away to Vedappar's temple. Tell the whole matter to the priest. He'll immediately do the poosai,[6] beat the rattle drum, and call Vedappar to come and sit down right there. He'll tell him, "She has come in the belief that I can get the job done. I have taken her money in the belief that you will do the job. Now please go and make a good, clean

---

6 Poosai (puja, or worship) and poosaari (pujari, or priest). Usually, the poosaari is not a Brahmin and the liturgy and ritual of the poosai have evolved in large part from local lore and customs.

job of it, or my name will be ruined, whether yours is ruined or not." That's how that poosaari will make Vedappar himself appear. What you want will get done. All you have to do is leave your petition with your request right there. He will take care of the rest.' Listening to the man speaking with such care and concern, Thangamani felt she should have gone directly to the Vedappar temple in the first place.

Should she try and go the next day? Considering the idea, she asked, 'How much will it cost, 'nga?'

'That poosaari is the one who attends on Vedappar as well as the others in his team. He's the one to tell you how much it will cost.'

'If only I had known all this before! I would have gone there!' Thangamani exclaimed and added, 'So now, should I go to the police?'

The man did not answer her question. He just laughed.

'Why are you laughing, 'nga?'

'Better than going to the police is to forget all about a thing that has already gone off and left you! And if you think the poosaari has cheated you, the police will cheat you a hundred thousand times more than that! You do whatever you have to do to make Vedappar happy. He will do the rest. He has a white horse! He's got a sickle in his hand! Police have nothing like the power he has! They're just a pinch of dust!'

'Then what will happen about my property?'

'For eight days, just be patient. If the thing doesn't come back to you, I'll tell you where to go, and it will come right back, all on its own. It is all because your family god hasn't visited your house lately, that's why it got stolen.' As the man was telling her how to get to the Vedappar temple, and which was the astrologically appropriate day of the week for her to approach the deity, along came the bus to her village. She waved it to a stop.

'I will do what you say, 'nga,' she told him, and got on.

Priyanka was sitting there, in the bus. 'Come sit here, aunty,' she said, making room for her, and asking in a voice full of concern, 'Where are you coming back from?' Priyanka lived on the street next to hers in the village and went to college in town.

No sooner had she asked, 'Where are you coming back from?' than it all came out from Thangamani, in a single breath – her daughter's turmeric-washing ceremony, her brother's ritual gift of a two-pavun chain, mortgaging that chain to pay back the loan taken to conduct the turmeric-washing, interest on it building up so much that she could not redeem that chain, the impending marriage, in just three days, of her brother's daughter, mortgaging her land to buy the bride the ritual gift of a chain, that chain being stolen, being thrashed by her husband, going to the Kolanji Appar temple and tying the prayer-chit … and all that the chit-dispenser had told her at the bus stand.

Priyanka listened to it all and remarked: 'So! Jewel gone, one day's wages gone, the money in your hand also all gone – right?'

A fury of despair came over Thangamani. 'Who-all must I listen to? What-all should I believe? Looks like they're all saying I will never get it back! And only three days left for the marriage! How good if I die before that!'

Hitting her head again and again on the handrail, Thangamani began to wail aloud.

Imayam is the pen name of V. Annamalai, a schoolteacher and one of the foremost contemporary writers in Tamil. He has seven novels, six short-story collections and a novella to his credit. He has won several prestigious awards, including the Agni Akshara Award (1994), the Tamil Nadu Progressive Writers' Association Award (1994), the Amudhan Adigal Literary Award (1998), the Thamizh Thendral Thiru.Vi.Ka. Award (2009), the Anantha Vikatan Award (2016), the Iyal Award for Lifetime Achievement (2018), The Hindu's Jayakanthan Award for Contemporary Tamil Literature (2018), and most recently, the Sahitya Akademi Award in 2020 for his novel *Selladha Panam*.

Vasantha Surya is a poet, journalist, and translator whose prose translations from Tamil include six novels, and an anthology of contemporary short fiction (*A Place to Live*). *The Stalk of Time* and *A Word Between Us* are her two poetry collections in English, while among her translations of poetry are *To Plunge Within*, a selection of verses from the Tamil classic, Nammaaazhwaar's *Thiruvaimozhi*, and several poems in *Tamil Dalit Writing*. *The Ballad of Budhni* is her translation of a narrative folk poem from Bundeli Hindi. Her works for children include *Mridu in Madras*, translated into Tamil by Prema Srinivasan and herself, and *Ramayana for Children*. Her articles and reviews have appeared in major Indian publications.

30 Years *of*

HarperCollins *Publishers* India

At HarperCollins, we believe in telling the best stories and finding the widest possible readership for our books in every format possible. We started publishing 30 years ago; a great deal has changed since then, but what has remained constant is the passion with which our authors write their books, the love with which readers receive them, and the sheer joy and excitement that we as publishers feel in being a part of the publishing process.

Over the years, we've had the pleasure of publishing some of the finest writing from the subcontinent and around the world, and some of the biggest bestsellers in India's publishing history. Our books and authors have won a phenomenal range of awards, and we ourselves have been named Publisher of the Year the greatest number of times. But nothing has meant more to us than the fact that millions of people have read the books we published, and somewhere, a book of ours might have made a difference.

As we step into our fourth decade, we go back to that one word – a word which has been a driving force for us all these years.

Read.